An unexpected visit from the daughter of an old mentor launches private detective Terry Luvello into one of the most intriguing cases of his career. Margaret Reasoner, the matriarch of one of Cleveland's wealthiest and most politically connected families, has recently passed away.

Not trusting any of her children, Margaret had added a clause in her will requiring a private inquest should her death take place under suspicious circumstances. Hired to investigate, Terry spends a week at the Reasoner's sprawling estate dealing with the increasingly hostile family as he unravels the mysteries of the mansion known as the *Shadow House*.

Terry recruits his partner and girlfriend, Cleveland police detective Hannah Page to aid in the investigation. The two uncover a web of secrets and lies that stretch beyond anything they have ever experienced. As the deceptions pile up along with the body count, a killer plans the ultimate revenge.

Terry's ingenuity and uniquely wry sense of humor help him navigate this complex case while juggling the demands of his clinical transition about to enter its final phase. In a household where no one is innocent, Terry must decide just how far he is willing to go to find the guilty party.

SHADOW HOUSE

Terry Luvello, PI, Book Three

Joe Rielinger

A NineStar Press Publication

www.ninestarpress.com

Shadow House

First Edition, May 2024

ISBN: 978-1-64890-758-6

Also available in eBook, ISBN: 978-1-64890-757-9

CONTENT WARNING:
This book contains fade-to-black sexual content, discussion of alcohol abuse, and description of seduction and sexual assault with the use of GHB, incest (past, off page), predatory masculine behavior, cheating, and gun violence.

To my wife, Lisa. You are the love of my life. Thank you for all your editing and story advice. I owe you everything, and you never even charge me interest.

To Rachel and Andy. Thanks for not laughing when your crazy father announced he was writing a book. I love you both more than I could ever say.

To Scarlett and Scout. Thanks for keeping me company when I write. Your plot suggestions can be a little off, but I appreciate them anyway. Your companionship is worth every doggie treat in the world, but I feel like I need to set limits—blame the vet, not me.

PROLOGUE

MY MOTHER WAS fond of folksy sayings, their subjects including pretty much any topic that struck her fancy. Regarding shadows, Mom told us we would never notice their gloom if we always chose to face the light.

My father would invariably grimace at Mom's optimism. Dad, a Cleveland arson inspector, had already grasped the lesson I would learn much later—shadows were everywhere, whether you faced the sunlight or not.

As a private detective, I work in a profession defined by shadows. Like my father, I have grown used to their gloom, a dark shade that might yield anything from a gun pointed at your head to a viable place of concealment. Detectives see shadows in the faces of everyone they encounter, even the clients who pay our bills. A famous TV doctor was known for saying that everyone lies. A private investigator assumes this without question, at least a detective aiming for a reasonable lifespan.

My PI mentor told me her shadows whispered with a language all their own. Although this pearl of wisdom came in hour two of a trip to Bernie's favorite bar, I grew to believe her nonetheless.

I once mentioned Bernie's observation to my girlfriend at the close of a particularly difficult case. With a practicality befitting a Cleveland police detective, Hannah told me I was full of shit.

After our stay in the Reasoner mansion, Hannah changed her mind. A 32,000-square-foot estate in the Cleveland suburb of Hunting Valley, the Reasoner home was perfect for shadows. The house was built in neo-Gothic style and dwarfed its Hunting Valley neighbors—a suburb where a million-dollar habitat was viewed as little more than a hovel.

No one would think "hovel" when describing the Reasoner estate. With a Zillow-estimated value of 28 million dollars, the mansion included twelve bedrooms and sixteen bathrooms, along with a 2,800-square-foot fitness center, an infinity pool, tennis courts, volleyball courts, and a stocked fishing pond. Remodeled at least three times since its 1929 debut, the mansion has maintained the original great room with its wood-paneled walls, vaulted wood-beamed ceiling, and a fieldstone fireplace designed under the watchful eye of its patriarch, Edward Reasoner.

Reasoner had earned his fortune transporting and selling illegal liquor across the Great Lakes during Prohibition. Likely under the influence of his wife, Edith, Edward eventually shifted his business to a more legitimate source of income, supplying industrial alcohol to the nation's early detergent and pharmaceutical industries.

As with many of the nouveau riche, Edward Reasoner had sought to cement his society bona fides by designing his mansion in what he saw as traditional European Gothic architecture. Unlike many buildings of the day, the Reasoner mansion was able to successfully duplicate the style it sought—its towers, battlements, oriel windows, and pitched roof making it appear castle-like in design.

Given its size and unique construction, the shadows cast outside the Reasoner mansion were to be expected. Its covered outdoor walkway bathed those entering the home in gloom, lending the oversized wooden front door an air of menace, as if the entryway to a movie haunted house.

As intimidating as those outdoor shadows might be, the shadows inside were far more striking. They had nothing to do with architecture and appeared in unexpected places—the bottom of the grand staircase, the entry door to Edward Reasoner's original study, even the space in front of the large window overlooking the infinity pool. The shadows in the windowed second-floor corridor seemed to dance, likely aided by the wind blowing the trees planted unusually close outside.

Those shadows were easy to find, as were the whispers. Their conversations included the voice of Edward Reasoner, who hanged himself from his mansion's wood-beamed ceiling just five years after his home's opening. Suffering from what would now be recognized as clinical depression, Reasoner committed suicide shortly after the death from cancer of his beloved wife, Edith.

If one listened carefully, one could also hear the cries of Albert Reasoner, Edward's six-year-old son. Albert drowned in the mansion's original pool after diving into water that was far too shallow. Twenty years later, the daughter of Albert's older brother died when she fell from the top of the mansion's grand stairway. After a brief investigation, the police could never determine whether she fell naturally or was pushed.

In the ninety years since, other deaths occurred, some natural, some not, all the deceased still eager to tell their tales out of school.

Those whispers, generated, I knew, by the paranoid part of my brain, were not the worst part of my stay at the estate. By the end of my visit, I realized it was only when the whispers ceased that madness overtook the Reasoner mansion.

When their whispers ceased, the shadows began playing for real.

CHAPTER ONE

I HATE ADULTERY cases—every private detective does. Tawdry and nasty by their very nature, they inevitably lead to pain for both the client and the accused. That's true even if the accused is one of those rare individuals who isn't actually screwing around.

So why do we take these cases? We take them for the same reason the men and women we follow choose to cheat. As cynical as it sounds, every private investigator knows that it's sex, not love, that makes the world go round. The two occasionally have some direct relationship, but those instances are not our concern. A PI's livelihood depends on the man who suddenly realizes his secretary is far more good-looking than his wife or the woman who decides she's just a little too lonely, waiting for her husband to come home after work. Their wronged partners pay our bills, and we take a deep breath, sigh, and spend one more night peering through a high-def camera next to yet another dirty hotel window.

Fortunately for my sanity, I didn't rely strictly on those cases. As Terry Luvello, PI, I had developed a good reputation for competence, much of that gained while assisting my police detective girlfriend on two high-profile cases.

Detective Hannah Page stayed with me through it all, though we had some rough moments after the conclusion of both investigations. We got back together after our last case on what Hannah called a "trial basis." Our reunion overjoyed my mother and my best friend. Hannah's parents—not so much.

Hannah had also stayed despite the complications and occasional wide-eyed stares caused by my transitioning to male. With just two months to go before my actual surgery, we were now living together in Hannah's Cleveland Heights home.

I loved her more than I could say, and I believed she loved me back. That love did not keep her from reacting negatively to my latest assignment.

Staring at me before I left that evening, Hannah asked, "Why do you take these cases? Trying to catch those shitheads in the act just depresses you, and we really don't need the money."

She wasn't wrong on either count, but I reminded her of our agreement. "When I moved in here, we said we would split the household costs. Like them or not, the adultery cases pay my part of those bills."

Hannah shook her head before giving me a kiss goodbye. "Get the hell out of here, but don't go getting any ideas. Just remember what I said I'd do if I caught you screwing around."

She had, in fact, told me exactly what she would do, a starring role in that scenario played by the woodchipper Hannah insisted on keeping in our backyard. I shivered despite myself—the cost of a self-assertive girlfriend who wouldn't dream of going anywhere without her Smith & Wesson.

Tonight's carnal shithead was one Seamus O'Donnell, a man who differed from the other shitheads I'd chased, if only because he didn't seem to be, on the surface, a shithead. A computer programmer at Cleveland's NASA Glenn Research Center, Seamus was outwardly the perfect family man—beloved by his wife, his three young children, and even his golden retriever puppy. I looked through both public and private records and found none of the usual indicators of infidelity. There were no unusual hotel bills, no significant cash withdrawals, and no sudden changes in wardrobe or hairstyle. When I spoke with his wife one week prior, she said Seamus had always been a model husband. Still, she had doubts.

It began with the napkins. Handing me the two

cheap paper cocktail napkins, his wife, Catherine, seemed almost guilty of her suspicions.

"Seamus is not the neatest man, and I often find candy wrappers and other crap in his pockets. Typically, it's nothing unusual. Then I found these."

I looked at the napkins. Both were for the Dorrance, a small dive hotel in Fairview Park. If Seamus was fooling around, he wouldn't be the first guy to do so at the Dorrance. Still, it wasn't much.

"Do you have anything else—unexplained absences, lots of late work nights, any unusual behavior? You said he seemed distant lately. When did that start?"

Catherine shook her head. "It started with the break-in. We went out to dinner with the kids about two months ago. When we came back, we noticed a broken window, and our TV and my spare laptop were missing— Seamus keeps his locked away in our bedroom. We called the cops, and they sent someone out to take a statement. Seamus has seemed unusually quiet ever since. I thought he was worried it might happen again. Now, I'm not so sure. You've got to understand"—she looked at me plaintively—"I've never seen Seamus even glance at another woman. I just can't imagine him screwing around."

Given her husband's work at NASA, I wondered about an employment-related secret. I then dismissed the thought almost as quickly as it had come. Spy movie conspiracies rarely occurred in real life.

I spent the next week following Seamus to all his after-work destinations. Unlike the spy caper that had once played in my head, those destinations were, in a word, boring. Seamus drove straight home for six of those nights. On the seventh, he stopped by the local Giant Eagle to pick up what looked like a bag of snacks.

Tonight, I hoped my luck might change. Catherine had called earlier that day because Seamus had told her he'd be late coming home. When she asked why, her husband said something about completing a report for senior management—unusual, Catherine said, because such reports were not normally a part of Seamus's job.

Hoping for a break, I pulled into a small drugstore lot across the street from a parking area used by NASA employees. My efforts were rewarded when Seamus exited the NASA building precisely at 5:00 p.m. Either he'd finished his report early, or the excuse he'd given his wife was, as she suspected, total bullshit.

The answer became clear as I followed Seamus for ten blocks down Lorain Avenue until we reached the gray concrete parking lot of the Dorrance Hotel. I parked just across the street and had a good view of Seamus as he exited his car and proceeded to an outside door on the hotel's first floor. I had my location, and I knew my target. Now, all I needed were pictures.

Whatever you've seen in the movies, residents rarely forget to close the drapes when they're in a hotel room. That maxim particularly held true when they're having an affair, and Seamus O'Donnell was no exception.

To get around this problem, PIs resorted to gadgets. Like most detectives, I owned a variety of cameras, all used for different purposes. After taking several pictures of Seamus knocking on the hotel room door, I pulled out a different camera, a thermal imaging model used by contractors to determine the structural integrity of a building behind its existing walls. Thermal imaging can't distinguish faces, but the camera's photos did outline human shapes. That was true even when those shapes were, in the vernacular of my girlfriend, "doing the nasty" on a hotel room bed.

With daylight fading and Seamus behind a closed door, I crossed the street and positioned myself outside the room's main window. I took several shots as Seamus and his unseen friend began screwing on the hotel bed. I took my last picture, but decided, for some reason, to take one more. I turned the camera back on, and that final image showed one figure, likely Seamus based on height, with his partner nowhere in sight. That was when things truly went south.

An older detective once cautioned me to listen to every word uttered by a client, particularly in adultery cases. Even if they were angry or lying, the person paying you still had a better idea than you what was truly going on. To be effective, that listening also needed to include a fair degree of interpretation—most clients weren't aware of how much they truly knew. It was a lesson I remembered almost too late.

I was trying for yet another shot when the hotel room door opened. That alone wouldn't have been a problem. If you followed enough carnal shitheads, you'd inevitably find yourself in a fair share of confrontations. The bigger problem—the right hand that emerged was carrying a gun.

My assailant was not Seamus O'Donnell. I've known only one other computer expert, and he'd never touched a weapon in his life. This hand belonged to a tall, well-muscled, half-dressed man in his mid to late thirties. I knew immediately what I'd missed.

Catherine O'Donnell had told me everything—I was just too dumb to put the pieces together. She said her husband never looked at other women, a statement I'd heard a hundred times before and discounted almost immediately. I never considered Catherine might be right. Her husband didn't look at other women because he was, in fact, a homosexual.

Catherine also told me her husband's behavior had changed after the police investigated a break-in at their home. A computer programmer might not know which end of a gun to hold, but a cop wouldn't be without one. I imagined a casual meeting after work to discuss the case—a meeting that unexpectedly led to other things. Hannah would call me an idiot for overlooking something so obvious. That assumed, of course, I stayed alive long enough to tell her.

Cops are good at reading faces, and I was guessing he read the shock on mine. It was time to return the favor.

"It's good to meet you, officer. I would at least button your shirt though. This March weather will kill you otherwise."

His own shocked look told me I'd guessed correctly. He still hadn't, however, put down his weapon, a Glock far bigger than my own. I needed to do some more convincing.

"Are you really going to shoot me with that thing? Seamus's wife knows he's having an affair, and she knows about the Dorrance. Who do you think hired me? My own police detective girlfriend also knows exactly where I was headed tonight and why. If I'm found dead somewhere, how long do you think it'll take her to find witnesses who saw you and Seamus enter your room together?"

Suddenly tired, I called out, "Seamus, quit hiding behind the goddamned door and talk some sense into your boyfriend!"

A chagrinned Seamus O'Donnell reluctantly walked out of the hotel room and stood next to his lover. Not looking me in the eye, he said, "Does Catherine really know?"

It was time to be blunt. "I'll give you one helpful tip—if you're meeting your lover in a hotel room, don't stuff the hotel's napkins in your pants pocket." I looked again at Seamus's boyfriend, still holding his gun. "I need to talk with Seamus alone. Unless you're still planning to shoot me, you need to take a hike."

Finally coming to terms with the situation, my anonymous police friend returned to the hotel room to gather his things. He exited two minutes later, said goodbye to Seamus, and turned to me one last time.

"You try and shake him down, and you will answer to me. A private investigator who looks like you won't be hard to find."

I waved my hand. "Relax, big guy. I'm just trying to let Seamus know the way I see this going. If he makes the right decision, it may actually work in your favor."

He finally left, and Seamus and I walked back into the hotel room. Seamus grabbed for his wallet, but I shook my head.

"While I don't think you're a bad guy, I work for your wife. She's paying me to tell her if what she suspects is true. I will not lie to her, but I will give you twenty-four hours. If you're smart, you'll use that time to sit down and tell Catherine what's going on."

Seamus looked utterly defeated. Sitting on the hotel bed, its covers still pulled down, he pled his case.

"I still love her, you know. I never cheated on Catherine before I met Brad. I never even contemplated cheating. I didn't know I was gay. Catherine and I—our sex life has never been great, but we were still active, you know? When I tell her, she's going to want a divorce."

He was probably right, but I felt like I needed to give him hope. I wasn't sure why, but I tried nonetheless.

"Maybe you two can come to some sort of an accommodation, one that takes into account both sides of the life you're now facing. I don't know how agreeable your wife will be, but I do know this—if you wait until I tell her first, she's going to divorce you for sure. I'll hold off talking to her, but one day is my limit. After that, she gets the pictures and my full report."

I stood to leave, but Seamus had a question.

"Do you really think she might stay with me?"

I had bet on the "how do you justify your shitty job" query I got from most of my wayward spouses. Seamus was one of the few carnal shitheads who didn't believe in blame-shifting. The truth was, I thought he was screwed. Who knows, however. Crazier things have happened.

"Tell Catherine you still love her. Even more importantly, tell her you're still attracted to her. In this situation, I suspect she'll need to hear that last part the most."

I left feeling hopeful. Seamus had asked the right question. With otherwise good people in just the right situation, guilt could be a cleansing thing. Those conditions were rare, but they occasionally did occur.

Far more often, I'd seen the opposite. Guilt left unaddressed could be a rot, a cancer that preyed on both the evil and the innocent.

For those caught up in that hell, sometimes death felt like a blessing.

CHAPTER TWO

I RETURNED HOME, and Hannah greeted me with a kiss. That kiss led to other things, and for the next hour, I forgot about Seamus, his wife, and his policeman lover. Afterward, lying next to Hannah, I told her the whole story.

"I can tell you feel sorry for this guy," she said, touching my face. "What makes him different, exactly?"

I'd thought about it while driving home. "Two months ago, Seamus probably couldn't have pictured himself screwing around. Then he meets this cop, realizes something about himself, and falls into an affair he'd never have previously imagined having. Is that something programmed into all of us—that potential for betrayal?"

Hannah looked at me closely. "I'm a cop, and you're a PI. We both know the answer to that question, at least for 90 percent of the population. That said, I like to think that you and I are part of the minority. You call yourself cynical, but at heart, you're a boy scout. You have your code, and you stick to it. I can't imagine you betraying me or anyone else."

Ironically, I found out the next day just how wrong she was. I had betrayed someone years ago. I just hadn't realized it at the time.

Hannah left for the Twelfth Precinct early the following day. I stayed home to write the O'Donnell report and do preliminary research on a new referral I'd received two days prior. That new case involved corporate theft; fortunate because I was in no mood for another philandering spouse.

The knock on the door came around one o'clock, just as I was finishing the last of my Subway meatball sandwich. I expected one of Hannah's busybody neighbors, but the woman standing on our porch was no one I'd ever seen. In her midthirties, she was short, maybe five-foot-two, with flaming red hair and a body like a fireplug.

My unnamed intruder regarded me with undisguised hostility. Usually, I have to at least say something before earning that reaction. I waited, and she finally spoke.

"You look exactly like she described you—more

muscular, more facial hair, but the rest is just the same. It took two years before my mother could even say your name without swearing."

I was still mystified, though something about the woman's hair did look vaguely familiar. If I was right about her age, her mother would be in her late fifties or early sixties. I couldn't think of anyone I had pissed off that fit that description.

My nameless visitor looked at me again as if amazed anyone could be this clueless. Shaking her head, she finally told me who she was.

"My name is Annabelle Moffitt. My mother was Bernie Moffitt."

Dear God, that's why her red hair looked familiar. I waved Annabelle through the front door and motioned her to sit on Hannah's Aliso sofa, the most expensive piece of furniture in our home. She sat, and I thought back to my time with Bernie Moffitt.

The State of Ohio required 2,000 hours of experience in investigatory work to obtain a private investigator license along with an associate's degree in criminal justice.

The degree was no issue. Though I already had a prelaw diploma, I added the required associate's certification without a problem. The work experience was considerably more challenging.

Twenty-three and just one year removed from announcing I was transgender, I was still getting used to the clothing, the new hairstyle, and the inevitable stares from virtually everyone I met. By the time I sought my license, I'd become less and less tolerant of the bullshit.

I walked into the corporate office of the Salinger Detective Agency in a surly mood. Located in downtown Cleveland, Salinger was, and still is, Ohio's largest private detective firm. To maintain that position, the firm typically accepted five new trainees each year. I was admitted into that trainee program sight unseen.

I was forced to meet with Harry Salinger, the firm's sixty-year-old founder, before being assigned a mentor. An allegedly famous midwestern PI, Harry had not investigated a case himself in the last twenty years. It was clear from the moment I walked into his office he assumed I was part of a joke.

"Who sent you?" he said, his patrician features almost comical in their disbelief. "Was it Mike?"

I was in no mood for an argument, having just encountered a similar reaction from the security staff downstairs. Figuring I had nothing to lose, I decided to be blunt.

"I understood this meeting was part of your training program. I have no fucking clue who Mike might be. I do know my friend John, a legal associate at Traber, Young, and Williams. He told me if you have an issue, his firm would only be too happy to undertake a discrimination lawsuit on my behalf."

In truth, John had a marketing degree and had just

begun assisting on one of his firm's local campaigns. My friend did, however, watch *Law & Order* reruns. I figured that was close enough for my purposes.

Harry sputtered something about being only too happy to have me on board. He then picked up the phone, a little too eagerly, to call my assigned mentor. Before my new boss arrived, he again turned to face me.

"Bernie's our best detective. You shut up and listen, and you might actually learn something. One other thing—you swear at me again, I'll have you escorted out of the building. I don't care if your friend is fucking Clarence Darrow; I don't put up with shit from trainees in my own office."

I nodded, having gotten all I had hoped for from our meeting. Salinger's door slammed open as if on time with that thought. It was then I met the unforgettable Bernie Moffitt.

The fact that Bernie was a woman wasn't my chief surprise. I knew at least five of Salinger's twenty detectives were female.

It was the overall Bernie package that was striking. No more than five-foot-one, Bernie weighed at least one-fifty pounds of pure muscle and had the thickest arms I'd ever seen on a woman. Her head, covered with bushy red hair, was held up by a barely discernable neck.

She looked at me, back at Salinger, and then pointed at me. "Who's the poof?"

Normally, I might have reacted to the insult, but I

was still staring.

"This," Salinger replied, "is Terry Luvello, your new trainee. He apparently thinks he's hot shit. I need you to disabuse him of that notion."

Bernie motioned for me to follow her, assuming I would do so without question. I hesitated, considering my options. I could leave, but that would get me no further down the road to my private investigator license. I also knew leaving was what Harry Salinger was rooting for, and I had no wish to give the dickhead anything he wanted. Beyond sheer spite, there was also Bernie herself. Unlike Salinger, I sensed this was a person who had some idea of what she was doing. I needed to learn—better to do so from someone knowledgeable. I followed Bernie out the door.

Still, I had to know just what I was in for. Walking behind Bernie into her broom closet–sized office, I figured I should explore the parameters of our relationship.

"You know, 'poof' is slang for a male homosexual. I'm a transgender male."

Bernie looked at me, her contempt evident. "First of all, I don't care who or what you are. You want us to get along? Just do what the fuck I tell you when I tell you to do it. Second, I call all my trainees poofs. That includes the women. You want me to stop? Prove you're worth something."

I could live with that, but I was still curious. "How

long did that take with your other trainees?"

"If I ever stop, you'd be the fucking first."

I soon learned that Bernie rarely uttered a sentence without an insult or a swear word.

I wasn't sure if she was telling the truth about her other trainees, but it took me three months to shed my poof status. Bernie and I had been having an unusually difficult time following a senior partner at one of Cleveland's many law firms. The man's highly suspicious wife had hired us one month ago, convinced her husband was screwing his twenty-five-year-old secretary. She was growing increasingly impatient at our inability to catch our target doing anything besides grabbing an occasional drink with colleagues at a downtown Cleveland bar.

Considering our problem, I had an idea. After waiting for the end of one of Bernie's frustrated rants, I said, "The wife suspects the secretary, but the only messages we could find between the two when we stole his phone were references to arranged meetings—the usual secretary-boss shit. What if that also applies to his private life? What if the secretary's not the other woman, just her boss's personal facilitator? The secretary arranges for a high-end hooker, and the asshole meets the escort in one of the apartments over that bar he's always at. We don't need his phone; we already looked through that anyway. What we really need is hers."

Bernie pointed to me. I was sure she'd say my idea

was stupid, but she nodded instead. "The secretary goes to lunch at Bennigan's at noon almost every day. You'll be waiting there. You'll do the lift because you're better at the sleight-of-hand stuff than I am. Once you have her phone, I'll be waiting outside in my car with Sam. Unless the bitch has some sort of way-out security, Sam should be able to download her messages. You can then return it before she realizes it's missing."

It was the first time Bernie had ever complimented me and the first time she had ever said more than two sentences without swearing.

I pulled off the lift at Bennigan's without incident and returned to Bernie's car, where I met Sam, Salinger's resident computer expert. It took him only two minutes to realize our target's secretary was surprisingly bad at deleting her messages. We learned she had arranged at least twelve meetings between her boss and someone from an outfit called Patterson's. Though the name could have indicated almost anything, Bernie had encountered it before.

"You have to give our guy credit. Patterson's is the most high-end escort service in the city. We're talking two thousand an hour for girls and guys who look like they could have walked in from a modeling agency. Quite a few of them probably did just that. We'll check the phone number to verify, but I'm sure that's what we're looking at. We can compare the Patterson's meeting times to when the wife says her husband was extra late. After that, I'll have a conversation with the shithead bartender.

That shithead bartender, quite impressed with Bernie's fake Cleveland Police badge, readily admitted his upstairs rooms might have been occasionally used for a tryst or two—totally without his knowledge, of course. He allowed us to stake out both the bar and the upstairs, with Bernie catching our mark in several photos, accompanied by a remarkably pretty girl who looked no more than eighteen years old.

Our lawyer's wife, married before prenuptial agreements became a thing, could not have been more elated. After that case, Bernie began calling me by my first name. I considered calling her Bernadette but decided against it—I had seen Bernie at the shooting range.

All those memories and more poured through my head as I stared at Annabelle Moffitt. I remembered Bernie talking about her daughter exactly once. She was finishing law school, and Bernie's only goal was to make enough money to keep her daughter away from the crushing debt faced by most law school graduates.

Annabelle had the same red hair and take-no-prisoners attitude as her mother, though she was probably at least an inch taller. With Annabelle now seated, I asked about Bernie. I noticed before she entered, that Annabelle had referred to her mother in the past tense.

"My mother is dead," Annabelle said, staring at me from her seat on the couch. "She was found five months ago near a pond below the Bridle Path Bridge in Hunting

Valley."

I was shocked. There were some people you assumed would never die, and Bernie Moffitt was one of them. I knew the Bridle Path Bridge area well. Hannah had pointed it out on one of our rare visits to her parents' home.

There are several high-end neighborhoods on Cleveland's east side. Bratenahl and Moreland Hills were only two. As beautiful as the homes were in those cities, the mansions in Hunting Valley were almost legendary. Small geographically, the village had a population of under one thousand. It was ranked in the top ten cities and villages across the United States for resident income. It was, in short, the last place I would have expected to find Bernie Moffitt.

I couldn't help asking, "Why was your mother mad at me, and what was Bernie doing in Hunting Valley?"

Annabelle looked at me in anger and disbelief. She really assumed I knew.

"Mom told me about the argument you two had when she took the Reasoner case. She wanted you to stay for at least one more month, but you refused—you had reached the end of your trainee hours and wanted to go out on your own."

It always amazed me how two people could live through the same set of events and yet remember things in a totally different way.

"Your mom did ask me to stay at least one more

month. She said she would speak to Harry Salinger about keeping me on as a full-fledged detective. I think part of her believed he might, but we both knew Salinger hated me. There was no way that dipshit would keep me on. I didn't fit his image of the gentleman private detective. Salinger liked to have parties and show off his staff. What would all his friends say when they saw me? I figured I should leave on my terms and not try to draw things out."

Annabelle snarled, "You think Mom looked like a gentleman private detective? Salinger may have been an asshole, but he wasn't stupid. People like my mother brought in clients. According to Mom, you would have done the same. You were the only detective my mother worked with that she thought was worth a damn. She trained you, and you wouldn't stay for one more case.

"My mother was obsessed with the Reasoners. Not at the beginning, maybe, but definitely by the time she died. I hated her a bit for that. I have a son; his name is Anthony. Mom missed the first birthday of her only grandchild to follow up some stupid lead on that cursed family. You want irony? Mom died two weeks before Margaret Reasoner. If you had agreed to help my mother, I have to believe things likely would have turned out differently."

I was in no mood for a guilt trip, and I knew there was more to the story. "I can't believe you came all this way just to berate me. You could have done that over the phone. Why don't you tell me why you're really here."

Annabelle bit her lip for a full ten seconds before responding. "What do you remember about the Reasoner case?"

"I was only involved for a few days, but the case was referred from Margaret Reasoner to Harry Salinger himself. I remember Salinger calling Bernie and me into his office to meet the old lady—I was amazed he would include me in a meeting with a client that rich.

"Margaret had turned eighty when we met. I gathered that her family was tired of waiting for her to pass on. That's not unusual in rich families, but Margaret was convinced one of them would try to speed up the process. With someone that old, it would have been easy. I don't think Harry believed a word of it, but Bernie seemed intrigued. When I left the firm, she was finishing the preliminary work—computerized background checks on the other family members, that sort of thing. I assumed Margaret was imagining things, especially when I heard she didn't die for real until last year."

Annabelle's face went from angry to dejected. "Margaret Reasoner didn't just die; she was killed. My mother kept up with the case on her own time, even when Margaret told her to stop. Before Mom died, she also spoke to Margaret's medical doctor. Margaret's last checkup was one month before she croaked, and the doc said she was in remarkably good health for a woman her age. I figured they held a pillow over her face until the old woman stopped squirming. That's one possibility. If they paid off the medical examiner, that would open up a hundred others."

I still wasn't sure where all this was going. Given Annabelle's mood, I was afraid to ask. Still, she was here, and I was curious despite myself.

"Let's say Margaret Reasoner was murdered. She died five months ago, so her estate has long since gone through probate. You came here to guilt me into doing something. The family already has her money and the mansion. What the hell were you thinking I could accomplish?"

Annabelle looked back at me, determination in her hazel eyes. "Probate has been delayed. It turns out Margaret included a codicil in her will no one else in the family was aware of.

"My mother had a copy of Margaret's will and all its details. You have to understand just how much Margaret despised her children. She viewed them as a bunch of ingrates who had no sense of what it meant to be a Reasoner. Her kids knew their mother's feelings and hated her back. When Margaret's lawyer informed her she would never get away with writing her kids out of the will entirely, the codicil was her fallback. I'm paraphrasing, but that provision stated if Margaret's death occurred due to unknown origins, any of the will's stakeholders could initiate a private investigation at their own expense. Once the clause was activated, the investigator would have thirty days to come up with enough evidence to prove, based on a preponderance of the evidence, that Margaret's death was due to murder. Did you ever hear of the slayer statute? While the will has passed the normal ninety-day probate period, that's what Margaret relied upon when she included the codicil."

That settled it. Annabelle was undeniably crazy. "The slayer statute says that a person or persons cannot inherit from someone whose death they intentionally cause. It was the Ohio legislature's way of saying that crime doesn't pay. You're right—if someone was implicated in the murder of Margaret Reasoner, the will would return to being contestable. If you think this is some sort of silver bullet, however, I will tell you why your plan won't work.

"To prove one or more of the Reasoners committed murder, I would need access to the medical examiner's files and the notes from the investigation the police performed when Margaret Reasoner died. More importantly, I would need access to the Reasoners themselves as well as the mansion where the death occurred. You're a lawyer. Why would the Reasoners possibly allow me that much accessibility when it could land one or more of them in jail? Who would need to sign off on the evidence, and who would benefit?"

Annabelle took her time answering. Clearly, she had given this matter a lot of thought. "Regarding the sign-off, I'm told the clause is pretty solid. The arbiter is someone Margaret Reasoner chose prior to the insertion of the codicil, a retired county judge. An alternate was also designated in case that judge died before the process was concluded. That person is another judge, one who's still sitting on the Cuyahoga County probate court. I checked with some people at my firm, and both are considered beyond reproach.

"About your second question, there is another stakeholder. Like many wealthy people, Margaret Reasoner was good at pretending she cared about those less fortunate than herself. The charity she spent the most time with was the Cranberg Institute for Children with Autism and Special Needs. Under the original terms of the will, Cranberg received one hundred thousand from the Reasoner estate. As you can imagine, that amount changes dramatically if any member of the Reasoner family is deemed ineligible to inherit. In that case, the school will receive the amount that would be due the guilty party. The estate's total value was almost four hundred million, split among the different family members. You can see why Cranberg is interested and willing to push the idea of an investigation. Before you ask, Margaret's lawyer made Cranberg aware of that detail in the will, something the Reasoners would have been happy to overlook."

Taking a deep breath, Annabelle continued. "Why would the Reasoners agree to an investigation? Quite simply, they don't have a choice. Stonewalling an inquiry, particularly with a charity involved, would result in publicity that would damage the family's name, not to mention the Reasoner corporate interests. That latter point is also why you are acceptable to all parties as the investigator. Your findings would be considered beyond reproach, particularly given the publicity surrounding your previous cases. The Reasoners, as much as anyone, do not want this thing dragging out."

The Reasoner name has always had a checkered past. For a family notoriously protective of their society bona fides, I could believe they would not want their name yanked further through the mud. Better a confidential inquiry than the humiliation that might arise with a newspaper investigation. Along with that consideration was Bernie—a woman who might have hated me, but I felt loyalty to, nonetheless.

More gently, I said, "Tell me about your mother's death. Surely you two talked about the same things you just told me. I'm gathering she kept up her own investigation in an unofficial capacity. Tell me what happened."

Annabelle looked away—this was a subject that still hurt. "Two days before she died, Mom told me she was going to try again to talk with you. Given her pride and how pissed off she was, I could tell she was desperate. As I mentioned, Mom's body was found at the bottom of the Bridle Path Bridge. The fall was at least thirty feet. The cops investigated for all of two days—claimed they could find no signs of a struggle, nothing that would indicate foul play. The fall was ruled accidental, though they clearly suspected suicide.

"I told the local cops Mom was investigating the Reasoners, but they looked at me like I was insane. And as far as the stuff I told you, Mom wanted no part in an investigation that depended in any way on the cooperation of that family. Before she died, I think she hated the other Reasoners as much as Margaret did."

I felt an obligation to Bernie, but I was still looking for reasons not to take this case. "If the Cranberg School is looking for an investigator, they may want someone else. Most charities would want someone more...mainstream."

Annabelle had anticipated this objection as well—damn her. "I already ran your name and credentials past their director. They'd heard of you and some of the work you did in the past. They sounded thrilled you might be working on their case.

It's good that one of us was. "What about the Reasoners? I'll need to spend a week at their house. That will include access to the family, their household staff, Margaret's physician, and the medical examiner's reports for both Margaret and your mother. I'm sure there are other things, but those will do to start."

"Does that mean you'll take the case?"

"I have one last question. You started our conversation by saying I betrayed your mother. With that in mind, why approach me? My reputation aside, Salinger is filled with detectives, many of whom knew your mother as well as I did. If you didn't want to go through your mom's own firm, there are plenty of smaller agencies around town."

Annabelle suddenly looked guilty. I realized then

why she had turned to me.

"The others turned you down, didn't they? You came hoping you could guilt me into taking this case. Your mom may have told you I was good, but the reputation thing was also a play to my ego."

Caught, Annabelle was again defiant. "This is my mother we're talking about. I will do anything to get back at those bastards. I'll ask again—will you help me?"

Manipulation aside, I nodded. I was as crazy as she was.

CHAPTER THREE

WHEN HANNAH CAME home that evening, I told her about my surprise visit with Annabelle Moffitt. Hannah could not have agreed more with my assessment of the case, though her reasons differed from my own.

"You're going under the knife in just two months. Don't wince," she said pointedly. "You know what I mean. Keep in mind, we still haven't even decided exactly what they're doing."

I knew what she meant all too well. Now that I had been on testosterone for some time, my surgical transition would occur in two phases. It would start with chest restructuring, essentially a mastectomy, to remove my breast tissue. Since I had been notably flat-chested my entire life, that seemed like a minor change. Phase two was where things got interesting.

My second procedure would start with a hysterectomy, then the removal and closure of my vaginal opening. With my phallus, I would have a choice between a metoidioplasty or a phalloplasty. The advantage of the second procedure was a more prominent male member, easily large enough for sex. The disadvantage—a phalloplasty would require a penile implant to become, as Hannah put it, "truly operational." That was a small price to pay, but Hannah had expressed concern.

Looking at me closely, she said, "Did you talk with John?"

John Travers had been my best friend since Saint Jerome's Grade School, and his maturity level had never progressed much beyond that point. Hannah had pushed me to speak with John, perhaps thinking he would suggest the more conservative route. She hadn't known my friend nearly as long as I had.

"John said, and I quote, 'go big or go home.' This is one time I have to agree with him."

"Does he know the skin's coming off your forearm?"

"I told him. He said he would have the same answer even if I had to give up the arm entirely. Remember—I warned you."

Hannah just shook her head. Returning to the case, I had another idea that might soften her reluctance.

"You told me you have four weeks of vacation the department is pushing you to take. If I'm going to pull off the Reasoner case, I'll need at least a week in the house to talk to the family and staff. Annabelle told me the Reasoners are open to me staying there for that timeframe. How about you come with me? You wouldn't be official, but I could use your eyes on this one."

Hannah thought I was joking. "You really want me to spend a week of my free time doing the same thing I would be doing if I was back at work? Why would I possibly say yes?"

With anyone else, that response would make sense. With Hannah, not so much. I motioned for her to sit next to me on the couch and tried my best to be convincing.

"You hate vacations as much as I do. There's a reason you have so much time accumulated. You love the hunt, and you love your job. You'd go nuts on a beach, and so would I. Let's do what makes us both happy. Let's catch a killer."

She gave me a very direct look. "If I say yes, there's something else that also makes me happy. Can we stay in the same room?'

"Since I'm suddenly in demand, I'll make it a condition of my employment."

Hannah seemed satisfied. After finishing dinner, we dispensed with a movie and went straight to bed, an added bit of happiness for us both.

Hannah went to work early the next day, which left me to plan our next steps. I started by contacting the Cranberg Institute to verify they were okay with both my involvement and my retainer. It turned out Annabelle hadn't lied. The director was not only aware of Annabelle's visit, he was markedly enthusiastic.

"One of our board members is Raymond West. He mentioned how you handled that insane robbery case at the Federal Reserve last year. He really couldn't say enough about you. Without your help, he said there would have been a catastrophe."

"Insane" was a good description for the events of last year. Something told me this case might be even worse—less far-reaching, but even more lunatic. I would have to thank Ray at some point, assuming I survived.

My role in the Reasoner case now official, I sat down at my computer to do some preliminary research.

The Reasoner company had come a long way since its Prohibition roots. Now called Reasoner Industrial and Pharmaceutical Products, the company's detergent and soaps division was currently third in the United States in overall sales. Since the nineteen-thirties, the soaps division had been the flagship of the Reasoner product line and was responsible for 60 percent of the company's overall revenue.

The company's pharmaceutical division, a relative newcomer to the Reasoner line, had become an increasingly important part of the firm's overall profitability. Now twelfth in the country in terms of sales, the division had made quite a name for itself while also gaining some favorable publicity. Reasoner

Pharmaceuticals had become particularly well-known in the field of orphan drugs, a line shunned by most major pharmaceutical companies due to its limited profitability. Beyond those drugs and the rare diseases they treated, the company had developed medications for more commonly diagnosed conditions, including anxiety and an alternative to epinephrine for severe allergic reactions.

The firm was listed as RIP on the New York Stock Exchange, a designation I found weirdly amusing. After a brief rise during the heyday of the pandemic, the company's stock had fallen about 5 percent over the past year.

The Reasoner clan themselves were a fascinating lot. The recently deceased Margaret had married Harold Reasoner when she was thirty-three. Children followed soon after, all still residing in the Reasoner mansion.

The oldest, Joshua Reasoner, was now fifty-six. He had been president of the combined Reasoner firm since his father's death almost twelve years prior. Joshua was married to Abigail Reasoner. The only reference I could find to Abigail came from a five-year-old profile done in *Cleveland Magazine.* According to the writer, Abigail was even more driven than her husband. She currently held the position of Marketing VP over all the Reasoner concerns.

Matthew Reasoner, age fifty-one, had acceded to his older brother's former position as director of the company's detergents and soaps division. Matthew's second and current wife, Emily Reasoner, unlike his brother's spouse, showed no sign of any connection to the Reasoner family interests.

Luke Reasoner, child number three, had no formal position within the Reasoner companies and, at forty-eight years old, no job anywhere else as far as I could determine. Luke did have an extraordinarily active social media presence, having been photographed at virtually every major Cleveland nightclub. One of those photographs came attached to a news story concerning a drunken rampage led by Luke and his friends in the Flats, a popular spot for Cleveland restaurants. Police had quickly broken up the melee, and there was no reference to charges for Luke or any of his pals. It seemed every wealthy family had a black sheep. Having chosen no other role, Luke had clearly assumed that position for the Reasoners.

Margaret's run of boys ended after Luke. Her next child, Judith Reasoner-Cairns, lived in the Reasoner mansion with her twenty-five-year-old son Mark and her twenty-three-year-old daughter Lydia. Judith, now forty-seven, was quite active in the Cleveland art scene. According to one article, she sat on the board for the Cleveland Institute of Art, a private college focused on art and design and known around town as the CIA.

I could find little about Judith's son or daughter. Lydia Reasoner had attended the CIA briefly, but I could find no record of her at any galleries or art events. Mark was even more of a cipher than his sister. After graduating from University School, Mark had no college record that I could find. Like his youngest uncle, it appeared Mark might spend his time living off the family fortune.

After I agreed to accept her referral, Annabelle stopped by a second time to deliver whatever Reasoner case notes and items her mother had kept at home. Those materials were sketchy at best, mainly covering what Bernie had dug up the year before she died. Annabelle also told me the Cranberg Institute had informed the arbiter that the will's dispute clause had been legally activated. That gentleman told the Reasoner family of my involvement.

After spending four hours in front of my computer and Bernie's private notes, I realized I'd exhausted my ready sources of information. I was also putting off the inevitable. I needed the Reasoner case file Bernie would have kept at the Salinger Agency. It was time to call Harry Salinger.

Chapter Four

TO MY SURPRISE, I was put through immediately to the great man himself. Our conversation did not go well. Once we got over Harry's false display of bonhomie, I described the case and what I was looking for.

Clearly taken aback, he said, "Bernie once asked me to hire you, but I always considered you an arrogant prick. Bernie was the same, but she was my meal ticket. I needed to put up with her attitude, but the thought of having two of you on staff was a nonstarter.

"I tell you this because you've proven me right. You want Bernie's case file? That's protected work product, which I assume you knew before you called. The fact that you asked anyway means those few high-profile cases of yours have clearly gone to your head. Before I hang up,

I'm curious—why the fuck did you think I'd give you anything at all, particularly on a case involving my wealthiest client?"

It was the reaction I'd anticipated. Fortunately, predictable people are always the easiest to manipulate. "You want to know why you should help me? I'll give you two reasons, both involving the Reasoners themselves.

"Reason number one relates to my next phone call. I will be speaking with Joshua Reasoner, who knows there are hundreds of millions of dollars on the line. The Reasoner company stock price will tank when the newspapers discover this story, something Joshua is also well aware of. Do you want me to tell him you're getting in my fucking way? Your richest client has options; the wealthy always do. He has no more say over your protected work product than I have, but are you sure you want to be the one to tell him?

"The second reason is related to the first, but it involves one of the few things you're actually good at. You are and always have been a shitty detective. That's why you sit behind a desk every day and let other people do the real work. What you are good at is politics. This case is a minefield. That's true no matter how it's resolved, even if the Reasoners are fully exonerated. There's a train headed down the tracks, Harry, and it's headed right for your firm. You give me what I want, and that risk is no longer on you.

"Still, it's your call. If you want to let your personal vendetta against me work to the detriment of your company, I can't do anything to stop you. Make a decision, but make it now. Just talking with you bores the hell out of me."

The sound of heavy breathing huffed over the line, and Salinger didn't respond for a full twenty seconds. Just when I thought I'd gone too far, Harry finally made up his mind. He would messenger Bernie's files to my home by tomorrow morning.

That job accomplished, I called Joshua Reasoner's office. Not shockingly, I was shunted to his secretary. I left my name, mentioning I was a consultant working on behalf of the school Joshua's late mother once supported.

I received a callback in just ten minutes. Joshua's secretary told me her boss would meet with me at his office at ten the following morning.

In anticipation of that meeting, I spent the next two hours going back through the information I had on the various Reasoner family members as well as the history and current status of the Reasoner financial interests. Joshua was not only the oldest Reasoner family member, he was the person to whom his father had entrusted the Reasoner corporation. He wouldn't give me much, but all I needed was access.

I'd just finished my re-review of the Reasoner family history when our front doorbell rang. A twenty-year-old kid carrying a large box stood on the porch. Harry Salinger had sent Bernie's files in near-record time. I assumed he was eager to avoid another phone call, but I'd take what I could get.

The box was surprisingly light given the time Annabelle told me Bernie had put into the case. Some of the pages were copies of the documents Bernie had kept at home. The case notes, however, were fascinating.

Bernie's aversion to computers was just one of her many idiosyncrasies. Unlike other investigators at the Salinger agency, Bernie wrote all her notes out long-hand, relying on her "poofs" to enter the notes into the agency's computer system. I carried out that task during the year I was in Salinger's employ, but all the notes from the period after I left were still in their original longhand. Fortunately, Bernie's handwriting was good, almost elegant—ironic for a woman once described as a female Mack truck. The notes painted a fascinating picture, far more nuanced than the one recounted by her daughter.

Whatever Annabelle Moffitt believed, her mother hadn't started out trusting Margaret Reasoner's story. Bernie's assessment of her new client—"potentially deluded and borderline paranoid"—left no doubt regarding her initial feelings concerning the case. It made me wonder why Bernie had pushed me so hard to stay. Why ask for help with a client you clearly thought was nuts?

Bernie spent her first few months on the Reasoner case doing background work as well as some basic surveillance, the highlight of which was a bug planted in Joshua Reasoner's Lexus. After an initial "nothing to see here" report to Margaret, she essentially dropped the matter, communicating with Margaret every six months or so to see if anything new had occurred. There was no sign Margaret was annoyed by the lack of progress.

Bernie's assessment changed late last year when Margaret invited her to the mansion. The invitation occurred just two months before Margaret's death.

Much of that visit was a walkthrough. Bernie's notes included a detailed description of Margaret's bedroom, the house's great room, and even the kitchen and staircase.

The rest of the Reasoncr family was notably absent during Bernie's visit. That left Bernie able to interview the household staff, always in the presence of the estate's manager, the unusually named Lawton Summers.

Based on her notes beforehand, Bernie expected nothing new from her visit. It was also clear she trusted the Reasoner's mostly silent house manager as much as she did most individuals, which was to say not at all. Bernie noted that Margaret excused herself during the middle of their walk. According to Bernie, that was when things grew tense.

What happened next was unexplained, but Bernie admitted throwing a teapot against a wall while touring the estate's elaborately ordained kitchen. That teapot exploded within inches of Summers's head. According to Bernie, Summers cleaned up the teapot shards and moved on to the next room as if nothing had happened.

Bernie left the Reasoner home convinced something was wrong, a conviction distinctly different than her mood on arrival. Her handwritten note on the bottom of the page, unsuccessfully scratched out, declared, "Maybe the bitch was onto something after all."

The remainder of Bernie's case notes grew almost comically perfunctory. They described places she had visited, a nearby grocery store, an auto repair dealership, and even a candy shop, without a hint of why she thought these locations were important.

That left me with two possibilities. Either Bernie had gotten spooked—hard to imagine of the always tough woman who had trained me—or she didn't trust her notes to remain private. I was betting on the latter. Given that all investigator notes were kept at Salinger's, Bernie must have thought her employer was compromised.

That possibility wasn't hard to imagine. Harry Salinger, the ultimate survivor, would have done the political calculus right from the start. Harry would have known Margaret Reasoner wasn't long for the world based on actuarial odds alone. If someone was trying to speed up that process, what were a few months to a woman that age?

Salinger would hope his agency could continue as the Reasoner's investigative firm of choice. The rich always need PI's. Once Margaret died, Joshua Reasoner would determine any future business. Providing Joshua with a little advance information on Bernie's investigation would be easy for Harry, not to mention potentially lucrative.

Bernie had no more regard for Salinger than I did. Rightly or wrongly, she would have assumed he was a rat and acted accordingly. The problem was—that left me no closer to determining what Bernie had seen that day in the Reasoner household. If her findings weren't recorded in her home files, just where had she hidden them?

I gave up my speculation when Hannah arrived home. She brought takeout, and we ate an eight o'clock dinner, early by our standards. While eating, I told Hannah where things stood and my frustration with the lack of information. As usual, her advice was on point.

"Bernie was your mentor. It's understandable you're looking at her notes for guidance. All the same, this is your case now. Meet with Joshua Reasoner tomorrow, try to avoid insulting him, and get a firm date for when you and I can visit the mansion. Treat this like it's an entirely new case. You are the investigator, and only your opinions matter. Whatever Bernie saw at that house, I have no doubt you'll see it too. It's only a matter of time."

She added, no longer looking straight at me, "I also have one other bit of advice, though it's not something you're going to want to hear. The people who live in Hunting Valley are unusually rich—that you know—but the village itself is small. The people who live there tend to interact only with one another.

"What if I talk with my parents? They aren't remotely as wealthy as the Reasoners, but I'm guessing they might know something. With my father in Congress and my mother a DA, I'm betting the Reasoners would have seen the advantage of playing up to them both."

Hannah's parents were, to put it mildly, not exactly my biggest fans. That feeling was particularly true of Hannah's mother, Amanda, who had appeared noticeably unhappy when informed that Hannah and I had "reconciled" after the violent ending of our previous case. Hannah's father at least made a show of being intrigued by my identity as a transgender male. Whether that was motivated by genuine interest or political calculation, he could usually manage a smile in my presence. Whatever my reservations, Hannah was right. If I didn't find her parents so god-awful, I might have thought of them myself.

"If you think your mother has forgiven you for getting back together with me, then call them. I thought rich people tended to be tribal. Do you really think they'll give us anything on the Reasoners?"

Hannah shook her head. "Don't overestimate the tribal nature of the rich. You haven't heard some of the conversations I have at my parents' dinner table. I'd say they'd do it for a nickel, but no payment would be necessary. The wealthy knife one another for sport."

Hannah called her parents after dinner, returning with at least one interesting nugget for her time. "I happened to catch both of them at home. My father didn't have much to offer, though he did call Joshua Reasoner a prick. Reasoner is apparently a Republican, so that could have been related to political differences.

"My mother had something more concrete. She said Reasoner Industrial might eventually find itself under indictment. Mom wouldn't give me all the details, but there's a whistleblower involved. Whoever that is identified two issues, both involving the company's detergent and soaps division. The first involves chemical dumping—more burial, really—in some land owned by the company adjacent to one of their Lorain, Ohio, divisions. The ground has been tested, but the Feds have come up empty. They're continuing to look because the site is huge, and the whistleblower wasn't very specific about where the stuff might be.

"The second allegation is a harassment complaint involving one of the two labs at the company's main headquarters. That case also isn't looking very promising. The Feds have made some inquiries, but no one will go on the record. Unless they do, Mom doesn't see much happening."

I was curious. "I would expect harassment to be a state issue. Why are the Feds involved?"

Hannah sat down next to me on the couch. "I asked the same question. All Mom would say is there might be a civil rights angle. Interesting if true, but I'm not sure it helps you much. Mom did say we should watch out. The Reasoners are rich and dysfunctional, a combination that makes them particularly dangerous."

I would take any information I could, particularly anything of possible use as leverage. Hannah and I went to bed, and I woke up early the following day for the hour-long drive to the Reasoner company headquarters.

Located in Elyria, the Reasoner corporation was housed in a fifty-year-old building constructed by Edward Reasoner's grandson after the firm's rapid growth made the original headquarters far too small.

Pulling into the Reasoner's giant parking lot, I found the main building depressingly nondescript. Whatever skills Edward's grandson had exhibited in growing the business, he had inherited none of his grandfather's architectural acumen. I parked my Volkswagen and went inside.

The downstairs security guard, eventually convinced I had no interest in shooting any Reasoner employees, escorted me to an elevator that looked as old as the building itself. After pressing the eighth-floor button, I quickly arrived at the Reasoner executive offices, the entrance behind an unusually large old-fashioned oak door.

It turned out the door was not only enormous but heavy as well. I gave it a considerable yank as the gray-haired secretary inside watched my effort with an apologetic expression.

"The door," she told me when I stepped inside, "was the only thing they saved from the original Reasoner building. I can't stand the thing myself, but Joshua likes it."

The Reasoner executive suite included five offices, with the door to Joshua's directly behind his secretary's desk. The security guard had already called upstairs to give them my name and warn them of my potential intrusion. After confirming my identity, the secretary made a quick call and waved me through.

Entering Reasoner's office, I was surprised by two things. The first was Joshua Reasoner himself. The man must have stood at least six foot five. Seated behind his desk, his head was still roughly level with my own. I could easily see why a mere wooden door would have presented little bother to someone his size.

My second surprise—we were not alone. The woman sitting next to Joshua Reasoner had short brown hair and appeared to be in her early forties. She was also noticeably pregnant.

Reasoner greeted me with what I assumed to be a smile. It was painful to watch, and I hoped I would never see the man laugh.

"My wife, Abigail, asked to join us when she heard we were meeting. Given that this is a family matter, I assumed you wouldn't object."

I nodded and sat in the large guest chair directly across from Reasoner's desk. Abigail Reasoner still had not said a word, so I figured I'd start things off.

"This is, as you say, a Reasoner family matter. My employer is the Cranberg School, but I'm coming into this job with an open mind. Your mother, Margaret, set all this in motion due to a fear she might be murdered. That being said, I have no reason at present to view her death as from anything other than natural causes.

"I see this as a fact-finding mission. To obtain those facts, I will need access to both your family and your mansion. I will need at least one week at your home to adequately build my report. While there, I'll also need to meet with your family, including your two brothers, your sister, your niece and nephew, and your respective spouses. I will also expect full access to all of the estate's employees, from your manager to the cleaning and kitchen staff."

Abigail Reasoner picked that moment to jump in. "You want access to our home and our family. How do we know we won't find your pictures and interview notes in some online rag? I have no idea why we're doing this. The old bitch died months ago. The medical examiner said it was natural causes. Why is this coming up now?"

I knew I'd get some form of pushback. I just figured it would come from her husband. I decided to shove right back.

"Why are we doing this? I assume you know the details of your mother-in-law's will much better than I do. I'm not a lawyer, but I have no doubt her instructions are bulletproof. How do I know that? Based on the simple fact I'm sitting here today. You may consider my demands to be an affront to your social station, but you will cooperate. I intend to be fair, but any lack of cooperation on your part will be noted in my report to Margaret Reasoner's designated arbiter.

"I have no wish to breach your family's confidentiality in any way that is not pertinent to this case, and I will sign an agreement to that effect. Besides yourselves, the only people who will be reading my report are my client and the arbiter."

Abigail Reasoner looked ready to argue further, but her husband waved her into silence. He had concerns of his own. The nature of those concerns told me just how far the Reasoner family would go to protect its interests.

"You spoke about your client. I have no doubt you checked us out, Mr. Luvello, but we also did our research. You learned about this case from a meeting with Ms. Annabelle Moffitt. Ms. Moffitt is the daughter of Bernadette Moffitt, an old acquaintance of yours and a woman who had been conducting a virtual war against my family, digging up supposed dirt wherever she assumed it could be found. I'm sure you also know of her mother's unfortunate death just a short distance from my home.

"You say that you will be engaged in a fact-finding mission. How do I know this isn't just about settling scores—one last favor to an old, now-deceased friend?"

Annabelle should have known. The Reasoners likely caught on to her inquiries almost immediately, no doubt from her first contact with the Cranberg School. From there, she would have been followed. I wonder if that job fell to one of Harry Salinger's band of merry men. Annabelle's visit to my home would have alarmed the Reasoner family. What else had they dug up?

Whatever his concerns, I knew Joshua brought up the Moffitts to see if I could be intimidated. Otherwise, he would have kept that knowledge to himself, currency to be spent later when needed. The fact that he told me now was an error on his part. It was essentially bullshit, and I decided to respond in kind.

"You appear shocked I get some cases by referral. Do you think they fall out of the sky? I'll give you something else that'll surprise you even more. The vast majority of my cases are referred by someone with an axe to grind, someone precisely like Annabelle Moffitt. I have to believe Annabelle isn't the first person to have a grudge against your family. If she bothers you, I have to ask myself why."

Joshua Reasoner paused before answering, perhaps wondering if he'd gone too far. When he finally did respond, his tone returned to the icily civil manner he used when I walked into his office.

"It seems like we're going to see a lot of each other. Do you mind if I call you Terry? About Ms. Moffitt, I have no issues with her referral. I just never understood her mother's obsession with my family. A daughter's negative reaction to her mother's death is understandable; I know how this must look from her perspective. My purpose in raising the issue is to ensure Bernadette Moffitt's death won't cloud your judgment to the same degree it has with her daughter."

More rich-person bullshit. "I have no issue with you calling me Terry, and I assume you will have no problem with me addressing you as Joshua. Regarding my objectivity, I have neither the time nor the desire to prove that to you. You clearly investigated Ms. Moffitt's activities, and I have no doubt your investigators gave you chapter and verse concerning my own history. If they'd discovered anything negative, you'd have had me tossed off this case right from the beginning."

Reasoner waved his hand. Whether he was agreeing or disagreeing, I really wasn't sure. There was one more thing I needed him to approve, which might piss him off far more than any perceived bias on my part.

"I assume you're okay with my terms, including full access to your home, family, and staff. Beyond those things, there's something else I'll need you to sign off on to more easily verify your family's innocence."

This time, it was Abigail Reasoner who made a "get on with it" gesture.

"When I go to your home," I continued, "I'll bring my partner with me. Her name is Hannah Page, and she is a detective with the Cleveland police force. I have no doubt her name came up on more than one occasion when you investigated me. Detective Page's instincts are exceptional, and yes, she and I have a romantic relationship. That relationship has never prevented us from successfully pursuing any of our cases. Her presence will not be in a police capacity; she'll serve as a consultant only."

I waited for the explosion, and I was not disappointed. This time, I guessed right—it came from Abigail Reasoner.

"My mother-in-law's will obligates us to go forward with your investigation. That being said, why would we possibly agree to allow a police detective in our home? No crime has been committed here. Ms. Page wouldn't even have jurisdiction if one had been. There are some in government circles who are jealous of the Reasoners and would love to come up with dirt on my family. That includes the police force. There's no way in hell we're letting your little girlfriend into our home."

I wondered briefly about Hannah's reaction if she should ever hear herself referred to as my 'little girlfriend." Holding her back would take a major effort. Before responding, I looked at Joshua Reasoner to see if he had anything to add. He remained silent; perhaps he realized how this might play in his favor.

I addressed my remarks to Abigail. "How you decide to play this is up to you and your husband, but I strongly suggest you reconsider. You're right; the terms of Margaret Reasoner's will do not obligate you to have a police presence in your home. You might, however, want to look at the bigger picture.

"You're worried about what might happen if this

investigation ends up in the newspapers. Such a leak would not come from me. I avoid reporters as much as possible, a fact I'm sure your background checks have already confirmed. Even if the disclosure didn't stem from me, however, that doesn't mean one wouldn't happen. NDAs aside, a leak could come from anyone connected with the Cranberg School or the arbiter's office. Given the number of people involved, a news story is inevitable.

"With that as a given, think of this as a PR campaign. Ms. Page is an investigator with an impeccable reputation within the Cleveland PD, and I like to think I have a similar reputation from my work as a private investigator. You want this matter cleared up as soon as possible, but you need to ask yourself what is more likely to accomplish that goal. An investigation performed only by me, even if it clears your family, could be challenged by competing parties. There is, after all, a great deal of money at stake.

"Now, hypothetically, let's say the results are attested to by both Ms. Page and myself. Under those circumstances, a challenge would be difficult to impossible. Although Ms. Page would not be acting in an official capacity, she knows what it means to lie under oath. With the word of a police detective and a well-known PI, your family's good name would be unassailable.

"If you get a call from a reporter, you can tell them you were so concerned about the integrity of the investigation that you authorized the presence of an off-duty police detective to ensure no doubts would remain once we vouch, as you are certain we will, for your family's complete and total innocence."

Joshua Reasoner remained quiet, and I could almost see the wheels turning.

I couldn't resist adding, "All of this assumes you and your family have nothing to hide. If that's wrong, then Mrs. Reasoner is correct. Having Ms. Page present would make no sense whatsoever."

Joshua Reasoner shook his head, a reluctant smile intruding on his previously grim face. "You should have been a lawyer, Terry. In any case, I'm beginning to see why you've earned your plaudits. I will grant your request. You'll have the access you requested, and Ms. Page can join you in your investigation. Can I assume one bedroom will be sufficient?"

He continued after my nod. "If it works with both of your schedules, you can arrive at the mansion one week from today. Will that be sufficient?"

I nodded once more and stood to leave. Before stepping out of the office, I addressed Abigail Reasoner.

"I want to congratulate you on your pending birth. Have you been trying long?"

I knew the question was intrusive, but I was genuinely curious. Abigail hesitated for only a second.

"My husband and I are looking forward to our son's birth, and yes, we know it's a boy."

She said no more, nor did her husband. I filed away that she never really answered my question.

CHAPTER FIVE

AFTER AGAIN DOING battle with the huge wooden door guarding the Reasoner executive offices—a skirmish Joshua's secretary now found highly amusing—I went home to tell Hannah about my visit. Unfortunately, I forgot about the time. It would be hours before my girlfriend returned.

I called Hannah's cell, worried that one week wouldn't give her enough notice to get the needed time off. Hannah's concern was something different.

"I can probably get the time off. HR has been pushing me to take a vacation for a while. Given that it's March, there isn't anyone else away in the precinct this month.

"The real question is Slovitz. The Reasoners are a political minefield waiting to explode. I'm not sure Slovitz will want me anywhere in their vicinity, and I'll have to give him a heads-up."

Anticipating my objection, she said, "Don't worry. He'll keep his mouth shut. I'm just not sure this is something he'll want me anywhere close to, particularly given the outcomes of some of the other cases you and I have collaborated on."

I could see her point. Captain Slovitz had been Hannah's boss since she became a detective. The previous cases Hannah and I had partnered on ended successfully, but the captain still didn't like me much. I don't think it had anything to do with me being transgender. The captain didn't like anyone outside the police force, and even there, he was a little iffy.

"Just remind him this isn't really a case. Tell him we're on a fact-finding mission, nothing more, nothing less."

Hannah snorted derisively, clearly thinking I was joking. "He knows you too well by now to believe that. I'll ask, but don't expect much."

We ended the call, and I returned to work on the Reasoner case. I first phoned the director of the Cranberg School to inform him of my progress and pending visit to the mansion. He sounded pleased, though I sensed he wasn't getting his hopes up.

Hannah arrived home that evening shaking her

head. "Slovitz signed off on our little excursion. He also said he still wasn't sure why I agreed to get back together with you again."

I couldn't help chuckling. I actually liked the captain.

"He hoped after the Federal Reserve case that you might have finally come to your senses. That I can understand, but he really didn't have any issues about you getting hooked up with the Reasoners?"

"Slovitz had two conditions. I need to make clear to everyone who will listen that my presence is unofficial, with no connection to the Cleveland PD. He also made me promise if we find any evidence that Margaret Reasoner had been murdered, I would immediately refer the case to the Hunting Valley Police Department. He considered informing them beforehand, but he eventually decided against it, figuring it wasn't necessary since I'll be there unofficially."

I spent the next seven days exhausting any additional sources of information about the Reasoners, mostly newspaper articles concerning the company's performance and its importance to the Greater Cleveland economy. The entertainment section articles were devoted primarily to Judith Reasoner and her forays into the art world.

On a more personal note, Hannah and I visited Dr. Sailor's office. I had been seeing the good doctor since the start of my hormone shots, but this visit would be different. My surgery was theoretically in two months. Before it could be officially scheduled, he was understandably pushing me for an answer about what I wanted done.

Hannah had been notably noncommittal on the subject, so I reached the decision on my own. Taking John's advice, I went big and chose a phalloplasty. With that done, we scheduled firm dates for my first two procedures.

Hannah noticeably exhaled after I made my announcement. I quizzed her when we left the doctor's office.

"Was that a good sigh or a bad sigh?"

Hannah shook her head, looking guilty to have been caught.

"It was very definitely a good sigh. I didn't want to say anything since it would have been self-serving, but the idea of you with a micropenis didn't exactly stir the imagination. I still don't love the thought of you getting a follow-up implant, but the final result sounds good to me."

"You know you can always tell me these things. I do value your opinion."

She still had that guilty look. "I know you do, and that's precisely why I didn't say anything. This is your body going under the knife. I would have gladly accepted either choice you made."

I kissed her, and we went home. As my thoughts

returned to the Reasoners, I considered and then rejected the thought of contacting Tomas.

When he wasn't with his girlfriend, Tomas O'Malley used to spend most of his evenings hacking into whatever company and/or computer system had annoyed him at any given point in time. He'd helped me extensively in two previous cases, neither of which would have been resolved without his aid.

That all changed when Tomas left his accounting day job and joined the police academy. He'd done so with the recommendation of Hannah and Detective Franklin Aimes, the computer specialist at Hannah's precinct. Assuming Tomas passed, he would take a similar position at whatever station the department assigned him.

His mother, Maria, hadn't been thrilled by her son's midcareer change. Believing I was to blame, my last dinner at the O'Malley household had included a string of angry-sounding Spanish epithets. I recognized only one—*gilipollas*, the Spanish word for douchebag. I was only aware of that one because Tomas had thrown it at me on multiple occasions. I knew better than to ask about the others. Aware of Maria's temper, I was just glad to walk out alive.

With Tomas tied up at the academy, I was left to my own devices. Having exhausted the few leads in Bernie's Salinger file, I again reviewed whatever newspaper stories I could find on the Reasoners. It was then that I had an inspiration.

The inspiration didn't stem from the stories; instead, I noticed their bylines. I'd reviewed the archives of the *Cleveland Plain Dealer* for the last five years, discovering eight stories that referenced the Reasoners from either a business or social perspective. One of them was a rather dry business article detailing the effect of the pandemic on the Reasoner detergent business. The other seven stories were more insightful looks at the family, all written by the same person.

Patrice Clairview had joined the *Plain Dealer* roughly twelve years ago after a stint at the *London Daily Mail*. I texted John to find out more about Ms. Clairview, hoping his advertising background might provide some further insight.

Though he'd never run into Patrice personally, John told me she had a reputation as one of the bulldogs of the local news scene. When asked why she'd moved here from London, John could only say it had something to do with a political scandal, the story blowing up more on the newspaper than the politician.

"I did some checking after you texted me," John said. "Clairview has a reputation for honesty, but she does nothing for free. If you want information, you'll have to give her something in return."

I had a feeling what that something might be. I called the *Plain Dealer* newsroom to leave a message for Ms. Clairview and received a callback five minutes later. Her accented voice sounded friendly, though I knew not to be fooled.

"Mr. Luvello, how delightful. I'd given up hope that any of us at the paper would ever hear from you. You probably don't remember, but I was the reporter who called you after the Michael Grieve affair. You pretty much ghosted me, then. Tell me why you're calling now."

I explained my interest in the Reasoners, a topic that clearly piqued her curiosity. Rather than give information over the phone, she requested that we meet. We picked a coffee bar next to the *Plain Dealer*'s Superior Avenue newsroom.

I arrived fifteen minutes early but found Patrice Clairview already seated and contemplating some sort of coffee drink that probably cost more than many of my meals. I sat across from her after ordering a Diet Coke, the only non-coffee option on the menu.

Clairview shook her head in mock amusement. "Here I am with the elusive Terry Luvello. You can't believe how thrilled my editor was when I told him we'd be meeting. A transgender detective who shot a serial killer and foiled a Federal Reserve robbery. Yours is a story I could truly sell."

I wasn't surprised, but I needed to redirect the conversation before it got out of hand. "I didn't do any of those things alone. I had a partner in both cases, not to mention the help of numerous others in the Cleveland PD."

She smiled once more. "I'm aware of your partner, the equally elusive Detective Page. She and I spoke once, shortly after the Grieve case. She told me to, and I quote, 'fuck off.' She said if I didn't, she would do certain things to my anatomy which I, though not a doctor, believe to be fundamentally impossible."

That did sound like Hannah, but I tried again anyway. "My real reason for contacting you has to do with the Reasoners. This isn't a case, per se. It's really more of a fact-finding mission. In my research, your name popped up on several news stories. I wonder if you can tell me anything about the family, either good or bad."

She laughed, then caught herself. "First of all, 'good' and 'Reasoner' should never be used in the same sentence. I can give you a bit, but I'll need some sort of quid pro quo. How about I get first dibs on the Reasoner story once the case is over?"

That was a no-go. I had promised confidentiality to both my client and Joshua Reasoner. Reasoner's lawyer had e-mailed me two copies of a nondisclosure agreement, one for me and one for Hannah, within an hour after I left Joshua's office. The agreement only made exceptions for my client and Margaret Reasoner's designated arbiter, and it wasn't something I could or would ever break. Although I had signed no such NDA with the Cranberg School, I'd also given them my promise.

"You're not getting anything about the Reasoners from me. If that's a deal-breaker, I'll just find out what I can on my own. I will, however, give you some background on myself and my past activities, within certain limits, including the two previous cases you mentioned.

That should at least give you a story. I'll leave it to your judgment whether it's worth speaking with me."

Clairview stared at me for a long minute before nodding. "Just remember—you back out on me, and you'll have a lifetime enemy in the press. You may not think that's important now, but you'd be surprised what a negative spin in the newspaper can do to any future business you might get."

We shook hands, and she began her narrative.

"I have one business story and one personal. I was assigned a profile piece on Joshua Reasoner about six months ago. The story was supposed to cover the family history, starting with Edward Reasoner and merging into Joshua as his current successor. I could, I was told, mention the good and the bad. I did my story; you probably read it when doing your research.

"That story did, however, leave something out. When the whole thing was almost ready to print, a whistleblower contacted me. I never got a name, but the man was someone high up within the Reasoner hierarchy. What he was alleging amounted to chemical dumping, but he refused to give me his name. Long story short, my editor refused to allow me to use that information without someone willing to go on the record. Now, we use unnamed sources all the time. It's a gray area, but it does happen. With a family as influential as the Reasoners, however, there was no way an allegation like that would ever get printed without proof."

It matched neatly with the story from Hannah's mother. "How did you leave it?"

"I gave the guy the number of someone I knew in the EPA. I have no idea if he ever followed up, but I heard a rumor the allegation went to the prosecutor's office. Should they indict, the Reasoner stock price can be expected to tank. You haven't told me what you're working on. If it involves anything with the potential for negative Reasoner family publicity, I would start checking underneath my car."

I shook my head. "I've been threatened before. It's an occupational hazard."

She looked suddenly grim. "These people play in a whole different league. You've had people point guns at you, scream at you. That isn't shit compared to what the Reasoners will do. Be careful; you still owe me a follow-up story."

I nodded. "I'm always careful. Sometimes it doesn't work out well, but at least I'm still breathing. Now, you also mentioned a personal issue."

"I'm not sure how important this is, but that family is as dysfunctional as it gets. The personal story stemmed from the same profile piece I just mentioned. For part two of the story, I interviewed Joshua and his wife—there's not much love lost between those two, by the way. We were seated in an open area, and halfway through the interview, Joshua's brother Luke walked through. I assume he was trying to get to whatever room was on the other side. I didn't think anything of it, but Joshua stood up without a word and promptly cold-cocked his brother before Luke even said a word."

Now this was fascinating. "What happened afterward?"

"His wife stepped between them, pointing at me for emphasis. Luke just stood up and left, still without speaking. Joshua sat back down. He started to mumble something in my direction but then caught himself while his wife went back to the last question I'd asked. They wanted to pretend nothing had happened and dared me to say otherwise."

"Did you ever speak with Margaret Reasoner?"

She paused for a second. "I did once. That woman is a sharp old bird. My impression? She's smarter than the rest of her family combined."

Ms. Clearview had no more insight on the Reasoners. We finished our drinks, and I handed her my card.

"I expect this to be over in two weeks, and I'll call you after it's done. We can arrange another meeting, and I'll give you what I can about some of my more notable cases. It won't include the Reasoners, but that's the best I can do."

Clairview had one more thing to add and caught up with me on my way out. "Just watch yourself. I said that already, but you don't want to find yourself face down in some stream in Hunting Valley."

We were almost to the door, and I stopped. "What

do you know about Bernie Moffitt?"

"Just what you do. She was investigating the Reasoners on behalf of their mother. As I said before, dysfunctional isn't nearly a strong enough word when describing that family. Like you, Bernie contacted me to see what I knew. Now she's dead, and I don't even remotely think that's a coincidence."

With those comforting words, Clairview walked out the coffee shop door.

CHAPTER SIX

DAY ONE

I TOLD HANNAH what I learned from Patrice Clairview after she arrived home that evening. Already aware of the dumping investigation through her mother, Hannah was far more interested in Joshua Reasoner's assault on his brother, particularly given the setting.

"It could just be typical brother-to-brother crap, but you have to wonder if this was something else. Luke Reasoner's not involved with the company, so whatever it was must have been personal. What happened afterward also speaks to Joshua's arrogance. A reporter wouldn't overlook something like that if they interviewed anyone else. For the Reasoners, the fight was just business as usual."

I had been getting dinner ready, and we sat at our kitchen table.

"You might have understated his arrogance based on what I saw during our meeting. That being said, Reasoner did promise his family would all be present for our stay. I asked about the household staff, and he gave me five names. All of them were working at the house at the time of his mother's death, and all are still at the house now. I expected more turnover, but Abigail Reasoner told me they pay the staff well."

Our discussion switched to packing. For me, that meant jeans and T-shirts, but Hannah's fashion decisions were more complicated. After being forced to look at three beige shirts, all essentially the same, I finally recommended she take her entire wardrobe and bring more suitcases. Sex was off the table that evening.

The following morning, Hannah finally pared her clothing down to two suitcases. When added to my one, our personal items easily fit into the back of her BMW. At Hannah's suggestion, we chose to take her car for this trip. Neither of us was sure they would even allow my Passat into Hunting Valley.

Hannah appeared thoughtful as she drove. "I know you'd like to find some nefarious plot, but the whole murder-the-old-lady scenario seems highly unlikely. Margaret Reasoner was in her eighties. She was looking at three to five more years tops. Why risk killing her off when her death was inevitable before too much longer?"

I had been thinking the same thing. "I agree, but there's something else that bothers me. I looked through all of Bernie's notes, the ones she kept at home as well as the ones in her Salinger file. We know Margaret Reasoner disliked her family, but Bernie never wrote down the reason why. One would assume it was the inheritance, but what if that's not it? From everything I read, Bernie first assumed Margaret was paranoid. Something changed Bernie's mind, and she became obsessed with finding the truth. I want to figure out what that something was."

With that, we pulled past an open gate onto the Reasoner's picturesque driveway. We then reached another gate, this one with a security booth. Hannah stopped and gave the guard our names. After checking a list, he raised the barrier and waved us through.

The house itself was breathtaking. It truly did look like a castle, and I expected to see archers on the parapet that ran along the mansion's gray roof. The word formidable came to mind, almost as if the Reasoner's massive home was sizing us up to see if we were truly worthy.

Hannah parked in a small open concrete lot just to the right of the mansion. The lot had space for at least ten cars, five of which were filled with older-model vehicles likely belonging to the household staff.

Hannah and I exited her BMW and grabbed our

luggage. As we approached the house, I heard her prolonged intake of breath. Her parents' Hunting Valley home was big, much larger than any I had been to previously. The Reasoner home was at least three times the size of the Page estate.

I envisioned an armed escort, but we made our way down the covered walkway unimpeded until we reached the front door. There, we were met by one of the Reasoner's uniformed household staff, a smiling blonde woman who introduced herself as Erin. When she escorted us inside, we met our first Reasoner sibling.

Judith Reasoner almost ran into us as we entered her home. She held a painting, and from the disgusted expression on her face, it seemed the artist had annoyed her somehow. Her grimace was so intense that I imagined the poor canvas headed for a bonfire.

Judith stopped when she saw us, likely wondering who let these interlopers inside her multi-million-dollar home, one of whom even dared to wear jeans. She looked at us, and Hannah and I looked back. Neither of us was sure what the social protocol was among the ultrarich.

Finally, Judith spoke, staring at me. "You're the private detective. Joshua told us you would be coming."

Hannah was still taking in the house, but I figured I should try to be polite. "I'm guessing you're Judith Reasoner. You weren't going to attack us with that painting, were you? We really don't mean you any harm."

Judith looked at the canvas as if she'd forgotten it was there. Her attention focused once again on her artwork. "I told the framer I wanted a gray matte boho frame. Does this look like a gray matte boho frame to you?"

I'd brought two pictures over from my old apartment. One was of my mother, and the other of Hannah. Both were in identical eight by ten metal frames I bought in a two-for-one sale at Walgreens.

Hannah might recognize a boho frame, but she'd decided to let me flounder. Luckily, I was rescued by the friendly Ms. Erin.

"I'm taking Mr. Luvello and Ms. Page up to their suite, Ms. Reasoner. I suspect they'll want to come down and speak with you after they get settled." Judith moved aside before I was forced to confess my ignorance. We mounted the grand stairway and followed Erin to our rooms.

Our suite was huge; there was no other way to describe it. With its own bathroom, a king-sized bed, and a small study, the space was three times the size of my old downtown apartment. Erin left us alone after telling us that dinner would be served at seven.

Hannah was snickering as I shut our door.

"All fun aside," I said. "What the holy hell is a boho frame?"

She shook her head in mock disgust. "Boho is short for bohemian. I can't believe you've been alive for thirty years and never run into a boho frame. The whole thing was rather hilarious. When we sit down with Judith for real, I'll make sure to mention you're a fan of the arts."

"You laugh, but if someone makes a sports reference, I'm going to turf that one over to you. For now, let's have a seat on our mammoth bed and figure this out."

Hannah joined me. "What's your plan, oh transgender Sherlock Holmes? I know you have one. You always do."

Transgender Sherlock Holmes? I did have a way forward in mind, but I wanted Hannah's buy-in to see if I'd missed something. Before I started talking, Hannah pointed silently at my suitcase.

I'd almost forgotten—Sherlock Holmes never would have. Hannah and I had discussed the possibility of our room being bugged. While she launched into a running dialogue about her impressions of the house, I pulled out a pen-like device from my suitcase.

I was, as Hannah had often noted, a tech junkie. Most private detectives are, if only as a matter of necessity. My limited budget kept me from going too far, but the seventy-dollar hidden microphone/camera detector had proven invaluable in the past. As Hannah continued talking, I circumnavigated our bedroom as well as the bathroom and study.

The device was multifunctional. It would search for signals from wireless bugs as well as miniature cameras. I wasn't so much worried about the latter, but the

Reasoners attempting to overhear our conversations seemed plausible.

Sure enough, I found bugs in the main room and the study. The bathroom was thankfully unmonitored. At the mild beeps from my device, Hannah responded as I knew she would.

"Before you get to telling me your grand plan, I'd like to take a shower. The one here looks bigger than our entire bathroom at home, so you are more than welcome to join me."

I agreed, even though I knew sex was not on her mind. We entered the bathroom—it truly was enormous—and Hannah turned on the shower. I closed the door, and we leaned against the marble countertop housing the five-foot-long double sink vanity.

Hannah turned to me. "You were right. Those bastards don't exactly play by the rules. Should I assume you want to keep the bugs in place?"

"Nothing in their family history told the Reasoners they need to play by the rules. That's how they got to where they are today. Let's keep the bugs operating. At some point, that may work to our advantage.

Hannah looked thoughtfully around the room. "Since constant trips to the bathroom will be taken as a commentary on their food or our sex life, did you also bring some notebook paper?"

"I brought four pads, two for moments like this and the other two for open use when we're interviewing the family and staff. For our conversational notes, just remember to get rid of anything you write. I wouldn't be surprised if the staff has been told to search our room when we're elsewhere around the house."

Hannah nodded. "That brings us back to my first question. Just what exactly is your plan?"

"We'll start at dinner this evening. That'll allow us to talk with the family as a unit just to ensure we're all on the same page. I want to begin with the staff interviews. They may be well paid, but the staff don't have the same stake in this investigation as the family. I'm guessing they may have noticed things, details that may help us when we get to our interviews with the Reasoners."

Hannah shifted slightly before speaking. "From what you told me, Joshua Reasoner's not stupid. He may insist on someone being present for the staff interviews, if not a family member, then at least the majordomo."

I looked at Hannah in disbelief. "That's why I bring you on these things. I thought majordomo was a word they made up for old movies. No one ever told me it was real."

Hannah shook her head, clearly reconsidering the whole Sherlock Holmes thing. "A majordomo, you idiot, is the head of household, essentially the house manager." She inclined her head toward the shower. "I thought that might have had something to do with why you brought me."

I was suddenly hopeful. "We don't have to be down

for dinner until seven, and I somehow doubt the Reasoners will run out of hot water."

Whether it was me or the promise of hot water, Hannah and I spent a very enjoyable hour in the Reasoner's oversized shower. Afterward, we dried off and dressed for dinner. That meant Neiman Marcus for Hannah, Lees and a T-shirt for me.

Hannah looked at me disdainfully on our way to the main dining room. "I can't figure out whether you're trying to make me look good or you really like that outfit. Do you own anything else besides T-shirts?"

We've had various versions of this conversation numerous times since Hannah and I met. She'd once bought me a Michael Kors polo shirt in the hope of improving my fashion sense. That effort ended when I wore it to mow the back lawn. I have received no further clothing gifts since.

"You don't need me to make you look good. As far as my outfit goes, I like jeans, and I like T-shirts. I've worn a suit on occasion, but if I did that too often, I'd lose my PI license."

Hannah shook her head, and we walked the rest of the way to the dining room in silence.

Like the rest of the mansion, the Reasoner dining area was massive, its table capable of seating your average football team. Though we got there at seven, it appeared we were the last to arrive. I counted eight Reasoners—the whole clan based on what I knew going in.

I had already met Joshua and Abigail. Joshua was seated at the far end of the table, no doubt where his father had sat before him, with Abigail at his side. Next to Abigail was Joshua's brother, Matthew, and a short-haired blonde woman I assumed was Matthew's wife, Emily. Luke Reasoner, the black sheep of the Reasoner family, was seated two seats farther down. I wondered if he'd been relegated to that position after his fight with Joshua.

On the other side of the table was Judith Reasoner, the only other family member we'd met so far. Next to Judith were her son Mark and daughter Lydia. Other than Joshua, Mark was the only Reasoner who looked up when Hannah and I arrived. As far as the others were concerned, we might have been the hired help.

Not for the first time, I was struck by the family's biblical first names. Joshua, Matthew, Luke, and Judith—it was as if Margaret had named them in the vain hope a religious tie might lessen the family's notoriety.

Not sure about protocol, Hannah and I sat away from the others toward the opposite end of the table. Joshua watched us closely and immediately insisted we move closer. That move placed us next to Lydia Reasoner, who, if she noticed the intrusion, gave no sign. Judith's daughter was extraordinarily pretty, much more so than her mother, with blonde hair and deep green eyes. Her quiet, almost solemn look made it appear she was contemplating some sort of tragedy. Wrapped in the solitude of her own thoughts, Lydia stared intently at her place setting.

Our entrance triggered the arrival of the food. I grew up in a meat and potatoes household. I wasn't sure what rich people ate, and I just prayed this meal would be recognizable.

Fortunately, my wish was granted. Two house staff brought plates filled with pork roast, au gratin potatoes, and green beans. It was surprisingly good compared to what I imagined we might be served.

I got in just three bites before the fun started. Joshua stood then and made the formal introductions. From there, he got to the reason for our visit.

"As you all know, Terry Luvello and Hannah Page are here to perform an investigation to satisfy the terms of Mother's will. You all know why, and I won't dignify her allegations by repeating them. They will be interviewing each of you, along with the household staff."

As he spoke, a tall, bespectacled man wearing a vest entered the room and stood to Joshua's right. I guessed this was Hannah's majordomo.

Joshua Reasoner glanced at us and pointed to the new arrival. "Standing next to me is Lawton Summers, our estate manager. I have asked him to take you on a tour of the house. For your convenience, I have also asked him to be present when you interview the staff."

"No." Not quite a shout, my answer still came out louder than I intended. Joshua Reasoner appeared more startled than angry. I was betting no one other than his mother had ever said that word to him in his household. His younger brothers also seemed confused.

Joshua stood up. "What do you mean, no? I will remind you this is our house, and we are setting the rules. You will follow them, or you will leave."

He stood, so I figured I should as well. I glanced quickly at Hannah, but she remained seated, still eating her pork.

I never even considered backing down. "You're forgetting something. The rules we're playing under were set by your mother, not either of us. Your mother's will specified an impartial investigation, and that's exactly what I'm here to conduct. I will certainly interview Mr. Summers, but that interview, like all the others, will be with him alone. That includes the house staff, your sister and brothers, and your niece and nephew.

"You can throw me out, though wasting this roast would be a shame. It would be even more of a shame if I had to tell my client and your mother's designated arbiter that I was not allowed to conduct a proper inquiry. I'm not a lawyer, but that would seem like a clear abrogation of the terms of the will. "

Matthew and Abigail both also stood. Who was I, dressed in jeans and a T-shirt, to challenge the eldest Reasoner? In the old days, they would have just had me shot. Given Bernie's fate, perhaps I shouldn't entirely discount that possibility.

Joshua gestured his wife and brother back to their

chairs and sat down. He waited, clearly expecting me to sit as well. I remained standing. I wanted to hear his answer.

He finally spoke. "You're quite correct. We are, for now, still living under our mother's rules. You will get your one-on-one interviews, but that deference will end once your engagement is complete. When would you like to start?"

It was subtle, but I recognized a threat when I heard one. I sat and decided to dial things down a bit. "Your offer of a tour with Mr. Summers is much appreciated. Ms. Page and I would like to see the entire estate, including your mother's bedroom."

Joshua had no objection. Hannah and I spent the rest of the dinner eating and answering non-case-related questions from the Reasoner clan. Most of them were aimed at Hannah, a number of those inquiries involving her parents and growing up nearby. The most interesting questions, however, came from Luke and Lydia Reasoner.

Seemingly unable to take his eyes off Hannah, Luke Reasoner asked if her looks were ever a detriment to her career.

I couldn't help being amused. If the question was a prelude to an attempted seduction, Luke Reasoner was in for a very rude awakening.

Hannah wasted no time in proving me right. "I've found that most guys who hit on me are trying to compensate for something. I brought the issue up once to the police psychologist after my first shooting. He said something about men seeking to substitute my gun for theirs." In response to the wide-eyed stares from around the table, Hannah added, "You don't have to worry about the shooting. I can tell you my bosses weren't. The second time I killed someone, they didn't make me see anyone at all."

Hannah had two sessions with the department therapist after shooting Michael Grieve. With the shooting justified and Hannah not the slightest bit regretful, those sessions consisted of check-the-box questions and a quick okay for her to return to duty. Still, it was a good story. Not surprisingly, Luke seemed to lose all interest in my girlfriend.

Lydia Reasoner did not. She turned to Hannah, shifting her focus from her now-empty dinner plate. "Growing up, did you ever imagine yourself in the position you're in now?"

Hannah glanced at me, not quite sure how to respond. I shrugged, so she tried her best.

"I didn't grow up intending to become a police detective. It was a career decision I made after college."

Lydia seemed surprised at the answer. "I think I'd like to become a detective. I've read all the Karin Slaughter Will Trent novels. I'm up to book nine already—unfortunate, because I think there are only two more.

"If I couldn't be a detective, I'd be a CIA spy or

maybe Mata Hari. I've never been quite sure which, but I always thought arresting someone might be fun."

Judith picked that moment to step in. "My daughter has quite the imagination. Her IQ was tested at 141, so I'm sure that plays a role." Turning to Lydia, she asked, "Would you like to return to your room and listen to music?"

Lydia stood up without a word and exited the dining area, headed, I assumed, for her suite. Her mother turned to Hannah in apology.

"You have to excuse my daughter, Ms. Page. Lydia suffers from what her psychiatrist calls a 'fantasy-prone personality.' It's a disposition rather than a disorder. It describes a person with a deep involvement in fantasy, what my mother would call an overactive imagination."

His words barely audible, her brother Matthew muttered, "A fancy term for saying she's delusional."

Judith's reply was pure ice. "She's not delusional, and it's not something that can be fixed. Despite what my brothers might think, I'm not sure you'd want to. It does make it difficult for Lydia to deal with the real world." Looking at her brothers, she added, "That isn't a reason for her to be on drugs."

Matthew turned away, and Joshua picked that moment to cut in.

"I'm assuming Lydia's...condition will not be part of your report?"

We were investigating his mother's death, and he

was concerned about me divulging his niece's psychological state.

"I see no reason why it should be. We'll only include those details relevant to your mother's death."

Joshua seemed satisfied with my answer. Everyone had finished their food, and the Reasoners excused themselves to do whatever the rich did at night.

That left us with the ever-vigilant Lawton Summers. He motioned for us to follow, still not having thrown a word in our direction.

I was curious. "What did you do before you joined the Reasoner household, Lawton? I was thinking stand-up comic or maybe motivational speaker."

My humor rarely worked in these situations, particularly with someone who likely made twice as much as I did for running a single household. We followed Lawton out of the dining area.

Our tour started in the great room. Once outside the hearing of the Reasoners, Summers turned into a veritable font of information. The tour included details about the current house as well as its history. This was the first time I'd heard the mansion's Shadow House sobriquet from someone associated directly with the Reasoners. He told us it was given to the home by one of Edward Reasoner's first guests, a friend from his old rum-running days across Lake Erie. The name seemed strangely appropriate, given the shadows both inside and outside the mansion.

Our tour also included the fitness center and the gourmet kitchen with an adjacent breakfast nook for the staff. We got our first clear view of the infinity pool through the great room's main window. Summers told us the majority of the rooms in the mansion had a view of the pool. Outdoors, we visited the fishing pond, the volleyball court, and the mansion's four patios. The grounds covered sixty-four acres, all remarkably tended with some of the most beautiful flowers I had ever seen, whose names I wouldn't even remotely remember.

After our walk outside, Summers took us back in to show us the rest of the home. The first floor included a twelve-seat movie theater and a large open room with a bar, a 150-inch TV screen, and what looked like the most up-to-date gaming equipment on the market. If I'd brought John, he'd likely never leave.

Joshua and Abigail occupied the primary suite, the only living area on the first floor. Their suite was not part of Lawton Summers's tour.

Our walkthrough also bypassed the occupied second-floor suites. I asked Lawton which of the rooms had been used by Margaret Reasoner before her death. Without a word, he led us to the suite at the end of the corridor.

Margaret's suite was larger than the one Hannah and I occupied. It was, Lawton told us, the largest on the second floor. That brought a question from Hannah.

"Margaret Reasoner was in her mideighties when

she died. Are you telling me she climbed that flight of stairs on a regular basis? She would have had to do it at least twice per day since I'm assuming she ate breakfast and dinner in the dining area. Why didn't she stay in the big suite downstairs?"

Lawton Summers had remained deliberate throughout our tour and took more time to answer Hannah's question. Before speaking, he pointed to a narrow door at the end of the hallway next to Margaret Reasoner's room. I'd assumed it was a storage closet.

"I should have told you earlier about the elevator." Summers opened the door to reveal a long compact lift. "It's not large; a tall man might have to crouch. It worked fine for Margaret's purposes, however. The elevator cage extends farther back than you might think. That allowed the staff to transport meal carts, laundry baskets, or anything else they might need to move back and forth.

"The elevator's location was one of the main reasons why, when Margaret gave up the first-floor suite, that Joshua insisted she take this set of rooms. Margaret used the elevator for the first few years after Harold's, death. As she grew more infirm, she chose to come downstairs less often. All her meals were brought upstairs by one of the household staff."

"You said the proximity of the elevator was one reason Margaret took this room," I asked. "What were the others?"

Summers hesitated. "The placement of the rooms

influenced Margaret's choice even more than the elevator. This suite was the only occupied one, other than your own to the left of the grand stairway. Margaret's children and grandchildren are all on the right. Things began to sour between Margaret and her children after Harold's death. Let's just say Margaret truly valued her privacy."

"You said she came downstairs for meals until the last year before her death. That must have been rather awkward, given Margaret's ill feelings."

"I may have been guilty of overstating just when that rift began." Summers now seemed eager to move away from the topic. "Margaret often got into arguments with Joshua and Matthew after Harold passed away. Those arguments were typically over company matters. When Harold was alive, he often included Margaret in business discussions along with the two boys. That made him truly ahead of his time, at least in many respects. From what little I observed, Margaret was a significant contributor to those discussions.

"When Joshua took over, business discussions typically were limited to Joshua, Matthew, and Joshua's wife, Abigail. I believe her exclusion hurt Margaret considerably and formed the basis for her anger. Still, Margaret continued to eat with her family during that period."

Summers paused before continuing, perhaps fearing he'd said too much.

"Margaret's behavior changed more markedly a month or two before her death. At that point, she chose to stay almost exclusively in her room. I'm not a psychiatrist, but my mother suffered from Alzheimer's disease. She became increasingly paranoid, convinced that some of the nursing home staff were out to kill her. I only mention this because I noticed the same level of paranoia from Mrs. Reasoner. The memory issues may not have been there, but the paranoia definitely was."

I looked closely at Summers and caught no signs of evasiveness. Was he correct? Was this a case of simple dementia?

Summers opened the door to Mrs. Reasoners' old suite, and the three of us went inside. Standing near the old-fashioned king-sized bed, he told us the suite had been unoccupied since Margaret's death.

Hannah and I began opening the dresser and desk drawers. Finding nothing, we did the same in the bathroom. We didn't find a single item that pointed to the previous occupant.

"What happened to Margaret's things when she died?" I asked. "I assume there must have been a considerable number of items. The desk alone looks well used. The carpeting is worn underneath, like a desk chair had been pushed back and forth."

"All of Margaret's personal effects were boxed and taken to the attic," Summers responded. "They were mostly clothing, books, and vacation pictures."

Interesting. I didn't realize the mansion had an attic. Hannah asked if Margaret had a computer or a diary.

"That's a definite no. Margaret had an older person's mistrust of all things technological. I don't remember her ever writing in a diary. If I'm wrong, that should have been stored with her other items upstairs."

We asked Lawton to take us to the attic, and he again hesitated, this time for more personal reasons. "The attic isn't pleasant, though we have had it fumigated recently. I'll take you up, but I'm a bit of a germaphobe. Beyond the addition of the elevator, the attic hasn't been renovated since Edward Reasoner originally constructed the house. I can show you where Margaret's items are, but you'll be walking on what are essentially loose floorboards. It happened before my time, but I'm told one of the staff fell between the boards and ended up knocking a hole in the ceiling of what is now Judith Reasoner's suite."

I looked at Hannah, who just shrugged. All cops and PIs have been in their share of old buildings.

Three people were a stretch for the Reasoner elevator, but we made it work. Summers pressed the old-fashioned push-button control panel, and we ascended slowly and quietly to the top floor.

Summers had, if anything, understated the condition of the attic. The room appeared to extend the length of the mansion, though very little of it seemed in use. Pull-string ceiling fixtures provided lighting. Summers turned them on as we moved forward.

Hannah and I followed our guide to the middle of the room, stepping carefully as the boards did, indeed, move under our feet. As we approached a pile of boxes Summers identified as Margaret's, my left foot went between two boards. I had a sudden image of falling through not one but two ceilings and ending up in Joshua and Abigail Reasoner's suite on the first floor. I figured I should wave to both as I landed. That seemed only polite after such an unexpected intrusion.

Summers apologized then, asking if he could be excused to attend to household matters. It seemed our distinguished household manager didn't wish to remain in the attic any longer than absolutely necessary.

Hannah and I went through the boxes one by one. Summers had been correct about their contents. Most contained clothing items, likely costing well over what I made in an average year. Pictures filled one of the other boxes. Many of those had been taken thirty to forty years prior, with Joshua, Matthew, and Luke in their middle teens. Primarily vacation photos, they showed the family smiling on what were clearly happier days. Hannah recognized one alpine resort as a place she'd traveled to with her parents.

"I'm amazed Summers left us alone with all this," she said. "Some of this clothing is really expensive. Either this attic must really spook him, or there are some kind of hidden security cameras up here."

I think she was joking about the cameras, though I'd put nothing past the Reasoners. Unfortunately, we found no diary or anything else used by Margaret Reasoner to record her thoughts. We put her items back in their designated boxes and retraced our route to the elevator, making sure to turn off the lighting. We returned to the second floor via the lift.

Now 10:00 p.m., Hannah and I decided to regroup in our room and plan for the next day. Joshua Reasoner had already provided me with the names of the house staff. With Lawton Summers's buy-in, we could set up a schedule for our second day.

As Hannah and I entered our suite, I motioned to the bathroom shower, our version of a cone of silence. Hannah had a different idea. At the far end of our living room, she opened the doors to a large cabinet we had yet to explore. There, we found a midsized TV with a remote sitting in front. Hannah pressed the power button, turned up the volume, and indicated I should join her.

"Summers said we're the only ones on this end of the stairway. If we turn up the volume, no one should complain about the noise. Not that I have a problem showering together, but this makes our intentions a little less obvious."

She was right. We sat on chairs in front of the TV, ironically an old *Columbo* episode, though the volume was far louder than I usually would have liked. That being said, it would confuse even the closest bug.

Since Peter Falk was in his "just one more thing" climax to the show, Hannah and I watched for a few seconds before we began.

Turning to me, Hannah said, "I have to buy you a raincoat."

I hoped she was joking. "You're going to buy your transgender boyfriend a *Columbo* raincoat? I couldn't walk fifty feet from our home without being arrested."

Hannah just shook her head and began in on the case. "Speaking with the help and the family is fine, necessary even, but we really need to talk with the medical examiner. A woman in her mideighties dies in bed; there almost certainly wouldn't have been an autopsy unless the family requested one. Still, I want to know if the ME noticed anything. That could be as little as a few fibers from a pillowcase."

I had already thought about the medical examiner. A few days prior, I'd applied pressure through the Cranberg School's always-eager attorney.

"You and I are meeting with the examiner at 2:00 p.m. tomorrow. That should allow us to complete our interviews with the staff and do any follow-up with Summers should that be necessary."

"What about tonight's walk-through with Summers? That wasn't as much a dead end as I thought it would be. The upstairs corridor is twice the length of our house. With Margaret the only occupant on this side, someone walking into her room could have easily gone unnoticed."

"It's not just the corridor," I replied. "The elevator door is right outside Margaret's room. A quick trip up, and you're right there. You wouldn't have to walk up the stairs, and the elevator is relatively quiet. You would never be seen unless someone was standing in the hallway.

"The other thing that struck me was how Summers described the sequence of events. Harold Reasoner dies, and Margaret begins arguing with Joshua and Matthew about the company's future direction. In some ways, that's to be expected. Joshua wants to put his stamp on the firm, and he doesn't want his mother looking over his shoulder. I suspect Margaret understood his motivation, even if she disagreed. If Summers is correct, Margaret continued dining and interacting with the family during that period.

"It wasn't until a month before her death that Margaret separated herself from her children. That could have been dementia-induced paranoia, but let's assume it wasn't. For things to change that dramatically, I'm guessing the family's disputes became personal. Something Margaret saw, heard, or did led to a conflict that might have resulted in her death. I could buy dementia or some misunderstanding, but Bernie had essentially the same reaction. Like us, she went on a house tour with the esteemed Lawton Summers. She entered the mansion convinced the case was nothing at all. By the time she left, Bernie was on a mission. I don't know what she saw here, but whatever it was persuaded her that Margaret was correct."

"It's thin," Hannah said, "but I think you're right. Something did change, and I'm curious if the staff might have noticed. I'm not sure they'll tell us, but it's worth asking. My parents have three people staffing their home, and I'm guessing those three could write a book about every argument my mom and dad have ever had. My parents pay them well just to ensure that never happens. From what you told me, the Reasoners do the same.

"We should ask Summers which rooms Bernie walked through. The bedrooms were off-limits for our tour, but Bernie went there by invitation of Margaret Reasoner. We need to know exactly what she saw."

Hannah was right, and I reminded myself to ask Summers that question the next time we met. Hannah then had one more observation about the evening's festivities.

"Before we go to bed tonight, can you stand up and shout "no" again? I thought that was super sexy, very *Mr. Smith Goes to Washington*. For a minute, I thought we'd get tossed out or fed to the dogs, but it was sexy nonetheless."

"One—I don't think the Reasoners have dogs. They'd be far too messy for their taste. Two—you think Jimmy Stewart is sexy? This is a whole new side of you. I'll have to try out that nice-guy stammer of his."

Hannah shook her head. "Get in bed before you entirely ruin the moment."

"Yes, ma'am, anything you say."

CHAPTER SEVEN

DAY TWO

HANNAH AND I went downstairs at eight for a Reasoner family breakfast of omelets and toast. Only some of the family were present. Joshua, Abigail, and Matthew had already left for work at the Reasoner headquarters.

That left us with Luke Reasoner, Judith, and her two children. Though Hannah and I would eventually meet individually with each of the four, I figured I might as well start asking questions. First, Mark and Lydia.

"I'm curious how you two see this whole situation. You've lived at the mansion your entire lives. Do you ever envision yourselves moving out?"

Mark answered first. "I want to go to Europe. European history was my best subject in high school, and I was also pretty good at French. I tried to talk my mother"—he pointed at Judith—"into the University of Paris. It's not like we don't have the money, but she wanted me to stay in the US."

Judith shook her head. "We've had this discussion many times. You want a history degree, but you have no idea what you'd do with it. Unless you want to teach, the degree itself is useless."

"You have an art degree, mother." Mark's voice turned petulant. "Are you really sure you want to use the word 'useless'?"

I'd hoped they would turn on one another, and this was a start. I turned to Lydia. "What about you, Lydia. Would you like to move out of the mansion eventually? Even if not, you've likely met some young men who'd gladly take you away."

Lydia turned to me, those emerald-green eyes twinkling. "I've decided I want to be a novelist, Mr. Luvello. This house is the perfect spot for me. Writing is the only profession where you get to lie for a living. I've learned so much about lying at the mansion. Everyone here is a liar, and my stories have grown quite vivid as a result. I just need to decide what lies I want to write next."

Her mother and uncle both moved to interrupt. I waved them off as Hannah followed up.

"Can we read any of your stories, Lydia?" I asked.

Lydia turned away from us as if worried she'd said too much. "Everyone here lies, and that includes me. I haven't really written any stories. They're all in my head right now, and they'll likely stay there. My narratives jump from one to the other—sometimes, they just blend together. I do enjoy my life here, however. It's been my version of an education, and I don't even have to go to Paris."

Hannah asked Lydia how she felt about her grandmother.

"Grandma always asked me questions about what I was doing and my plans for the future. I don't think she ever understood writing. The idea of placing yourself in another world where you called the shots—Grandma thought that was too much like Mark's video games. I think part of her was tempted to toss Mark and me out the door. She would have convinced herself it was for our own good."

A curious answer from an even more curious person. I turned to Mark, but Luke picked that moment to stop staring at Hannah and cut our inquisition short.

"You'll have one-on-one time with all of us, so breakfast and dinner should be for more relaxing conversation. Joshua told me your first visit this morning would be with Carol Anne from our kitchen staff. Since you both appear to be finished, I can introduce you to her right now. I assume you'll want to meet in your room."

I couldn't resist. "You're what now, forty-eight, Luke? Isn't that a little old for your brother to still tell you what to do?"

Mark appeared to snicker, while Lydia seemed not to notice. As for Luke, he held his temper.

"We all have our crosses to bear, Mr. Luvello, the price of being born in a family where so much is expected. Walk with me, and we'll go find Carol Anne."

Carol Anne Hemmings proved to be two rooms away, in the breakfast nook finishing her own breakfast. A friendly-looking woman with gray hair, she could have been anywhere from her midfifties to early sixties. After Luke introduced Hannah and me, I suggested we have our conversation outside in the sunny weather.

Luke looked annoyed, no doubt thinking of the bug in our room. He couldn't come up with a good reason to turn down my suggestion, however, so Hannah and I headed for the door to the nearest patio. It was then we noticed Carol Ann remained staring in my direction.

"Have no fear, Carol Anne," Hannah said helpfully. "The dead guitarist on his shirt is just one of several from his collection. It has nothing to do with his paranoid schizophrenia. That manifests in different ways, but I'll be there to keep you safe."

She still looked doubtful, perhaps thinking Hannah was telling the truth.

Finally, Luke Reasoner snapped. "You'll be fine. The

sooner you answer their questions, the sooner we can get rid of them and have our lives return to normal."

Carol Anne followed, and the three of us abandoned Luke for the great outdoors. It really was a gorgeous spring day. We sat on one of the patio benches and listened to the suddenly disgruntled birds in the trees around us.

Maybe it was the birds, but the once reluctant Carol Anne grew surprisingly talkative now free of the indoors. I had deliberately placed her first to interview on my list of household staff. Bernie's private notes had mentioned that she was assigned to Margaret during the last year of her life. That care included meal delivery and any other home care she might need. As a certified nurse aide, Carol Anne also made sure Margaret took her pills when required.

Margaret had apparently liked Carol Anne. According to Bernie, she and Margaret often talked well into the night. I began by asking her about the evening Margaret died.

"Margaret was quiet that night, calm and not appearing overly sick. I took her through the usual routine before she went to sleep. I gave Margaret her pills, something she always hated, then I closed her window. It was early October, but it was still warm overnight. Margaret would use the bathroom a lot during the evening. She had a bladder inflammation that just wouldn't go away.

"Margaret must have opened the window during

one of her trips because I found it raised the next morning. That wasn't unusual for her in the slightest. She liked to hear the damn birds yammering, and they'd start around seven thirty. They would have driven me crazy, but Margaret enjoyed the noise. She said they were better than an alarm clock.

"The birds were making their usual racket that morning, but I found Margaret still lying in bed. I was sure she was sleeping. I shook her twice before checking her vitals."

Hannah asked if Margaret had spoken much the evening before she died.

"She was pretty quiet. It seemed like she wanted to rest, so I gave her the evening pills and got out of there."

This next question would be tricky. I hoped that being outside would make Carol Anne less guarded when answering.

"Tell us about Margaret and her children. We'll keep your answer entirely confidential. Margaret was clearly afraid of something, and I'd like to know what that something was. Did you ever observe any arguments between Margaret and her children or grandchildren? She cut herself off from her family just before her death. Was there something you noticed that might explain why?"

"I heard arguments between Margaret and Joshua almost from the day I arrived at the mansion. Part of that was just Margaret being Margaret, and the rest was due to her husband's death. I started here shortly before

Harold died. From everything I heard, the two of them were extremely close.

"After Harold passed away, Margaret was the senior voice in the family. For the sake of the family's legacy, I think she felt obligated to give her two cents. That said, Harold had left Joshua in charge of the Reasoner corporation, and Joshua wanted to run it the way he wanted."

"What about Abigail Reasoner?" Hannah asked. "While Joshua and his mother were fighting, did she get involved?"

Carol Anne shook her head. "Mrs. Reasoner not only got involved, I think she instigated a lot of it. To Abigail—and she'd kill me for using her first name—being a Reasoner was a status thing. Understand, a lot of what I'm about to tell you now is secondhand.

"Abigail was a midlevel marketing manager when she first arrived at the mansion. It was actually Matthew who brought her home. The two had been dating for about a month.

"Now, Matthew is better-looking than Joshua, though Luke is by far the most handsome of the Reasoner boys. Their looks didn't matter much to Abigail, however. Joshua was number one in the pecking order, and he became her top priority. I heard that Abigail started flirting with Joshua while still dating Matthew."

"The switch in her affections couldn't have gone over well with Matthew," Hannah said.

"It didn't, but Joshua was still the number one son.

There was a family conference between Harold, Abigail, and the two boys to resolve matters. From there, it became a business decision, and Abigail began openly dating Joshua. They were married a year later. When the previous marketing VP resigned, Abigail was promoted in his place."

It was like some demented soap opera. I was fascinated, but we had limited time. "Let's go back to the fights between Margaret and Joshua. Margaret ended her life as a virtual recluse in her own home. If I understand you correctly, you're saying those fights weren't the reason why."

Carol Anne nodded. "You're right about that. During my time with Margaret, she would swear up a storm and tell me Joshua would ruin the company. Later, I'd see the two of them laughing it up at dinner. Matthew would usually be involved as well, despite his past history with Abigail."

"What about Luke?" Hannah asked.

"He's a strange one. He'd never talk to me or any of the other staff. When I brought in the food for meals, it seemed like he just watched everyone else. Abigail was the same way. In her case, I think it was resentment. At what, I was never sure."

"Last question," I said. "What can you tell me about Lydia and Mark?"

"Lydia is what my daughter would call 'spacy.' When I first met her, I thought she was on drugs. Now,

I think it's her personality. Something in that girl's mind isn't connected in the same way as yours and mine.

"Mark is your average rich asshole—assumes he's entitled to everything because of his money. Olivia is part of the kitchen staff, and you'll be meeting with her after you're done with me. Make sure to ask Olivia about Mark. The two of them had quite the run-in."

Hannah and I thanked Carol Anne for her time and candor, promising everything she said would be kept confidential. We then followed her back to the kitchen, where she introduced us to Olivia Santos. A pretty Hispanic woman with long dark hair, Olivia appeared to be somewhere in her late twenties. Figuring we shouldn't fool with a good thing, Hannah and I chose to interview her on the same patio we used with Carol Anne.

Olivia had less to say than her workmate, though she was quite forthcoming when we asked about Mark Reasoner.

"I was on the housecleaning staff when I started with the Reasoners. I'd just turned twenty-one, and Mark was seventeen. When he saw me in the hallway that morning, he told me he'd spilled a drink in his room and asked if I could help him clean up.

"I knew I was in trouble when he closed the door behind me. I saw right away there was no mess on the floor. Mark moved to his bed and asked me to sit next to him. I started to leave, but he said if I didn't do what he wanted, he'd report my family to immigration. Rich people assume all Mexicans are illegal. My mother is Mexican, but my father is a US. citizen. They met when he was working at the embassy in Mexico City.

"I told Mark all this, but he said it wouldn't matter. He said the Reasoners had so much pull he could make it difficult for my mother no matter who she was married to.

"I still didn't move, and he made a grab for my breasts. I'm not proud, but I slapped him hard on the side of his face. The little shit actually started crying. He said I hurt him, and he begged me not to tell anyone else in the family. Mark promised to never do anything like that again.

"I knew he was lying. He might have taken his time, but that asshole would have set me up for something as an excuse to have me fired. It was a Saturday, so I left his room and tracked down his uncle, Matthew. He told me to give him one day to fix things. I figured I'd get thrown out for sure, but Matthew came back before the end of my shift with a proposal. Rather than the cleaning staff, I was reassigned to the kitchen. With that change, I wouldn't have to interact nearly so much with Mark. My salary was also bumped up by seven dollars per hour. The only condition—I could say nothing about what happened. If you tell them I told you, I'll probably be fired on the spot."

From what little Carol Anne had told us, I'd assumed we'd be looking at some faux innocent rich kid grope. As nasty as that would have been, this was something far worse.

Hannah asked if Joshua or Margaret had ever spoken to her about Mark.

"I assume Joshua knew about the arrangement, but he never said a word to me. I'm guessing neither son ever said anything to Margaret. I'm not sure if she would have murdered me or her grandchild, but someone would have gotten killed."

Olivia continued, "I probably should have just left and reported Mark to the cops, but I figured they wouldn't do anything, and I really needed that extra money. I'm only going part-time, but I'm studying at Tri-C to be a physical therapy assistant. I couldn't have done that if I didn't have that bump in salary. I'll be finished in six months. After that, I'll be through with the Reasoners forever."

We thanked Olivia, promising nothing she told us would ever be repeated. Olivia turned to us one last time as she rose to go back inside.

"I probably wouldn't have told you any of this if I wasn't planning on leaving. When Joshua told us you'd be coming, it was pretty clear he didn't trust you. I think that made me believe in you more. If I thought you were working for those assholes, I never would have said anything. I don't know what Carol Anne told you, but I suspect the same is true for her and everyone else working here."

We spoke to four others on the staff that morning. Three were full-time employees, with the fourth working ten hours per week. Rosario, the cook and only male in the group, could tell us nothing about Margaret and the family beyond their menu favorites. The others weren't much more forthcoming, though all confirmed the arguments between Margaret and Joshua regarding the company's future. The most interesting tidbit from those later conversations came from Chloe, a diminutive maid who seemed hesitant to even look in my direction. She told us Abigail Reasoner was always "egging on" her husband.

"I always thought Abigail and Margaret hated each other," Chloe said. "When Joshua's father passed away, I think Abigail viewed that as more of an opportunity than a loss."

We finished our staff interviews at noon. Rather than eat lunch with Cleveland's most affluent dysfunctional family, Hannah and I decided to dine at a nearby restaurant. We informed the ever-present Lawton Summers of our decision, then Hannah drove us to the Benyard Grille, a barbecue place only fifteen minutes from the mansion.

Between bites of a pulled pork sandwich, I asked Hannah what she thought so far.

"We've identified three people with at least something of a motive. Joshua was involved in several disputes with his mother over the company. If his mother found out about the dumping the Reasoners are accused of, that could explain her actions in the months before she died. Abigail is also a suspect. From everything we've heard, she seems like your classic cold-hearted bitch. She started off as a social climber, moving from Matthew to Joshua. Now that she's entrenched near the top of the food chain, who knows to what lengths she'd go to stay there.

"My third person is more of a reach, but what about Mark? Olivia said she didn't think Margaret knew, but maybe she was wrong. Margaret viewed the Reasoner name as a legacy—something to be lived up to rather than be taken advantage of. If Margaret learned about Mark's little rape fantasy, she might have threatened to cut him out of the will. To a shithead like Mark, a man who never worked a day in his life, that might have been a call to action."

I'd been thinking about Mark. "That would also explain what else we heard. Margaret's arguments with Joshua, while heated, were apparently about professional issues. Neither one appeared bothered by their disagreements. Margaret's decision to hide away upstairs seems different somehow, almost visceral in nature. If she learned Matthew and Joshua knew about Mark and swept everything under the rug, that might have been enough to push her over the edge. Would she have gone so far as to threaten one or both about the will? From what we've heard of Margaret's temper, it's at least possible."

Clearly troubled, Hannah put aside her sandwich

and pointed out the biggest flaw in our speculation. "We're sitting here trying to figure out who might be responsible for a murder we don't even know was committed. We can throw around possibilities, but none of them will mean a rat's ass unless we have a crime. You said our meeting with the medical examiner is at two. Unless you intend to finish those fries you're dawdling over, let's get the hell out of here and do some real investigative work."

We drove from the restaurant to the Geauga County medical examiner's office. After a brief stop at the front desk, we were ushered into the office of Dr. Morgan Ho, the chief medical examiner for the county.

Trying to avoid the appearance of an official visit, Hannah didn't show the doctor her badge. I'd already explained the reason for our interview over the phone, so Dr. Ho had come prepared with the file on Margaret Reasoner. After introducing Hannah and myself, I asked about an autopsy.

"Unless they have a knife sticking out of their abdomen, we generally don't perform autopsies on eighty-five-year-old women who die in their sleep," Dr. Ho replied. "If you ask around, I suspect you'll find the same is true of every medical examiner's office in the country. My predecessor, Dr. King, was the examining physician. Under the circumstances, I couldn't agree more with his decision not to perform one."

I looked at Hannah. "That's a good pro tip. If you're

going to kill someone in Geauga County, avoid the abdomen at all costs."

Hannah ignored me, as did Doctor Ho.

I tried again without the humor this time. "I understand only a small percentage of cases indicate the need for an autopsy. Still, your predecessor was present and did an examination. Do you mind sharing with us what he wrote in his notes?"

Dr. Ho looked further through the file. "It appears Dr. King was very cognizant of the potential political impact of this case. Though he didn't perform an autopsy, he took pictures of the body both at the scene and in the lab. He also took blood samples. I can only assume he was looking for poison of some sort. Interestingly, it appears Joshua Reasoner requested the testing."

That was unexpected. Either Joshua suspected something, or he knew what the samples would show. I motioned for Dr. Ho to continue, and he leafed through three pages of lab results.

"I'm finding nothing here out of the ordinary. There are no signs of poisoning by household products or more esoteric toxins such as arsenic, pain medicines, or sedatives. It appears Mrs. Reasoner was taking medication for diabetes, but there was no indication of an insulin overdose."

Despite myself, I was disappointed. Hannah asked about the pictures. There were several, and Dr. Ho laid them on his desk for review.

The first few apparently showed nothing interesting, but he paused on photo number four.

"Hmm." He tapped his pencil on the desk.

Hannah and I waited, both of us holding our breath.

"What do you see?" I asked finally. Dr. Ho looked up. It was as if he had forgotten we were in the room.

"When human beings die, blood pools in their lower extremities. You've probably heard of rigor mortis. The pooling effect is known as livor mortis. This effect results in a discoloration of the skin, which is normally dark purple. Look at this picture and tell me if you notice anything interesting."

Hannah and I studied the photo. Having had much more exposure to autopsy photos than I, she spotted the anomaly first.

"You said dark purple, but her skin is almost blueish gray."

Dr. Ho practically beamed. Hannah, he liked; me, not so much.

"You're right about the color, and it's something you typically don't see. It often gets overlooked, particularly in cases where no autopsy was performed. That color is an indication of methemoglobinemia. I won't go into details, but it's a blood disorder where the hemoglobin in your blood can't release oxygen to body tissues."

He paused there, perhaps expecting us to see the implications. I didn't have a clue. From Hannah's expression, she shared my confusion.

Realizing he was speaking to two cretins, Dr. Ho finally chose to enlighten us.

"The condition can result from many factors, pain killers and herbicides being only two. Most of those conditions would have shown up in the decedent's blood tests. Given that they didn't, my suspicions would turn to the other likely possibility.

"I'm talking specifically about carbon monoxide. CO poisoning seems unlikely given where she was found, but that is my opinion nonetheless."

I looked at Hannah, the wheels turning in both our heads. I asked Dr. Ho just how sure he was of his diagnosis.

"If we had done an autopsy, the poisoning would have shown up for sure. The organs and muscles in a carbon monoxide case tend to take on a distinctive cherry-red coloring. Given what I do have to go on, I can say for certain Mrs. Reasoner did not die of natural causes. The color shown by the livor mortis is a dead giveaway. As far as carbon monoxide is concerned, I would say the odds are 60 to 70 percent. The only thing lowering those odds is the circumstance of her death. If carbon monoxide leaked into Margaret Reasoner's bedroom, the person who found her body would have noticed it immediately. They certainly would have been overcome themselves."

"It's unfortunate," he added, "that CO poisoning

wasn't suspected from the start. Although exposure does affect the blood—that's actually how it kills—the particular blood test used to diagnose the condition is only performed when carbon monoxide is suspected. Dr. King ran all the standard blood work, but I'm sure he didn't even consider CO as a possibility. I can't blame him. Under the circumstances, I wouldn't have myself."

It sounded like an excuse, and I couldn't help asking, "Why wouldn't Dr. King have noticed the livor mortis? You saw the color discrepancy right away."

Dr. Ho shook his head. "You have to take into account the totality of the circumstances. Mrs. Reasoner was in her mideighties. To a medical examiner, a death at that age is routine. Then you add in the fact that her blood tests were normal, and she died in a house where carbon monoxide poisoning would appear unlikely, if not impossible. Doctors are as guilty as anyone else of making assumptions. Based on the facts I cited, those assumptions would almost always be correct. This was the one time in a thousand where they were not. Was the livor mortis missed? Maybe it was, but, again, I might have done the same."

Remembering my flawed assumptions from the Seamus O'Donnell case, I was more than sympathetic. I looked at Hannah. "Carol Anne said she closed Margaret's window that evening before she died, but she found it open the next morning."

Hannah knew where I was going. "She said Margaret sometimes opened it up herself during the night, and

Carol Anne assumed that's what happened in this case. What if she was wrong? What if someone entered Margaret's suite and opened the window after making sure Margaret was already dead? That would have eliminated any trace of the gas. Carol Anne wouldn't have noticed a thing."

I turned again to Dr. Ho. "If a window was opened, how long would it take for carbon monoxide to clear from a room?"

He looked surprised by the question. "I'm not an expert, but I would imagine it would dissipate fairly quickly. A fireman could give you a better idea, but I can tell you that Margaret Reasoner could not have opened that window herself. She would have been overcome long before reaching it, and whoever entered the room the next morning would have found Margaret lying on the floor. If there was carbon monoxide present and the window was opened, that would indicate someone else opened it."

I had one last question. "Given how long Margaret's been dead, I'm assuming even an exhumation couldn't provide definitive proof of carbon monoxide poisoning. Is that correct, or is there something that I'm missing?"

Dr. Ho shook his head. "Unfortunately, you're not wrong. There's no way I'm aware of that you could get proof at this late stage."

Hannah had that predator smile of hers. There was blood in the water, and we both could sense it. Rather than take up more of his time, we thanked Dr. Ho and asked him to keep our conversation confidential. That wouldn't necessarily keep him from talking, but Hannah's mother had vouched for his professionalism. While I wouldn't trust Amanda Page for much, I knew she didn't hand out votes of confidence on a whim.

As we walked to her car, I asked Hannah what she thought.

"It's a possibility, a real possibility. Short of a space heater or something similar, carbon monoxide just doesn't leak into a single room in a house. We need to check back with Carol Anne. I want to know if she noticed anything unusual that morning. If this was deliberate, we'll also have to figure out how the gas was introduced into Margaret's room. It's not like you can buy bottles online."

I checked online as Hannah drove. As it turned out, my girlfriend was wrong. You could buy tanks of carbon monoxide on the internet from any number of suppliers. The uses for the compound were also interesting.

"Carbon monoxide has several industrial applications, including metal fabrication. More importantly, it's also used to manufacture chemicals, including acids and alcohols. Now who do we know that runs a chemical firm?"

Hannah looked grim. "We say nothing about this to the Reasoners until we have some sort of proof.

We arrived at the mansion, and Hannah pulled into

the guest parking area. Exiting her car, we were interrupted by a shot.

To those who haven't heard both, a gunshot seems almost indistinguishable from a firecracker. On a superficial level, they truly are similar. Both are loud cracks, but the sound from a gunshot tends to be deeper and considerably more deafening. The noise from a gun can cause permanent hearing loss depending on one's distance away. Assuming there is more than one, gunshots are also more rhythmic—a human being typically depresses a trigger at a somewhat regular interval.

Being depressingly familiar with both, Hannah and I had no issues recognizing the sound of a rifle. The noise came from the back of the mansion, and we ran to find who or what was being sacrificed to the uncertain whims of the Reasoner family.

We found the answer behind the volleyball court. There, Joshua Reasoner faced a target alongside his brothers, Matthew and Luke. All three held rifles. It was the first time I'd witnessed any sign of camaraderie within the family.

Matthew was the first to see us approaching. He said something to his brothers, and they also turned to face us.

"Relax, detectives," Joshua said. "We may be too old for volleyball, but we have quite an extensive collection of rifles. Some are vintage, and others are new. One or more of us comes out to the range, weather permitting, at least once a week. We've all gotten to be quite good. Even Judith and Lydia use it occasionally, along with Mark."

"Just where are these guns kept?" Hannah asked.

It was Matthew who answered. "There's a walk-in gun safe just off the smaller kitchen. Lawton may not have pointed it out in your tour, but it holds both rifles and pistols. We use the rifles when we're at the range. The handguns are for self-defense should someone break into our home."

Luke then pointed to me and laughed. The sound was not particularly pleasant. "I think Mr. Luvello expected to see his picture on the target. You can relax. Our ancestors weren't beyond shooting a poorly performing servant, but nowadays, we just fire them. We haven't experienced too many deviants, however. I guess we'll just have to wait and see."

I was always amused by people who thought I might care about their insults. Allowing that to happen would require a level of concern I've never been able to reach.

"Actually, Luke, I was worried for your safety when I noticed Joshua holding the rifle. I heard he once punched you during a newspaper interview. From what I understand, it doesn't sound like you're especially good at defending yourself. I guess that's to be expected from someone still sucking off the family tit."

Luke's sneer grew savage, and I reminded myself to stop insulting people holding semiautomatics. Sensing trouble, Joshua and Matthew both stepped between us.

"Families will have disputes," Joshua said, "but it doesn't mean we're not there for one another. Perhaps you and Detective Page should go inside. Dinner will be served at seven."

With nothing more to say, Hannah and I turned and walked away. When we were safely out of hearing range, Hannah turned to me and smiled.

"Sucking off the family tit? Where did you pull that one from, some book of ancient insults?"

"It was something my dad used to say when we visited my Uncle Jack. He was always borrowing money from any relative dumb enough to give him some. Dad finally told him off, though he and my mom got into a big fight afterward."

It was still two hours before dinner, and Hannah and I returned to our room. After cranking up the volume on the TV, we sat on the bed and talked strategy.

"We still don't have enough to go on," Hannah said, stating the obvious. The carbon monoxide angle is fascinating, but it's totally unprovable at this point."

"It is unprovable, though it wouldn't have been if the test had been performed after Margaret died. Dr. Ho told us Joshua requested the bloodwork his predecessor performed postmortem. If this was a planned killing, and Joshua was involved, he'd have been taking an enormous risk. How could he have known what tests would be run? If Dr. King had noticed the odd coloring of the livor mortis, he likely would have tested for carbon monoxide. If that had happened, the whole plan would have been blown right there.”

“While Joshua may be innocent,” Hannah said, “it still doesn’t tell us why he requested the testing. Was he simply trying to forestall any future inquiries, or did he suspect one of his own family members? We’re meeting with Joshua tomorrow, and maybe we should just ask him. He won’t admit anything, but it’d be interesting to see his reaction. We don’t have to mention the carbon monoxide thing at all.”

Her suggestion made sense, but that still left us with a ton of unanswered questions. Hannah and I sat silently for a while, considering our options.

Still frustrated at where things were headed, I began to pace. Hannah watched me for a while before finally breaking the silence.

“Your point about Joshua is a good one. If he suspected something was off with his mother’s death, someone else in the family might have picked up on the same thing. Remember Lydia telling us everyone in her family lies? Even if that’s true, none of them will admit to anything unless we get creative. No matter what we saw at the outdoor range, it’s clear this family has trust issues. You need to turn them against one another and get them to react without thinking. You’re good at pissing people off—it’s kind of your superpower. Figure out their weak points and go after them. I’ll do whatever I can to help.”

She was right, and I thought I knew where to start. Still, there was another side to the problem we also needed to address.

"You're not looking well," I said. "I think by tomorrow you might feel worse, too ill to go down for dinner."

Hannah appeared confused before her smile returned.

I started pacing again. "Bernie saw something in her mansion walkthrough, something that convinced the most cynical person I knew that Margaret might have a real reason for feeling paranoid. We weren't allowed to see the family bedrooms, but I'm guessing Bernie had no such restriction since she was there at Margaret's invitation. Dinner is the only time we can count on the entire family being downstairs. While I'm with the group, you should be free to explore upstairs. If someone's missing from the table and you need to abort, I'll send you a text."

"Why not do the dinner thing tonight?"

"I want to wait until after our interviews with Joshua and Abigail. There's something about the relationship between those two that isn't quite right. I'm not sure what that something is, so it's more of a gut feeling. I'm hoping if I poke a bit, I might be able to find out more."

"What if someone on staff catches me sneaking around?"

"Near as I can tell, the only staff present in the

evening are the kitchen workers and Lawton Summers. He has his own room in the mansion, but Summers appears to stay downstairs during dinner to supervise the staff."

"What about my meal?"

"I'm amazed you survive on stakeouts with your appetite. I'll try to sneak you some food. Worst case scenario—there's always food by the breakfast nook. If anybody sees us, we'll tell them you're feeling better."

Hannah shook her head. "I just noticed you didn't volunteer to be the one sneaking around."

"That's because the family doesn't like me. You, they're not so sure about. Luke wants to sleep with you, but for the rest, it's a class issue. They know about your parents and your upbringing in Hunting Valley. To their minds, you're one of them."

It was nearing seven, so we headed downstairs to dinner. The seating arrangements were the same, with us sitting next to Lydia, who stared absently into the distance. Watching Luke, I wondered if his anger at the shooting range would carry over to the dinner table. He seemed quiet, however, still observing Hannah while barely looking in my direction. Perhaps one of his brothers had warned him before we came downstairs.

Dinner was excellent, a beef roast with potatoes and carrots. Unlike yesterday, the questions for Hannah and me were few and far between. Joshua shared a story about his dealings with the Reasoner company board of directors and a potential new detergent product line. I waited for a break in the conversation. The three hotheads in the family appeared to be Abigail, Luke, and Joshua. I'd already pissed off Luke. I figured it was time to work on Abigail.

"How is the pregnancy going, Mrs. Reasoner? I was wondering if you've had any difficulties given you are—and I apologize for saying this—a bit older than the average expectant mother."

It was, admittedly, a low blow. I wasn't just trying to piss Abigail off, however. My other target was her husband. I was laying the groundwork for tomorrow's interview.

Lydia Reasoner smiled for the first time since our arrival. Gazing around the table, Luke Reasoner also seemed amused. Joshua and his wife just looked angry.

"We were forced to have you as our guests, Mr. Luvello." Joshua's tone was pure ice. "That invitation should be considered a privilege, not a right. Issues over my mother's will aside, I will have you thrown out of here on your ass should you ever insult my wife again."

Having achieved the desired effect, I walked back my comment immediately. "Your husband is correct, Mrs. Reasoner. I overstepped without meaning to. While my question was worded in the worst way possible, I'm really just curious how your pregnancy is progressing."

"I am six months along, Mr. Luvello." Abigail's tone was as icy as her husband's. "My age aside, the doctor has informed me the baby's health is quite good. Joshua and I have been trying to have a child for some time. We're having a son, as I mentioned when we first met. I view him as nothing but a blessing."

So, they had been trying for a while. That saved me from another landmine question. I then turned to Judith, who'd been unusually quiet.

"Judith, at the risk of causing further insult, could I ask you a question? As part of my research, I came across biographical information about virtually everyone in the Reasoner family from Edward on down. That includes all of you seated at this table. The one person I couldn't find any background on was your husband, Calvin. You still hyphenate your last name, so I assume he's deceased or your split was amicable. I'd have guessed the former, but I couldn't come up with a death certificate in the name of Calvin Cairns."

"Can you tell me why this is important, Mr. Luvello?" Judith said, hissing. "You're investigating my mother's death. Calvin hasn't been a part of our household since Lydia was in her early teens. Surely you don't think he's a suspect?"

Hannah had been quiet throughout dinner. She appeared to be concentrating on her second helping of beef roast, perhaps fearing this would be her last dinner for the next two days. Clearly on my own, I turned my attention back to Judith Reasoner.

"I'm a private detective. We tend to be curious by

nature. The lack of information on your husband stood out compared to the reams of newspaper stories on the rest of your family. If you don't wish to answer, I won't push any further.

Judith didn't answer, but her daughter did.

"Daddy went cuckoo," Lydia said, staring straight ahead at some invisible object on the dining room wall.

She pronounced the last word with an almost child-like lilt. Her mother's face went white, as did the faces of every other Reasoner except for Mark. Lydia turned to her mother.

"You might as well tell him. Whatever Terry says, he'll never stop prying until he gets his answer." She then turned to me, again, a youthful earnestness on her beautiful face.

"You won't stop, will you? I've often considered becoming a detective, so I looked you up when Uncle Joshua said you were coming. All the newspapers described you as relentless. I'm guessing that makes you good at your job, though it's likely annoying for those closest to you."

Hannah spoke up for the first time. "You don't know the half of it."

That seemed to break some of the tension. Everyone at the table but Luke smiled. Judith finally gathered herself and addressed my original question, this time to her oldest brother.

"My understanding is the NDAs they signed prevent

them from disclosing any information not pertinent to the case. Is that right?"

Joshua had clearly hoped we could avoid this topic. Finally, he nodded.

Judith turned again in my direction. "I sense my daughter is correct in her appraisal of your talents, so I'll tell you the whole story. My ex-husband Calvin is currently living in an institution. Calvin was an excellent artist, and he loved sketching the outdoor scenery here at the estate. That fondness aside, he never felt comfortable living in the mansion. His episodes started when Lydia was a young girl. I assume you're familiar with the nickname for this house?"

Hannah had told me even before I started looking things up online.

"I know the locals call it 'Shadow House. That was based, I was told, on the number of family members who have died here."

"You're right about the name," Judith said. "We've all heard it, even from those who tend to depend on our family's money. My husband took it a bit too seriously. I started finding him in our room, talking to the walls while pacing back and forth. Eventually, Calvin refused to come downstairs for meals. One of the kitchen staff would take his food to our suite, though even they had grown spooked by Calvin's behavior.

"Ultimately, we had a family conference. My parents felt the best solution would be to send Calvin off for some rest. We did so with the expectation he would be gone for a period of months. As you can guess, that turned out to be wildly optimistic. The facility we sent him to is the best in the state. It's located about two hours from here, just outside of Columbus. Even so, Calvin continued to slide downhill. The last time we saw him, he barely recognized me or the children.

Hannah asked how often they visited.

Judith looked guilty. "Usually, about two or three times per year. We used to go more often, but there just doesn't seem to be a point. Calvin and I are now divorced though I chose to still hyphenate my name."

"Mother's afraid," Lydia said, "that I'm a chip off the old block. I think my grandmother worried about the same thing."

"That isn't true!" Judith said, likely worried we were getting too far afield. "Your grandmother loved you and Mark. She always used to tell me how smart you are. She wished you had more of an interest in the business."

Lydia turned to me. "I am smart, you know," she said matter-of-factly. "I have an IQ of 141. I never understood just exactly what that meant though. What good is intelligence for someone in my situation? I might be much happier with an IQ thirty points lower."

Looking at her mother, Lydia added, "I once overheard Grandma tell you I was looney tunes. She thought Mark was lazy, but she figured he could be fixed."

She had the most curious way of bouncing from

topic to topic. Mark, likely hearing this for the first time, reacted angrily.

"You're lying. She told me I reminded her of Grandpa."

"That's true. She said you reminded her of Grandpa just before they got married. Grandma said it was her influence that turned him around. She hoped some girl could do the same for you."

The tension around the table had risen considerably, precisely what I'd hoped for when we sat down. Despite that success, however, I couldn't help but feel discouraged. I had thought the family turning on one another might lead to some answers. Instead, I'd only managed to expand the field of suspects. If I kept going, I might manage to implicate the entire table. I wanted to ask Lydia about her education, but Hannah beat me to it.

"My mother wasn't in favor of me going away to school, but I have two online degrees from Johns Hopkins University. The first is in biology, the second in English literature. They'll let you take anything if you have the GPA and the tuition money, especially the latter. I completed the requirements for both degrees in just three years."

I don't know what I expected, but it wasn't that. I wondered if Judith might contradict her daughter, but she didn't say a word. Lydia was as smart as advertised.

For a change of pace, I turned to Matthew's wife, the

quietest member of the Reasoner clan.

"Emily, I was curious how you met your husband. I couldn't find any record of you working for any of the Reasoner entities. How exactly did you two meet?"

Matthew was about to object, but Emily waved him off.

"Your instincts about the corporation were spot on; you're just wrong about the person involved. My father was an assistant vice president within the Reasoner detergent division. The company hosts a Christmas party every year for high-ranking employees here at the mansion. My mother had just passed away, so my father brought me instead. Matthew and I literally bumped into each other at the punch bowl. We spent the rest of the evening talking, and that, as they say, was that."

"Since we're discussing personal backgrounds," Luke said to Hannah, "can you tell me just what was in yours that would lead you to date a transgender male? I heard you two met on a case, but why would a beautiful woman like yourself spend time with someone"—he pointed derisively in my direction—"like that?"

He was far too obvious, and Hannah appeared entirely unfazed.

She shook her head. "If you really want to know, it's the sex. None of the so-called real men I met before Terry could even begin to compare. The ones who spend all their time staring at you are the worst. From the ridiculous looks on most of their faces, I figure their manhood is more than questionable."

I couldn't help chuckling. Both of Luke's older brothers did the same. It seemed a good time to excuse ourselves, and Hannah and I went upstairs. After first turning on the TV, I started things off.

"Tell me your thoughts about Lydia."

"That is one weird, mixed-up girl. Assuming what she said about college is accurate, she's also brilliant. Do you think she hated her grandmother enough to carry out this scheme? Which assumes there was even a scheme to carry out."

I'd been pondering the same thing. "By herself, I don't think so. Lydia speaks about her grandmother in a very unemotional tone, almost as if she's come to terms with her situation here. For all her talk about everyone in the household lying, she also seems incapable of telling anything but the truth."

I sat down on the bed. "When we meet with Lydia, I want to ask about her love life. She's a beautiful woman who's never spoken about a male or female partner. She could be asexual, but I'm not sure. She's your classic gothic mystery character."

"Did you notice one of her degrees was in biology? She would be aware of the effects of carbon monoxide, though every adult on the planet knows it's nothing you want leaking into your home."

I again started to pace, then pointed at Hannah. "I

still want to know motive. If carbon monoxide was involved, I also want to know how someone leaked the gas in Margaret's room."

I finally sat down. "It's the motive angle that's really bothering me. This whole situation was personal; at least, it was for Margaret. She separated herself from her family after accusing them of planning her murder. When confiding her fears to Bernie, Margaret never said why they would want her dead. Bernie eventually found that out on her own, and I think that knowledge might have killed her."

Hannah had started taking off her clothes. She was still discussing the case, though my own reasoning skills took a sudden nosedive. "Who are we meeting with tomorrow?"

Suddenly, I didn't have a clue. I searched my memory. "Tomorrow is brother day. We're meeting with Joshua, Matthew, and Luke. Just saying that makes me feel like I'm back in Catholic grade school. Are you still up for doing a little dinner hour exploring?"

"I am, but you better make sure I get something to eat later. The Reasoners may be dysfunctional, but their chef is damn good."

Now naked, Hannah climbed into the king-sized bed. I took my own clothes off quickly, a sudden thought interfering with my mood.

"After what you told Luke, how much pressure am I under to perform?"

"I'll be more than satisfied as long as you don't forget that trick with your tongue. You also have to promise me you won't lose it when they install your newly functional appliance."

My appliance? I felt like a soon-to-be renovated kitchen. "I may need frequent practice to maintain my skills, but I promise I won't forget how."

Hannah spread her legs. Practice tonight would not be an issue.

CHAPTER EIGHT

DAY THREE

OUR MEETING WITH Joshua was scheduled for seven a.m. He'd informed us previously that we would have only one hour, his work schedule dictating the early appointment.

Our on-time arrival required me dragging Hannah out of bed, a task I accomplished after listening to an impressive number of expletives aimed in my direction. After a quick shower, we threw on some clothes. Hannah asked about my strategy before we headed downstairs.

"Nothing special—I'm just going to ask when he found out his wife was having an affair."

She thought I was joking. We knocked on the door of the first-floor suite, half expecting to see Abigail. It was Joshua, however, who opened the door. He saw me glance inside and anticipated my question.

"Abigail left a few minutes ago. We knew you wanted to speak with me one-on-one, and she had an early meeting anyway."

I was struck by the sheer size of Joshua's suite. Beyond the living room we were standing in, the suite included a master bedroom, two offices, and, for some odd reason, three bathrooms. Joshua told us all of this, seeming quite proud of the space he had inherited.

After the mini-tour, Joshua pointed to a couch next to the indoor fireplace, and I got right to it.

"I want to start by asking about your relationship with Luke. As you already heard, I spoke with a reporter who did a profile piece on you about six months ago for the *Cleveland Plain Dealer*. She told me Luke wandered into the room where you were meeting, and you stood up and punched him in the mouth. She said you never explained the assault—you just continued on with the interview.

"Both the nature and timing of that incident made me curious. People don't typically throw punches over business disagreements. This seemed like a personal matter between you and your brother. That always bothered me, and it's only since we came here that I put two and two together. Your wife was in the room when the fight occurred, and she had just learned that she was pregnant. Abigail said you two had been trying for a child for quite a while.

"Forgive me, but I must ask—did you suspect your wife and brother were having an affair? Your wife is a pretty woman, and your brother doesn't seem like the type who would hesitate to take advantage, even with a family member. The way I understand it, that's a trait he shares with you. I know Abigail was dating Matthew when the two of you first met."

Joshua stood immediately, and Hannah's right hand moved to her side, a reflexive shift since her gun was locked in one of her suitcases upstairs. To describe Joshua's face as red would hardly do it justice. His skin tone was just short of purple. I expected an explosion, and I suddenly remembered the family gun safe was no more than fifty feet down the hall. Lucky for me, this blast was of the controlled variety.

Joshua stepped directly before me. "You little shit, how dare you impugn my wife. If even a word of this gets out to the public, I will dedicate every dollar I have to ruining you. That shouldn't be too hard with the state of your finances."

Joshua said all the right things. He defended his wife, and he threatened me. The only thing he didn't do was deny the two had an affair. I decided to keep on pushing. Since Joshua was already standing, I figured I'd join him.

"If you're saying I'm wrong about the affair, tell me why you punched your brother."

Joshua stepped back toward his seat. After his outburst, he seemed able to look everywhere but in my direction. "Disputes between my brother and me are not within your purview, Mr. Luvello."

I was back to being Mr. Luvello again. "I'm afraid you're wrong. Look at the timeline. You and your brother get into a fistfight over an issue affecting your family. Right about that time, your mother chooses to divorce herself from all of you. Margaret was no longer willing to even take meals with her children. I'm guessing your mother might have found out whatever drove you and your brother to fight. I think it affected her to the point where she just got tired of the lot of you."

Joshua shook his head and laughed, a grating, caustic sound, angry and sad at the same time. "You think an affair drove my mother from the family? You have no damn clue what we grew up with. Do you want affairs? My father slept with at least ten women I know of, including the nanny my mother hired to take care of us when we were younger. My mother knew about all of them, including the nanny. She even joked about how that woman also took care of my father. When I was eight, I asked my mother why I saw Daddy kissing Alice before they walked into the master suite. My mother told me, 'Alice sings daddy a lullaby before he takes a nap just like she does with you.' As long as my mother could keep up the charade of being Harold Reasoner's wife, the rest of it was fine with her. I swear the family name was more important to her than it was to my dad."

That might explain why Luke was the way he was. Still, I wasn't about to let Joshua Reasoner off the hook.

"You still haven't told me why you hit your brother. An affair might have meant nothing to your mother, but I suspect it would have to you. If it wasn't that, tell me why you hit him."

"It was...nothing. Just a brotherly spat that went a little too far. It had zero to do with my mother's death, that I guarantee you."

He hadn't expected the question, so he hadn't prepared a lie. I didn't believe him, but I pursued a different topic.

"The upstairs suite your mother stayed in has a fireplace. Yours does as well. I'm assuming they're all electric. Is that correct?"

I had surprised him once again.

"The fireplaces in individual rooms are all electric," he said. "What the hell does that have to do with anything?"

Joshua had already proven he wasn't a good liar. I decided to risk it.

"Just what do you know about carbon monoxide?"

He looked even more confused than when I asked about the fireplaces. "I'm not a chemist, but I know it's a chemical compound. You don't want it in your house, but it has a variety of industrial applications."

He continued, "Before I took over the firm, I ran the company's detergent and soaps division. I believe we used carbon monoxide there, though the chemical processes involved were not a part of my day-to-day routine. If you want to know more about that, you'd have to ask Matthew. My brother is more familiar than I with the chemistry side of things."

He looked straight at me when he answered—no blinking, no hesitation, none of the usual signs a person wasn't being truthful. I decided to push further.

"Is there a person at the firm I can speak to regarding the carbon monoxide you do use? I'm looking for someone who would be familiar with the firm's chemical inventory. Would you be willing to connect me with such an individual?"

"I could connect you with our inventory manager," he said, suddenly suspicious, "but I won't unless you tell me exactly why you're asking."

I sat back down, and Joshua did the same. "Before I answer, I need you to tell me one more thing. The medical examiner told us you requested that blood samples be taken from your mother after her death. Normally they would have performed just a cursory exam on a woman in her mideighties who dies in her sleep. Assuming that led nowhere, they would have signed off on the death certificate with nothing more involved. Why did you request the bloodwork? What did you suspect?"

He again looked away and paused before forming his answer. "With a family as rich as ours, I knew there would be conspiracy theories. I suspected nothing. I just wanted to forestall any questions that might come up through the press or anywhere else."

He was lying. Returning to his earlier question, he asked me again why I was interested in the Reasoner chemical inventory.

If he could lie, I could lie. "I'm interested for the same reason that you requested your mother's blood-work. I just want to cover all my bases."

Hannah started to cough just then, and I remembered our plans for the evening. Joshua looked concerned, but Hannah waved him off.

"It's nothing, really. Just a little cold. It's likely just a twenty-four-hour thing."

She was, as usual, way ahead of me. Joshua turned back in my direction.

"If you're done with your half-assed slimy innuendo, I am going to my job. And if you repeat any of your insinuations to my wife, I will destroy not only you but Detective Page as well."

I couldn't resist. "Actually, innuendo is the wrong word. Innuendo is an allusion. What I said about your wife and brother—that was right out in the open."

We stood to leave, but Hannah stopped and faced Reasoner before we reached the door. "You know, whenever I'm threatened by some shithead during an investigation, I always view that as a sure sign I'm on the right track. Think about that before you ever consider threatening me again."

I'm not sure anyone had ever dared call him a shithead in his own home. I looked at my girlfriend as the door slammed behind us.

"That was fun. I'm still not sure Joshua killed anyone, but he is hiding something."

We climbed up the grand stairway, a journey my Fitbit always insisted on recording as three flights of stairs. Hannah stopped before we reached the top.

"I don't think he committed murder, but I agree—he knows something. He requested those blood tests for a reason, though he showed no reaction when you mentioned carbon monoxide. I was surprised when you brought it up, but I understand now why you did."

We continued up the stairs and finally reached the door of Matthew Reasoner's suite. My plans for Matthew weren't as clear-cut, but there were still things I could probe. Matthew opened his door after my first knock, his wife Emily nowhere in sight.

Matthew's suite was considerably smaller than his older brother's. Beyond the living room with the seemingly mandatory electric fireplace, the suite included one bathroom, a single bedroom, and a study, the latter larger than any of the rooms in our Cleveland Heights home. After a brief tour, we returned to the living area.

Hannah and I sat next to each other on one of the

two couches, with Matthew sitting on the other. Purely on instinct, I decided to switch the order of my questions.

"Tell me about your relationship with your mother. From everything I've heard, Margaret could be a difficult, if not a controlling woman. How did you two get along?"

Matthew hesitated, understandable given the circumstances. "My mother was a driven woman, committed to maintaining the Reasoner legacy. She could be hard on us, particularly Joshua, but we all understood her motivations."

I leaned forward. "I imagine that drive could be challenging to live with. I understand you were the one who brought Abigail home only to have her end up marrying your older brother. The way I heard it, that switch was due to your mother's intervention. She sat you down and told you this was how it needed to be. How did you feel about that? It couldn't have been easy. Joshua got your girl, not to mention the company presidency when your father died. I would have been pissed."

Matthew waved his hand in a "nothing to see here" gesture. He was either more easygoing than his brother or a much more accomplished liar.

"It's true. I did bring Abigail home first. I knew pretty quickly, however, that she would never be the woman for me. You described my mother as controlling and committed to maintaining the Reasoner legacy.

Both those things are undoubtedly true, and I believe her commitment even exceeded my father's.

"I bring that up because those same two personality traits also apply to Abigail. I'm not trying to speak ill of either my sister-in-law or Joshua, but I never wanted to be one of those guys who ended up marrying his mother. I love Emily, and I am grateful she has no direct involvement with the company."

Having interacted with Abigail, I actually believed him. "Tell me about your own involvement with the Reasoner corporation. I know you direct the company's detergent product line. I understand nothing about detergents except for the pods I put in my washer every week. I imagine the chemistry and research involved can be daunting. Could you tell me about your own background? Do you get involved with the nitty-gritty details, or do you leave those for others?"

"I actually like the nitty gritty, as you put it. Before I took over for my brother, I earned my bachelor's degree in chemistry at Case Western Reserve. While my parents insisted on the major—they always saw me as the heir to the detergent line—I found I liked my coursework. I no longer have the time, but I used to sit in during the company's research and development meetings. I'm curious, though, why you're interested."

Matthew would know all about carbon monoxide and its use in the company's manufacturing processes. I also had no doubt he could obtain a tank or two anytime he wanted. While I had alluded to my theory with

Joshua, I decided to keep quiet with his brother. If Matthew had requested the CO, he could easily have falsified the paperwork.

"I'm just trying to get a feel for what you and Joshua do within the company. Call it due diligence or an obsessive need for information. I want to ensure my investigation is as thorough as possible."

Matthew nodded. Thoroughness was something he clearly understood. I tried a new approach.

"Tell me about the day your mother died. It must have been a shock. Despite her age, I understand she was in reasonably good health at the time of her death."

Matthew looked troubled for the first time in our conversation.

"It was a surprise, to be perfectly honest. While mother had done a pretty good job of separating herself from the family, I had the opportunity to speak with her in the hallway the morning before she passed. She was actually quite calm, friendly even. She still had that same determined quality she always possessed, but she didn't appear in quite the same state of turmoil as when I spoke to her on previous days."

Hannah took that moment to break in. "You mentioned your mother's break with your family. When did that occur, and did she ever give you any hint as to why?"

Matthew's troubled look returned. "I would say it was maybe a month or two before she passed away. Joshua and I tried speaking with her when it happened, but she could barely look at us, she was so angry. I still have no idea what caused the rift, only that she seemed calmer just before she died."

I wanted to ask about Luke, but not in the same direct way I did with Joshua.

"Let's talk about Luke. Your mother and father clearly had well-defined plans for you and Joshua—they even chose your major. How did Luke get away with being, shall we say, not so well grounded?"

Matthew stood up and began to pace. His younger brother was a difficult topic.

"I said I wouldn't speak ill of Joshua, but my brother Luke is an idiot. I guess every family has to have one, and that is the role Luke chose to play. My parents did have plans for Luke. Given my brother's creative tendencies, they figured Luke would slide into the VP of marketing position that Abigail eventually assumed.

"Luke, however, would have nothing to do with real work. My brother interned one summer after college, working in the marketing department. That almost became a major scandal after Luke groped one of the marketing secretaries against the wall in his office."

Hannah was appalled. "You said it almost blew up. What happened?"

"My father was still alive at the time. He paid the secretary a significant sum in exchange for an NDA. At her request, she was also transferred to another department. She left the company of her own accord about five years ago."

I had to ask. "Given Luke's history, did you or Joshua ever worry about him being around your own wives? Emily would seem especially vulnerable since she stays here while you're at work.

Matthew hesitated as if deciding how much to tell us. His dislike for his younger brother finally won out over any perceived need for discretion.

"Luke did come up behind Emily once while she was getting something from the kitchen. Emily told me he never actually touched her; he just stood close enough so that Emily was forced to brush past him to get out of the room. From what she told me, he was leering all the while.

"I confronted Luke in his suite that same evening. He denied everything, of course, and said Emily must have been imagining things. I reminded him I was a much better shot than he was. I told him if Emily ever 'imagined things' again, my next visit would come after a stop in the gun closet."

Not a bad response. "Did Luke ever try anything after that?"

"My brother is a coward. No, he never bothered Emily again. For the family's sake, I chose to forget about the incident. We've even had some outwardly friendly gatherings, like the one you saw at the gun range. Still, your brother hitting on your wife is something you never forgive. If Luke bothers Emily again, I will kill him. Family only goes so far, even among the Reasoners."

While I understood his perspective, it was interesting how he so casually mentioned killing a family member. The most outwardly easygoing of the Reasoner boys, Matthew was, by training, a chemist. Could he have planned and executed Margaret's death? Given the right motivation, I had no doubt he could.

Hannah and I stood to leave, thanking Matthew for his time.

He escorted us to the door and said, "I assume this conversation will stay between us? Joshua is always harping about nothing coming back to impugn the family's reputation."

Grateful for his honesty, I felt the need to offer him some reassurance.

"Neither Detective Page nor I will ever speak about anything not directly related to your mother's death. I realize these questions are difficult. I just wanted to get a more complete picture of the family dynamics. Detectives look for patterns—that's what we do. If I have any additional questions, I will let you know.

We exited, and I turned to Hannah. "Do you remember when I said your parents were the craziest rich people I knew? They're now in second place, way, way back in second. Is there anyone in this godforsaken house who isn't a suspect?"

Hannah shook her head. "Aside from you and me, I

would say no."

Our next interview was with Luke Reasoner. I still had no idea who had caused Margaret's death, but it was Luke I desperately wanted to be guilty. Knowing that, I reminded myself to be dispassionate. Before proceeding to Luke's suite, Hannah asked if we could take a detour to our own. She had one more question she didn't want to ask in the hallway.

When we were safely in our room, Hannah flipped on the TV and asked, "Before we came here, you told me we would meet with Margaret's lawyer. What day do you have that penciled in for? I want to find out when Margaret added that codicil to her will."

I checked my iPhone calendar. "We're meeting with the lawyer at nine tomorrow in his downtown office. Afterward, we return to talk with Abigail, Emily, and Judith Reasoner. Think of it as ladies' day."

We left our suite then and maneuvered down the long corridor toward Luke's apartment.

I knocked four times on his door without a response. "Do you suppose the idiot ditched us? He knew we'd be coming. I wonder what bullshit excuse he'll have for this."

My impatient girlfriend wasn't fond of idiots. She tried the door and found it unlocked.

The layout of Luke's suite was very similar to Matthew's, though his living room was littered with liquor bottles. We were both annoyed, so Hannah and I walked unbidden into the bedroom.

Hannah spoke first. "Holy shit!"

Holy shit, indeed. As it turned out, Luke had a good reason for not answering his door. Lying naked on his king-sized bed, Luke Reasoner was quite dead.

The bloody hole on the side of Reasoner's head made it immediately obvious just how he had died. Next to the body lay one of the oddest handguns I'd ever seen. Had it come from the Reasoner gun closet? Once we got over our shock, Hannah called 911. While she waited, I went to notify his family.

Matthew wasn't in his suite, but I tracked him down just as he was about to exit the front door. Seeing my face, he asked what the hell was going on.

"You need to come back upstairs with me right now."

Matthew didn't waste time asking for explanations. He followed me as I ran back up the grand stairway.

As we reached Luke's suite, I warned him to be prepared. He said nothing, and we continued to the bedroom doorway. Hannah stood just inside to properly secure the crime scene. Luke's body was visible from the door, and Matthew's face drained of color.

"How...how did this happen?"

I would have thought the hole and the gun made that obvious, but Hannah explained the likely sequence of events, finishing just as Judith appeared and stood behind Matthew.

"I heard the commotion," she said. "What did he do now?"

Finally noticing our faces, she caught a glimpse of Luke's body. "Oh, my God! Was it drugs? Did you call an ambulance?"

Hannah took Judith by the arm and maneuvered her and Matthew back into Luke's living room. I walked with them, and Hannah again explained our discovery of Luke's body. We were joined then by Lydia and Mark, both of whom said they heard us talking from their rooms. Lydia stood next to her now-sobbing mother.

Hannah, in full cop mode, gave everyone the lay of the land.

"I called 911. In one or two minutes, you'll hear the sirens. The EMTs will come in first to confirm your brother is dead. Once they do that, they'll be joined by the medical examiner and the local cops. Depending on what the ME determines as time of death, the cops will have some very direct questions about where you were and what you may have heard."

"I assume my brother committed suicide," Judith said, no longer crying. "Why would they question us?"

The police and ambulance sirens were now growing louder, and I spoke more quickly. "I'm not a forensics expert, but the location of the gun and his body face down with his hands by his side does not spell suicide. The cops will investigate, and they will have questions."

To Hannah, I said, "I'll go downstairs and let in the crowd. They should be here in about sixty seconds based on the sirens."

As I was leaving the room, Judith Reasoner said, "How do we know you didn't do it? You and my brother argued in front of everyone. I assume you own a gun. Why couldn't you have killed him?"

I stepped back into the room; I knew someone would ask this question. "I do own a gun, but not the one lying next to your brother. You want to know why else I'm innocent? I'm guessing the gun that killed him came from your gun safe. I don't know how many of you have keys, but I don't. Do you want another reason? If I was going to kill your brother, I wouldn't have done nearly as half-assed a job of faking his suicide."

Judith looked stricken, and I suddenly felt terrible. She'd just lost her brother—a dick, no doubt, but her brother nonetheless. I would apologize later, but the pounding on the front door was now unmistakable. I ran downstairs, followed closely by Matthew.

As it turned out, Lawton Summers had beaten us to it. He'd been busy in the kitchen and now looked stunned by the horde of EMTs and cops rushing through the doorway.

I directed the group upstairs, where Judith waited to escort them to Luke's suite. Outside, at least two ambulances and three Hunting Valley police cars had pulled up. Given the small size of the village, I suspected our call had been answered by the entire village police force.

Turning around, I faced a small man, fortyish, with prematurely gray hair dressed in a dark-blue off-the-rack suit I suspected no Hunting Valley resident would have ever considered. Clearly not an EMT, he was likely the village police chief.

He confirmed my guess with an introduction. I was looking at Chief Connor Reilly. I gave him my name, and he looked at me with suspicion.

"Just what the hell is going on here?"

I gave him the bullet-point version, explaining my involvement as well as Hannah's. Rather than question-ing the appearance of a detective from another city, he seemed intrigued by her presence. I offered to take him upstairs and introduce him.

He followed me up the grand stairway, as did Mat-thew, who was now speaking with Joshua on his cell phone. Joshua and Abigail, having already gone to their company offices, would have had no other way of know-ing about Luke's death.

Hannah stood outside Luke's suite, engaged in an animated conversation with Judith and her daughter. I introduced Chief Reilly to all three. Now facing someone official, Judith launched immediately into a string of questions. The chief sidestepped all of Judith's queries with a quick look at the murder scene and then asked Hannah and me if he could speak to us somewhere alone. Not wishing to be overheard by the listening device in our room, we took him back downstairs to the TV room.

"Though well-funded"—the chief spoke mainly to Hannah—"the police force in Hunting Valley is likely smaller than any you've dealt with—just myself and three officers. That's due in part to the size of our village, but it's also the way the community wants things. People here have secrets, and none of our ultrarich residents want the police looking into their drug habits, sexual proclivities, or anything else that might embarrass them.

"For that reason, we primarily try to keep tabs on the obvious—kids racing the cars Daddy and Mommy gave them for their birthdays, breaking up outdoor parties that might get too loud, that sort of piddly shit.

"We have little or no experience with murder. I've been here for six years, and we've never had one. We've rarely even had an assault. That shitstorm you've got upstairs? We don't have nearly the resources needed for that sort of thing. The Geauga County ME is on his way. I called him on the drive here."

He pointed to Hannah. "I could use you on this. You and Mr. Luvello have been here for several days. You know the family and all their peccadilloes. This isn't your jurisdiction, but there are ways around that. If your captain gives his permission, would you be willing to take over the case?"

Looking then at me, he added, "Deciding Mr.

Luvello's role is up to you. Use him or send him home—I'll support any decision you make."

Hannah, no idiot, knew what was really going on. "How much of this is being driven by your lack of staffing, and how much by your desire not to antagonize the Reasoners? Don't answer that because I think we both know the truth. I'll give you the phone number of my captain all the same. If he gives his okay, I'll consider going ahead. While you're contacting him, I need to talk with Mr. Luvello alone. I'm assuming you'll be here for the next few hours. We'll meet you back at the crime scene when we're done."

If the chief was offended by Hannah questioning his motives, he showed no reaction. Hannah gave him Captain Slovitz's number, and she and I exited to the same outdoor patio we'd used to meet with the cooking and cleaning staff. We sat on one of the benches, and I led off.

"You're right. This is a CYA move, nothing more and nothing less. Are you sure you want to take official control over this investigation? The chief called it a shitstorm, and he was absolutely correct."

Hannah looked thoughtful. Picking up my habit, she stood and began to pace.

"I know this puts me at risk, but it also gives us access to resources we haven't had to date. Do you want to search rooms? We could do that openly without me pretending to have some sort of illness."

She continued without waiting for my answer, "That's not the only advantage. Joshua refused to give you access to the company's chemical inventory to check on their carbon monoxide supply. If I get a warrant, we can look at anything you want. I'm not sure we have a need at this point, but I'll also push Slovitz to let me use Aimes should there be any computer issues."

Neither Hannah nor I possessed anywhere near Detective Aimes's level of computer expertise, so it would be good to have him on hand if needed. I was still skeptical, however.

"What about Slovitz? He's a good cop, but he's also a political animal. He would know better than anyone else the minefield you'd be stepping into." As if on cue, Hannah's phone picked that moment to play "Easter Parade."

I shook my head. "I can't believe you change your ringtone with every holiday."

"It's better than playing the same outdated blues song."

Robert Johnson outdated? No longer willing to debate ringtones, Hannah picked up the call.

Captain Slovitz invariably spoke so loudly over the phone that I never had any difficulty hearing his end of a conversation. All the same, he hadn't reached this volume level since the day Hannah first told him she and I were back together.

Slovitz asked to be put on speaker, though I could

hear him perfectly well without it. I tried to be polite.

"Captain, how are you doing this fine March day?"

"Luvello, shut the hell up for once and listen. I knew letting Page go with you to investigate those crazy-ass rich people was a mistake. Whenever you and she team up, it always ends up nuts. I swear you're the whole reason I can't keep on any weight."

The captain was anorexic, an admission he finally made to both himself and his staff. Hannah told me he was doing better these last few months, but gaining weight was still a struggle.

Taking my silence as a hopeful sign, Captain Slovitz finally told us why he called.

"The chief down there told me, without using these exact words, that he would rather throw himself in front of a bus than deal with the Reasoners. The exact words he did use involved the need for cooperation, your stellar record on closing big cases, and the far greater resources Cleveland can bring to bear on an investigation like this. That aside, it amounted to the same thing. The Reasoners help pay his salary, and the Reasoners are pricks, la di damn da. Before I call him back and tell him to go fuck himself, I need your perspective on this, Page."

Hannah paused for only a second. "I know the risks, but I'd like to follow through. Terry and I believe this family has committed one murder and quite possibly two. The second happened on my watch, which really pisses me off. I want the asshole or assholes who did this because I feel like they've been laughing at us the whole time we've been here. I'll let Terry speak for himself, but I want payback. That being said, I'll need departmental support. That may include subpoenas for Reasoner company information. It may also include Aimes, but I'll let you know if and when that becomes necessary."

Slovitz never hesitated. "I'm sure we can find some judge the Reasoners have pissed off. Aimes is involved in another case, but that should be winding down. I'll let him know you might be calling."

He continued, "Luvello, you've been awfully quiet. I know Page wants to continue. What do you think?"

I was surprised by the question, especially since he'd started the conversation by telling me to shut up. "I'm with Hannah on this one, Captain. We're not only convinced Margaret Reasoner was murdered, we're 90 percent certain of the means.

"With the Luke Reasoner murder, the killer did a slipshod job of faking a suicide to the point I'm not really sure they were trying that hard. We have the murder weapon, and the medical examiner can tell us the time of death. The only problem with both killings is the sheer number of suspects. Give us a few more days, and I think we can wrap this up."

"Just remember," the captain responded, "officially, the police are investigating the Luke Reasoner murder only. You may be sure Margaret Reasoner was killed, but right now, she died due to natural causes. You'll have to split responsibilities unless the medical examiner changes his ruling. Page, that means you're on the Luke Reasoner case with Luvello taking the mother. Remember that when you're asking for corporate records. Unless your subpoena has a Luke Reasoner angle, even the friendliest judge will tell you to screw yourself."

Hannah started to protest, but I waved her off.

"We can make that work," I told the captain. "This family is ultra-dysfunctional. Both killings are clearly related. With a little more work, I think we can prove that to any judge."

The captain said he would call Chief Reilly with the news. He had one more reminder before ending the conversation.

"Luvello, do you remember what I promised you after your last case?"

"I'm paraphrasing, Captain, but you said if I screwed up one more time, you'd arrest me in a millisecond."

"I'd like to add to that. If you get Page involved in any more of your insane theories, I'll forget about the arrest and move right to the execution. Do you understand what I'm saying?"

He ended the call before I could answer.

Hannah looked at me. It was not a happy expression. "You want to tell me just what the hell you're thinking? Assuming the person who killed Margaret Reasoner used a carbon monoxide tank from the Reasoner corporation, we'll need a subpoena to see which of the brothers might have ordered one. The captain's right. With Luke's death the only homicide, we'll never get anywhere near those records no matter which judge we approach."

Now I was the one pacing. "Don't think of what we don't have; think of what we do. The medical examiner believes Margaret's death was likely due to carbon monoxide poisoning. We know the fireplace in her room is electric, not gas, and the window was open when her caregiver checked on her the following morning. That tells us someone came into the room after the CO had its intended effect, hoping no one would ever figure out how she died.

"So we know Margaret was killed, and Luke was murdered before he could speak to us. Putting those two things together, how hard do you think it'll be to convince a judge the killings were related—that the person who murdered Margaret also killed her son?"

Hannah looked thoughtful. "We'll need a written statement from the medical examiner, but you're right—we may not be as screwed as I thought we were." She stood up and started toward the house. "We need to get back in there. Once the ME gives his okay, this house is officially a crime scene. That means we can search anywhere we want, including the gun safe and the individual suites. I want to do both before the person who killed that bastard gets around to destroying evidence."

We made our way back upstairs to talk to the medical examiner, the same Dr. Morgan Ho who had first clued us into Margaret s likely death via carbon monoxide.

"The ruling is homicide by gunshot; that much is obvious." Dr. Ho had arrived just fifteen minutes before, but his opinion was immediate and definitive. "We'll analyze the gun from the bed, but it looks like a Ruger MK II, one of the quietest handguns you'll ever find. That detail explains why no one else in the home heard the shot. You can be sure whoever killed Luke Reasoner chose the weapon for that reason."

Hannah asked if his homicide ruling was official, and Dr. Ho nodded.

"The victim is lying face down on his bed. That doesn't preclude suicide, but his hands are palm down by his side. Someone doesn't shoot themselves in the head and put their arms down in that way. Not seeing any signs of a struggle, I wonder if he wasn't drunk, on drugs, or taking some kind of sedative. We'll do a thorough autopsy, but I don't think he ever saw his killer."

While Dr. Ho and his staff arranged for the transport of Luke's body, Hannah and I spoke to Chief Reilly in one of the empty bedrooms, with Hannah starting.

"I talked with my captain, and he okayed me taking over this case. I'm also going to take you up on your offer of assistance. Given what the three of us just heard, I want to search every room in this house. That includes the suites, the gun room, and even the goddamned kitchen. I need your help with that, Chief, and the two officers you have onsite."

"We'll get right to it," he said. "Let me just explain things to my men."

With Chief Reilly out of earshot, Hannah said, "The Chief and I will take the rooms on the left-hand side of the corridor. I want you to supervise the two officers searching the other side. I have no idea how competent either of them is, but their experience level in something like this is probably minimal. I don't trust them, but I do trust you. I need you to make sure they don't miss anything."

I noted the word "supervise" and started to object.

Hannah waved her hand. "You're not a cop, remember? Anything you find would have questionable admissibility if and when this thing goes to court. Just watch them like a hawk. Point out if they miss anything, but let them do the searching."

This was her world, and she was right, as usual. We returned to the bedroom to find Chief Reilly talking to Joshua and Matthew Reasoner. We joined them, and the chief informed both brothers about the ME's homicide ruling and Hannah's expanded jurisdiction.

Joshua transitioned from upset to ballistic. "Why the fuck do we even pay your salary," he said, his voice rising, "if you can't handle a case like this?" He then pointed at Hannah. "Why have some outsider looking into my brother's killing?"

He was speaking to Chief Reilly, but Hannah answered. "I'll give you two reasons. The first is I'm very good at what I do. I'm sure the chief is as well, but I'm guessing there've been maybe two homicides in Hunting Valley in the last ten years."

The chief raised one finger, and Hannah continued. "I've investigated twelve homicides in the last year alone. As I'm sure you know, a few of those were with Mr. Luvello here.

"Think about it. Throughout Terry's investigation, you've emphasized the need to keep our findings out of the newspapers. With your brother's killing, that hope is dead and gone. The papers will get ahold of this; that much is a certainty. Your best hope of putting this behind you is a quick resolution led by someone the press believes is experienced and impartial. My investigation will not be painless, but it will be thorough, and it will be fair.

"The second reason is even more practical. Quite simply, I'm already here. I was scheduled to stay at the mansion over the next few days, assisting Mr. Luvello concerning your mother's death. Do you really want two parallel investigations taking place in your household? You've been a CEO long enough to know the best solution is often the simplest. I'll lead the investigation into your brother's killing and continue to assist Mr. Luvello in the matter of your mother. Let's deal with both deaths in the most straightforward way possible."

Joshua walked away without replying, but Matthew still had one question.

"You said this will inevitably hit the news, but can we at least avoid any press conferences until this mess gets resolved? Newspaper speculation will hurt the entire family, not just the person who did this. You talked about being fair. That's all I'm really asking."

Hannah shook her head. "I will not meet with the press while the investigation is ongoing. My superiors, however, almost certainly will. If they avoid the local reporters, it'll look like stonewalling. I won't encourage it, but there will be some interaction between the department and the press. That's just inevitable."

As Hannah spoke, I returned to Luke's suite to talk with Dr. Ho and caught the doctor as he was in the final stages of preparing the body for transport.

"I know you still need to do an autopsy, but what can you give us as to time of death?"

Dr. Ho looked thoughtful. "You have your hands full, so I won't give you the whole song and dance about body temperature, rigor mortis, etcetera. Bottom line—we're probably looking at eight hours. Given it's now about two o'clock, I'd say Mr. Reasoner was shot between 5:00 and 6:00 a.m. I'll let you and Detective Page know for sure when I get the body back to the morgue."

The time of death ruled out precisely no one, so Hannah and I were still dealing with a whole family full of suspects. Dr. Ho was eager to return to business, but I had one more request.

"You said Reasoner was likely drunk or drugged before he was shot. I didn't smell alcohol, so I'm assuming it was the latter. Can you let us know ASAP what you find in his system? Given his history, the drugs may have been self-administered. All the same, I'd like to know for sure."

Dr. Ho nodded. "I didn't notice any needle tracks, but that still leaves a number of possibilities. I understand you and your partner are now running this investigation, so I'll let you know my findings right away."

I thanked him and went back to Hannah. Finished with the Reasoners, she was in the process of telling Chief Reilly and his officers her expectations for the second-floor search. I began knocking on doors to lead the family downstairs, knowing she wouldn't want them present.

Lydia and Mark were together in Lydia's suite. After some grumbling from Mark, both agreed to go downstairs to the kitchen area. I then found Matthew and his wife still outside Luke's suite. Joshua had already retreated to his first-floor living area, accompanied by Abigail.

With all the Reasoners congregated on the first floor, I realized we had one other problem. I went back upstairs to track down Hannah.

"While we're up here checking out rooms, the family

will be downstairs alone with access to, among other things, the gun safe. I'd still like to be involved in the search up here, so how about sending one of the uniforms downstairs to keep an eye on things? Our search might take longer, but it'd be worth it not to give that group free access to God knows what on the first floor."

Hannah nodded, but I had one other request.

"The ME thinks Luke may have been knocked out, possibly by a sedative. We need to check the medicine cabinets in all the rooms to see what the killer might have had access to."

Now impatient, Hannah said, "Anything else, or can we get on with things?"

I had nothing more, so Hannah sent one of the uniforms downstairs. She and Chief Reilly then began searching the suites on the left side of the corridor while my designated flunky and I started searching the right.

Luke's suite had already been examined by the Hunting Valley cops under Hannah's watchful eye, so I started with Judith's suite next door.

Once inside, my flunky introduced himself as Officer Kenneth Styles. If Officer Styles resented my oversight, he was diplomatic enough not to say so. He pointed to the now-closed door. "She's kind of scary, isn't she?"

"Kid," I said, "you have no idea."

"Is it true her parents live in Hunting Valley?"

I nodded, and he shook his head. "Somehow, that explains things."

Though young, Styles proved surprisingly adept. We began with Judith's bedroom. After pausing briefly to gaze at a particularly lacy set of lingerie, he continued his search, even lifting up the mattress to look underneath. From there, he shifted to Judith's walk-in closet and, finding nothing of note, moved on to Judith's study.

He discovered the first item of interest in the top drawer of an expensive-looking mahogany desk. Styles pulled out a small leather journal, opened it and, after a brief glance, said, "It looks like this is some sort of diary. I'm guessing you'll want to look at this."

I took the journal, but I'd need to read it later. We then moved to Judith's bathroom. I pointed to the medicine cabinet, and Styles obediently opened the small metal door and began poking through Judith's rather impressive collection of medications.

Two of them were sedatives, the prescriptions written by different doctors. Both were interesting but not by any means definitive. I suspected we might find a similar set of meds for anxiety and/or depression in some of the other suites as well. I checked to see how many pills were missing, but both bottles were nearly full. Having finished Judith Reasoner's suite, we moved to the one occupied by her son.

Mark's living area was, to put it mildly, adorned differently than his mother's. Multiple video game systems were placed prominently in his living room. A bookshelf with at least fifty disc containers flanked them, unusual since most video games were now downloaded directly. Curious if those containers might be hiding anything besides games, I directed Styles to open each one, a task he performed with a look close to wonder. I couldn't blame his reaction. If John had been here, I might never have gotten him to leave.

The discs were a dead end, and we found nothing else of interest in Mark's bedroom, study, closet, or bathroom. Mark did have an impressive set of porn magazines hidden under the mattress in his bedroom, quite old-school since virtually all that content would have been accessible online. And Mark was apparently not the anxious type; the only meds we found in his bathroom were aspirin, decongestants, and eyedrops.

While I would have loved to find an empty carbon monoxide container, Ruger shell casings, or something else tying Mark to the murders, I wasn't shocked that we were unsuccessful. These killings, particularly Margaret Reasoner's, involved a degree of sophistication well beyond the capabilities of Judith's son. Officer Styles and I finally gave up and moved on to Lydia Reasoner.

Lydia's suite could not have presented a more noticeable contrast to her brother's. Four bookshelves surrounded the living room's Sony television. The set was apparently little used based on the thin layer of dust on its remote control.

Lydia's bedroom was frilly and pink, two attributes

that would have appalled my down-to-earth girlfriend. Styles conducted a thorough search of both areas before we moved on to Lydia's bathroom.

Rummaging through her medicine cabinet, Styles pulled out aspirin, antianxiety meds, and a sheet of other pills he examined with a puzzled expression. He tossed them to me. "They're in four rows of seven, and the last row is a different color from the others. Do you have any idea what the hell these are?"

Despite never having cause to use them, they actually were familiar. "You don't have a girlfriend, do you, Officer Styles?"

I hoped he wouldn't take offense, but I was genuinely curious.

"I do have a girlfriend," he answered with enthusiasm. "We met three years ago in our church choir."

A church choir—that explained it. "What you have here are birth control pills. It looks like Ms. Lydia may be in a relationship. Her rather insulated life raises the question of with whom."

Styles didn't appear embarrassed. That was good— I liked the kid. I asked him to toss me the antianxiety pills, which he did before moving on to the rest of the room.

The half-full bottle proved nothing beyond Lydia's likely treatment for depression, though the combination intrigued. Depression and a boyfriend—Lydia's life was far more interesting than I'd have guessed.

We finished our search of Lydia's suite after examining her closet, its contents yielding an eclectic assortment of dresses and casual wear. Thinking about the boyfriend, there were only a couple of items that could even remotely be defined as sexy.

Styles and I proceeded to the vacant rooms on our side of the corridor, our search of the occupied suites complete. Each of them followed the same floor layout as the other suites. All were empty, almost spotless, in terms of evidence.

As we left the final set of rooms, we found Hannah and Chief Reilly waiting in the hallway. I looked at Hannah, and she shook her head—Styles and I weren't the only ones who had come up empty. I asked Hannah where we were headed next.

"The Chief and I are going downstairs to check Joshua's suite and the other first-floor areas. If you and Officer Styles come along, that should substantially shorten the time involved."

I was also thinking about next steps. "Officer Styles can go down with you. I'd be superfluous, and I have one more place up here I'd like to check."

Hannah frowned, but she trusted me enough not to ask and proceeded downstairs with Chief Reilly and Officer Styles. Wondering if I was only wasting my time, I headed for the attic elevator.

I've always hated attics. It wasn't the mice. My father was pretty good at keeping those out of our house.

The majority of the bugs also left me unafraid. The spiders, however, scared me shitless. If there is a God, those eight-legged demons from hell must have been a product of quite the heavenly bender.

I was determined to look nonetheless. I hadn't told Hannah where I was headed, though that had more to do with the danger of others overhearing. Beyond the Hunting Valley cops, those "others" included Lawton Summers, who had picked that moment to step out of Mark's suite upstairs.

"Lawton, this floor is a crime scene," I told him. "You need to go back downstairs with the others."

"I'm sorry, sir. I was actually checking on the whereabouts of Mr. Mark. His mother noticed he wasn't downstairs and thought he might have walked back up here to get one of his portable game consoles. I didn't think a quick check would do any harm. Sometimes he wanders by the fishing pond outside. I'll check there next."

I waited, but Lawton didn't move. He'd seen me about to press the button for the attic elevator.

"Are you headed upstairs, Mr. Luvello? I can come with you if you like, though it's not my favorite place. Let me tell Ms. Judith about Mark, and we can go up together."

I shook my head. "There's no need for that, Lawton. I've been in attics before. If the spiders get too rambunctious, I even brought my gun."

He didn't crack a smile. Did he ever? "It's not the

spiders, sir, but the rats. Ms. Emily noticed droppings last week almost right where you're standing. This is an old house, and the exterminators aren't always effective. I placed several traps in the attic at Mr. Joshua's directive. Just be careful you don't accidentally run into one. I wasn't here then, but I understand Ms. Lydia did that when she was five years old. Two of her fingers were broken as a result.

His phony concern was starting to get annoying. "I'll survive, Lawton. Why don't you go find Mark and make sure he knows his room is off-limits."

Summers simply nodded before retreating down the grand stairway. I had no doubt he'd let Joshua know where I was headed, but I suspected the oldest Reasoner brother would have his hands full downstairs, trying to keep matters from spiraling any further out of control. Pressing the elevator button, I proceeded to the Reasoner attic.

Once there, I pulled the string for one of the overhead lights, then paused as I remembered the layout of the Reasoner's second floor.

With all our efforts to figure out who had killed Margaret, we'd forgotten the question of how it was done. Since our first conversation with Dr. Ho, my working assumption had been that someone obtained a tank of carbon monoxide, likely from the Reasoner chemical division, and somehow placed that tank in Margaret's room.

It hadn't occurred to me until later how ridiculous the assumption was. If that had been the killer's plan, the sound of the door opening might easily have been enough to wake Margaret. Even if she didn't wake immediately, Carol Anne told us she tended to make bathroom trips at night. The CO canister would have had to remain in the room for a reasonable period of time to be effective. Margaret might trip over the tank before she even saw it.

There was also the issue of the tank's size. I'd found a handy online safety website listing the typical dimensions for gas tanks used in industry. With few exceptions, most tanks were over four feet tall. The tank would be plainly visible if someone like Carol Anne entered the room at the wrong time. A late-night visitor to Margaret's room might also be spotted by another family member. There'd be no easy explanation for that visitor wheeling a gas tank.

That left the elevator. The outdoor grounds of the Reasoner mansion were so extensive that someone could easily have hidden the container nearby to be brought inside when the time was right. Luke had a reputation for nighttime partying. I guessed both he and the other Reasoners often kept late hours.

Carrying out the attack from the attic had another advantage, one that went beyond the elevator and the lack of foot traffic on the third floor. Summers had mentioned that one of the staff had fallen through the boards and through the ceiling of Judith's room.

Margaret's killer could have moved one of those boards and drilled a narrow hole through the ceiling in her suite with a small, relatively quiet hand drill. If it had been me, I'd have chosen Margaret's closet or study, areas where a hole might have gone unnoticed. All you would need then was the gas container and some plastic tubing. The tubing would direct the vapor with no danger of the killer being overcome.

No one would have noticed a tiny opening in the ceiling with all the uproar over Margaret's death. A few days later, the killer could have plastered the hole to make sure it was invisible.

Once the gas was in Margaret's room, the killer would have simply replaced the loose floorboards and waited an hour or two for the carbon monoxide to have its effect. It'd be a matter of returning to the second floor, donning a rudimentary gas mask, and entering Margaret's room to open the window. Getting the empty container back downstairs for eventual disposal would have been the riskiest part of the plan, but that too would have been doable using the elevator.

As scenarios go, it was the most plausible. The only problem I could think of was logistical. There was a reason most industrial gas tanks came with wheels. Even someone as big as Joshua Reasoner would have a problem carrying one. Rolling the container across the loose attic floorboards would have been noisy, not to mention the risk of the tank itself falling through to the floor below.

The location of Margaret's suite, closest to the attic elevator, might have mitigated the noise issue. The floorboard risk might have also seemed negligible, assuming the killer moved carefully to their chosen location.

With the latter problem in mind, I maneuvered to where I judged Margaret's room would be. I could have used Hannah, but she'd be busy coordinating the first-floor search and pacifying the increasingly restive Reasoner clan. That brought to mind the young and competent Officer Styles, and I returned to the elevator to head downstairs.

It was the first time I'd taken the lift to the ground floor. I exited in the main kitchen, somewhat to the surprise of the staff preparing the evening dinner.

Figuring I should say something, I asked what was for dinner. Rosario, the cook, pointed to the unrecognizable mess in front of him and told me it was sushi.

It really was turning into a bad day. Not wishing to bother the staff further, I simply nodded as if eating cold fish was the most natural thing in the world and went to hunt down Officer Styles.

I found him in the dining room, standing in the background among a group of Reasoner family members, observing a notably belligerent Hannah explaining to Joshua why a search of his suite was not open to question. Knowing she wouldn't need my help, I tapped Styles on the shoulder.

"How would you like to get back to doing some real police work?"

He shook his head and muttered, "Dear God, yes."

I led him through the kitchen to the elevator. On the way, I waved to Rosario, "Any chance you guys have some leftovers from yesterday?"

He just stared as if I was speaking a foreign language.

I tried again. "Have you ever considered cooking the fish just to change things up?"

Rosario's stare remained unchanged.

Maybe Hannah and I could order takeout.

Culinary concerns on the backburner for now, Styles and I proceeded to the second floor, where I stationed my young friend in Margaret's former room. Explaining my plan, I gave him my cell phone number and returned to the attic.

After maneuvering my way to where I had judged Margaret's room to be, I removed some of the floorboards and began tapping on the ceiling. Styles texted back with just one word, "bathroom."

With his assistance, I worked my way around the surrounding area until I'd marked the ceiling over Margaret's bedroom, bathroom, living room, and closet.

I texted Styles to release him from ceiling tap duty, having mapped out my workspace. Hearing the mechanical whir of the elevator gears, I expected he'd returned downstairs to rejoin his cohorts. To my surprise, the elevator was headed my way, and Officer Styles emerged seconds later.

"I figured you might need some help. Do you mind if I join you, Mr. Luvello?"

"Only if you call me Terry and let me call you Ken. Are you sure you don't want to rejoin the downstairs crowd?"

"I was standing around trying to keep from falling asleep before you came to get me. I've been a cop for two years. Searching those rooms with you was probably the highlight of my career. This is a nice village, quiet, if a bit pretentious. For a cop, that adds up to boring as hell."

I'd underestimated him. This churchgoing, small-town policeman was far more intelligent and ambitious than I realized. I pointed to the ceiling above Margaret's bathroom, and the two of us got back to work.

We hit paydirt above Margaret's bedroom, the place I least expected to find success. In what would roughly be the middle of the room, I found clear evidence of plaster dust and a small hole, maybe an eighth of an inch in diameter. Near the hole were two small screws, both of which looked like they'd been there for some time. I tried shining my pocket flashlight through the opening, but it seemed to be blocked just below ceiling level. I called to Ken, currently surveying the bathroom ceiling.

I showed him my discovery. "Any chance you'd be willing to go back to Margaret's room? There's something underneath this hole, and I'd really like to know what that something is."

Glancing at his radio, Ken said, "The chief hasn't called me yet, and he knows I'm helping you. I see no reason not to keep going."

I waited until I heard him disembark from the elevator and began tapping around the hole with a loose piece of wood. The text came almost immediately.

You're directly over a standard First Alert smoke detector. Do you want me to take it off?

I texted him to wait. I was playing a hunch, and I wanted to be there to see if I was correct. If so, I'd also need to grab Hannah, busy or not, from whatever she was doing on the first floor.

Entering Margaret's room, I found Ken standing precariously on Margaret's rolling desk chair.

"Is there any chance you have a small Phillips-head screwdriver?" he asked.

My father taught me to always travel with a small set of screwdrivers. I'd never understood why as a child, but some lessons take a while to absorb. I'd used these screwdrivers in my detective work more times than I could count, once as a makeshift weapon. I hustled back to our suite and grabbed the set from my suitcase.

I returned to Ken and handed him a tool I figured might work. As it turned out, he didn't even need one.

Ken removed the alarm cover as any homeowner

would do when changing the batteries. With the cover off, it was easy to see the hole drilled directly through the base, a fraction of an inch from the far side.

Ken looked at me with a quizzical expression. I just felt vindicated.

"Ken, I need you to go downstairs and grab Detective Page. She might resist, and she will call you names you never heard before in church. Just tell her Terry has something she'll definitely want to see, and she needs to get her ass up here ASAP."

Ken obediently left, though he still looked dubious. Thirty seconds later, he returned with Hannah, who was more than a little disgruntled.

"Junior here told me I needed to get upstairs as fast as possible," she said, staring disdainfully at poor Ken Styles. "That means I left Chief Reilly with the family from hell. That doesn't particularly bother me, but this better be damn important."

I told Hannah about my theory that the attic was the delivery room for the carbon monoxide gas and then showed her the hole. She was notably unconvinced.

"The attic does make a ton of sense, but the hole is a reach. How do you know that wasn't just another opening someone drilled for a different smoke alarm or something else on the ceiling?

I shook my head. "I found plaster dust by the hole on the attic side. If someone drilled that hole from Margaret's room, the dust would have fallen to her floor. The hole itself was an eighth of an inch in diameter. How many fire alarms or ceiling fixtures are hung with bolts that size? If that doesn't convince you, look at the alarm cover. There are openings along the side to help detect smoke from a fire. I think the killer used those openings in an ingenious way. Instead of smoke rising from the room to the alarm, he or she pumped carbon monoxide down through a tube to dissipate throughout the room."

Officer Styles had his own objection. "You're pumping gas through a smoke alarm. Why wouldn't it have gone off?"

"It wouldn't have gone off because it's not a CO detector," Hannah answered, as if speaking to herself. "This is a standard smoke alarm, and those functions typically require separate devices. Some catch both, but this one doesn't look like one of those—it would say so on the side. The mansion almost certainly does have CO detectors, but I'm guessing those are mounted in the corridor. The gas from Margaret's room wouldn't have leaked that far with the door closed."

She turned to me, smiling this time. "Jesus, Terry, I think you figured it out, the 'how' anyway, if not the 'who.' This, and a revised statement from the ME about Margaret's death, should be enough to get us a warrant for the Reasoner chemical supply records. Linking the two murders won't be difficult, then, even for the most dimwitted judge."

She spoke again, this time to Styles. "We'll need to take pictures of the ceiling from Margaret's room and the attic. We'll also need to unscrew and bag the fire alarm. It's evidence now."

Styles went downstairs to get a camera from his black-and-white. Alone now, I looked at Hannah.

"As much as I despise the idea of sushi, I think we need to eat with the family tonight. That way, we can make them aware of how we see this going. That should include continuing with our planned interviews. On the nonfamily side, we still need to speak with both the ME and Margaret's lawyer."

Hannah sat on Margaret's bed. "I know you want to talk to the lawyer about the codicil that brought us here in the first place. What else are you aiming to tie down?"

I started to pace. "We need to know just when she placed that codicil in the will. There's a sequence of events here, starting when Margaret walked into the Salinger office seven years ago, claiming someone might try to kill her. You would have thought that would bring things to a head, but the dynamic in the family stayed amazingly status quo. Margaret was still eating with her children. She got into arguments with Joshua, but those appeared to be business related. Bernie is an absolute bloodhound when she smells something, but she essentially gave the case up for dead.

"Everything changed about six months ago when Margaret contacted Bernie and had her come to the house. Once here, Bernie became convinced something bad might really be going down.

"Six months ago, Margaret also began to separate herself from the family, with her no longer even eating dinner with her children. Margaret was the family fixer. She put up with her husband's numerous affairs, all in the name of maintaining her power within the family hierarchy. When Matthew first brought Abigail home as his date, it was Margaret who smoothed the way for her to marry his older brother. Whatever caused Margaret to back away from her children must have shaken her to the core.

"Lastly, there was the punch. Joshua, for some unknown reason, coldcocks Luke in front of a newspaper reporter. That attack fit right into this same timeframe. The fact that Luke is now dead doesn't mean that Joshua killed him, but it is one more piece of the puzzle we need to fit together."

"Don't forget Abigail's pregnancy," Hannah added. "She's six months along, which puts it right in the middle of everything we're discussing. If her baby isn't Joshua's, that could explain his assault on Luke. It doesn't explain Margaret; affairs were something she often overlooked, but it's one additional factor we need to consider."

Officer Styles, Ken to his friends, returned with his camera. He took several pictures of the ceiling before moving to the smoke alarm, making sure to get close-ups of the hole in the screwed-in base.

"Don't forget," Hannah reminded him, "to get some shots from the attic side."

Ken told her that was already done. "That's why it took me so long to get back here. If you don't have anything else, I need to get going. The chief wants me at the station."

Somewhat surprised, Hannah said, "Very efficient, Officer Styles. Let me know if you ever want to consider a Cleveland transfer."

Ken just nodded and left to rejoin his chief.

Hannah and I were interrupted only minutes later by a knock on Margaret's door. Lawton Summers had come to remind us it was 7:00 p.m. A little thing like murder wouldn't get in the way of a prompt dinner at the Reasoner home.

I wasn't sure if I wanted to eat sushi, but I got lucky. The Reasoner's chef earned my eternal gratitude by serving both sushi and baked salmon, the latter dish something I could actually keep down.

Hannah and I faced a barrage of "where do we go from here" questions pertaining to the investigation. Their brother had just been killed, but I saw no sign of grief. That was even true for Lydia, seemingly the most empathetic member of the clan. Instead, I saw only calculation, the family's predator-like shrewdness mixed with no small degree of fear.

After glancing at Hannah, I filled them in. "We'll keep to the schedule we laid out before. Tomorrow, Hannah and I will meet with Judith, Abigail, Emily, and Lydia. We'll also want to see an inventory of all weapons purchased and kept in the gun safe. I assume such an inventory exists and can be obtained easily.

"With the upstairs search completed, you're all allowed to return to your suites. Luke's will be off-limits until we tell you otherwise. That prohibition also applies to the cleaning staff."

Hannah and I had discussed informing the family about our suspicions regarding carbon monoxide and its role in Margaret's death. With the family all together, now seemed like the perfect time. We waited for the inevitable question. It came, not surprisingly, from Joshua.

"You two were upstairs a damn long time. Do you mind letting us in on just what you're thinking?"

"Your home has been the scene of not one murder but two," Hannah replied. "While your mother's death was initially ruled due to natural causes, we now have direct evidence this was not the case."

"Bullshit!" The cry came simultaneously from Joshua, Matthew, and Abigail, all appearing angry enough to dive in our direction. The rest stayed quiet.

Hannah remained calm. "Based on postmortem photos of your mother's lower extremity, the Geauga County medical examiner feels she likely died of carbon monoxide poisoning."

"Even if you're right," Abigal sputtered, "people die of carbon monoxide poisoning all the time. Why the hell would you think this is murder?"

I figured it was my turn. "People do die of CO poisoning quite often. Those deaths typically stem from devices that burn fuel. I'm talking about gas heaters, fireplaces, gas stoves, that sort of thing. The problem with such a scenario is that your home is all electric. I verified that with your house manager just before we came downstairs. The conversion was done about five years back."

"We believe," Hannah continued, "the CO was leaked into your mother's room through a hole drilled through her ceiling from the attic directly above. We found the hole, and we now know how it was disguised. That was the cleverest part of this affair—the hole was drilled partway through the smoke detector bolted to her ceiling. The gas essentially leaked through the alarm, something it would have never sensed since it was only designed to detect smoke from a fire. As an aside, Margaret's room and the attic are also off-limits without my permission."

I looked around the room as Hannah talked. Everyone at the table appeared surprised, no one more so than Joshua and Matthew. If the Reasoners were acting, they were doing it well. Hannah and I had gone this far. I figured we might as well tear the bandage off completely.

"Given what you just heard, we'll also be requesting your cooperation in gaining access to the company's chemical inventory. We can get a warrant if you like, but that would go through a judge with the possibility of leaks from any number of sources. With your sign-off, we can find the information we need in as nonpublic a way as possible."

"Assuming you're correct about the carbon monoxide," Joshua said, thinking things through, "canisters can be obtained from any chemical supply company. How do you know it came from ours?"

Never the most patient of people, I was running out of what little I had. "Let me be blunt. Your mother's murder was almost certainly committed by a family member. Why the hell wouldn't we look into your company first? If we don't find anything, then you're right. In that case, we would have to get a new warrant to search your financial records for any outlays to outside chemical firms. That search would be exhaustive with no limits whatsoever on what records we examine. Given that, you should pray we find what we're looking for at your corporation."

No one, especially a person of means, wants the police combing through their financial records. Joshua looked at Matthew, who nodded silently. We'd get our look at the inventory records. I noticed neither brother even glanced at Abigail. The other Reasoner senior VP sat next to her husband, quietly seething. If looks could kill, Joshua would have joined his youngest brother in the morgue.

In giving us his permission, Joshua had one, not entirely unreasonable, caveat. "Our inventory records are stored within the Reasoner computer system. I'll notify our manager tomorrow, and you or your computer expert can look through our chemical supplies. Just to be clear, the inventory is all you will be looking at. I need your word in writing that this will not be a fishing expedition."

Considering the other investigations swirling around his company, I wasn't at all surprised by that restriction. Neither Hannah nor I had any problem agreeing since the other cases weren't our concern. With our agreement, Joshua gave us his inventory manager's name and telephone number, asking that we wait until tomorrow morning to make the call.

Hannah and I then excused ourselves to return to our room. Hannah had received at least three messages from Captain Slovitz, likely impatient at being kept out of the loop. We first turned up the sound on the TV, a nightly habit that now seemed routine.

Hannah spoke to the captain while I attempted to put some sort of order to the events of the day. Ten minutes later, Hannah put down her phone and joined me on the side of the bed.

"After he again reminded me I should never have gotten back together with you, Slovitz agreed that Aimes could help us go through the Reasoner's computer system."

"Whoever killed Margaret," I said, "did so with a degree of elegance you almost need to admire. What are the odds we'll find a transfer record in the Reasoner's computer files?"

Hannah looked determined. "I have to believe we'll find something. If not, we may be relying on your income for a while."

"Our joint income may be the least of our issues. If this case goes south, you and I might join Bernie at the bottom of the Bridle Path Bridge."

CHAPTER NINE

DAY FOUR

HANNAH ROLLED OUT of bed the following morning and called Detective Aimes, giving him the name and number of the Reasoner corporation inventory manager. Aimes promised to call us back before noon. We then grabbed a brief breakfast downstairs, some type of muffin the cook swore, correctly, that we would like.

Following breakfast, we then went to meet Judith Reasoner. As with the first day we entered the mansion, Judith greeted us holding a painting.

"Look at this," she said with disgust, "and tell me what you think."

I was facing a cow. It was, admittedly, a very lovely cow, but I had no idea why Judith was showing us one at that particular moment. I assumed the painting must be "important." I glanced at Hannah for guidance, but she just shook her head.

I took a stab. "The cow is alone and appears very well-fed. The barn next to it has its door open. Is the cow about to be slaughtered?"

I was, apparently, a philistine. Judith threw the painting on a desk, her disgusted expression now aimed in my direction. Part of me was happy—I liked that cow. I was glad I guessed wrong about her killing.

Not one to worry about livestock, Hannah said, "Perhaps we could get to the reason for our visit. Do you mind if we sit down in your living room?"

We moved to the couch, Judith sitting across from us on a small loveseat. I started things off.

"I wonder if you could tell us about your relationship with your mother. We heard she could be rather demanding, particularly when focused on maintaining the family's reputation. That couldn't have been easy to live with."

Judith nodded. "The word easy would never be used in conjunction with my mom. I know this isn't something I should say after her death, but my mother would sacrifice anything and anyone to maintain the Reasoner family name. In a tragic way, that even included herself. My father had numerous affairs and did very little to keep them hidden. My mother knew and never said anything. When I was just entering my teenage years, I made the mistake of asking her about Daddy and how she could keep living with him. She slapped me without saying a word. Then she told me how disappointed she was and that there were some things I just couldn't understand.

Judith looked down at the floor as if confronted by a memory she had no wish to face. "Don't get me wrong, I loved my mother. I think she always felt she was doing the right thing by acting the way she did. That said, I could never find it in myself to like her very much. When she insisted Calvin be sent away, I thought that was the last straw. I later came to see it as the right thing, so maybe I'm more like my mother than I'd care to admit."

Hannah went next. "How about answering the same question, now regarding Luke.

There was no hesitation this time. "Joshua and Matthew always thought of Luke as an idiot. I understood why, at least on the surface. Both of them were tall, popular with girls, and good in school and sports. Luke just never measured up, other than maybe with the girl thing. As the youngest child and the only daughter, I got to see the other side of Luke. Saying my brother was an idiot was like saying a cobra is dumb. No matter the size of its brain, it can kill you quite efficiently.

"When I was seven years old, I got a game for my birthday. I don't even remember the name, just that it was some kind of toy operating room. Luke decided it was something he wanted, and he was pissed I wouldn't let him play with it. About a week later, I found the game burned in our outdoor firepit. I remember when I discovered it, turning around and seeing Luke watching me out the nearest window. He was laughing that nasty laugh of his.

"I told my parents, but they pretty much ignored the whole thing. I think they had the same opinion of Luke as my brothers. To them, Luke was a nonentity, completely unimportant in the larger scheme of things. I never made that mistake. It wasn't that I gave into him, but I avoided my brother whenever possible."

I asked about her life outside the mansion. "Your children are young, and you are by no means old. Are you able to get out, to date, to have fun?"

"I have attended numerous art gatherings, and I have dated several men from those events. None of them meant as much to me as my ex-husband, but they had the virtue of being available. Sometimes you need that, even at my advanced age."

"What about Lydia?" Hannah asked. "She's a beautiful young girl from an extraordinarily rich family. Not to sound too nineteenth-century, but part of me is surprised she isn't married already."

Judith laughed, not altogether pleasantly. "Lydia dated several boys in her high school, not to mention a few she met at social events organized by the online college she graduated from. While I think Lydia liked a few of the boys, she always seemed to cut things off before getting too close. In the last few years, she's hardly dated anyone at all. Mark is just the opposite. My son is always falling in love, often to his own detriment."

"Explain that," Hannah requested. "If you're worried, remember we did sign an NDA."

Judith hesitated before replying. "Mark has a daughter, a girl he fathered when he was just eighteen. Megan is now seven years old. She stays with her mother, someone Mark met when he was a senior in high school. Mark drives over to see her once a week.

"As you can imagine, there were financial arrangements involved. One of those stipulated that Megan would never come to the mansion. That was not," Judith added hastily, "a condition of our choosing. For whatever reason, Megan's mother had no wish for her daughter to meet the rest of Mark's family."

A wise girl.

Hannah had one last question. "Who do you think killed your mother and brother?"

Judith shook her head. "I have trouble believing any of us did. My family is very damaged. I'm sure you've noticed that even in your short time staying here. Being a Reasoner has always meant a certain 'us against the world' mentality. Now you're asking me to believe it's us against us. Despite what I told you about Luke, I never saw him resort to physical violence. He could be as vindictive as hell, but murder? I never would think that of anyone in this family. Are you sure it couldn't be someone on staff?"

I had been cruel to her once; I would need to be again. "How many people on staff have a key to your gun closet? Other than Lawton Summers, how many of your staff have access to your home at night to move the CO cylinder up to your attic? We need your input here, Judith—not your artistic imagination."

She just shook her head, now staring down at the floor. We would get no more from Judith Reasoner this morning. After thanking her for her time, we moved on to her daughter.

Lydia's suite was next door to her mother's. She opened the door immediately, wearing a sheer nightgown.

We told her we would wait, but Lydia seemed surprised by the suggestion.

"I don't usually wake up until closer to noon. I typically wear my nightclothes until I have to go downstairs. If this bothers you, I can change."

I looked at Hannah, who simply shrugged. Before we could even sit down, Lydia had a request of her own.

"Promise me you'll tell me where the investigation stands so far. I know it's inappropriate to ask, but this is quite the murder mystery. We have two killings within a family that lies incessantly, along with simmering hatreds barely under the surface. It's an Agatha Christie story, except neither of you resembles Hercule Poirot."

She looked at me more closely. "You should grow one of those upward-curled mustaches, Mr. Luvello. That would make the whole thing quite perfect."

Her tangents were exhausting. Hannah and I moved to Lydia's couch and sat down. Lydia remained standing as I tried to pull us back to planet Earth.

"You spoke about simmering hatreds just below the surface. Can you elaborate on just what those are?"

"I would think it'd be obvious. Let's start with Joshua and Matthew. Joshua fears Matthew is gunning for his job, and Matthew feels Joshua is taking too many unnecessary risks. They try to hide it, but they don't mind arguing when I'm around. They think I'm a twit. Do you think I'm a twit, Mr. Luvello?"

"I would say that's the last thing you are, but keep going. Tell me more about the hatred in this house."

"Well, there's Uncle Luke. No one ever took him seriously, with the possible exception of my mother. She once described him as a snake, but I think that gives him far too much credit. I thought of him more as one of those pitiful burrowing rodents, a house mouse, if you will. They create nests and hide, hoping none of the other residents realize they're around. Before you know it, they're eating your food and tunneling into your walls. That's bad enough, but the real problem are the ones that spread disease. Even with Uncle Luke gone, I think a lot of his disease is still here."

"Tell me about your grandmother," Hannah said.

"From everything we've heard, she was dedicated to maintaining the family name and reputation above all else. How did she react to all of this disease you mentioned?"

Lydia brightened slightly at the mention of her grandmother. "I'm not sure I realized it then, but I think Grandma tried to face the hatred. She just got worn down. Eventually, she could only die."

"She didn't just die, though, Lydia," Hannah said. "Your grandmother was murdered."

Lydia showed no reaction. Hannah might have been talking about the weather. "Grandma was murdered, wasn't she? Who do you think did it? I know you're looking at my entire family, but I think it was the house. People call this the Shadow House, but I think it's much, much worse. Shadows can't hurt you, but this house is corrosive, almost like acid. I once told Uncle Joshua we should burn it and start over. What's the good in having money if you can't burn something down now and then?"

I was sure there was a term for Lydia, but I wasn't a therapist and had no idea what that term might be. I tried a different tack.

"A few months before her death, your grandmother began spending almost all her time in her room, including when she ate her meals. What do you think drove her to do that? She was the family matriarch. Even with Joshua leading the company, Margaret's position in the family hierarchy was unquestioned. Why would she just give that up? Did you talk to her after the split?"

Lydia shook her head. "I think Grandma had bigger concerns than speaking with me. As to what drove her to it, who could tell? Maybe it was anger; maybe it was guilt; maybe she no longer liked her place at the family dinner table. I wouldn't dare to hazard a guess."

I had hit a sore point, and I decided to switch topics. "Does it ever get lonely here at the mansion? A beautiful woman like yourself, I'm sure you have plenty of suitors, male or female. Even if you're not interested in romance, I'm sure you think about getting away now and then. If you don't drive, what about walks?"

"How nice of you to ask about my love life, Mr. Luvello. Are you inquiring for yourself? If it's the night-gown, I really can change. I also doubt Detective Page would appreciate our tryst."

Hannah looked amused rather than offended. Lydia was the most curious combination—childlike and a se-ductress at the same time. The mix seemed vaguely fa-miliar, and I wondered again about consulting a thera-pist. Unfortunately, the only one I knew specialized in transgender issues.

Hannah was starting to look bored and made a slight sideways motion with her right hand. I recognized the gesture; she thought we were wasting our time. Still, I had one more question.

"Your Aunt Abigail is obviously pregnant, and I

understand she and your uncle have been trying for some time. With all the talk of affairs running through the Reasoner household, was there any suspicion about how Abigail may have gotten pregnant? Forgive the question, but I do need to ask."

I saw that flirting glint in her eye once more. "You're asking how Abigail got pregnant? I assumed it was in the usual way." Lydia laughed then, suddenly sounding much older than her twenty-three years. "Don't worry, I know exactly what you mean. You're asking if I ever noticed any furtive glances or sudden exits from a suite that wasn't her own.

"Do you know the advantage of being thought a twit, Mr. Luvello? People tend not to notice when you're around or worry about what you might have seen. Aunt Abigail is a strong woman. She started with my Uncle Matthew and moved quickly to someone she knew could better benefit her career. Would she take advantage of an opportunity with someone who could offer her more in other ways? I have no doubt she both could and would."

"And who would this other man be?" Hannah asked the obvious question.

Lydia laughed again, stood up, and moved to the door. Clearly, we had overstayed our welcome. "I can't solve your case for you, Detective Page. If I did that, you and Terry wouldn't have any fun at all."

Before our next interview, Hannah and I ducked

into our room and turned on the TV.

"You went to a therapist last year," Hannah said. "Do you have any idea what someone like her is called?"

"Batshit crazy comes to mind, but I suspect that's not a clinical term. I'm just wondering if anything Lydia told us can be relied upon. The therapist thing is not a bad idea though. Do you know anyone we can call?"

"I'm not sure where you're going, but the department shrink is Dr. Carl Baxter," Hannah said. "I'll try calling him after we're done today."

"I'm not sure where I'm going either; it's just that Lydia reminds me of someone from one of my former cases. I'm not sure who; it's an old memory."

"Do you really think Abigail and Luke were screwing around?" Hannah said, returning to the other, more obvious point from our interview. "Matthew told us Luke came on to Emily. What if he did the same with Abigail, but she showed some interest? Adultery has driven more than one spouse to murder. The whole thing would be particularly tough if Joshua suspected his child was fathered by the brother he always looked down on. As you pointed out, Joshua punched Luke during his newspaper interview for reasons that were likely personal. What's more personal than adultery?"

She was right, and yet there was something that didn't quite add up.

"If Joshua suspected Luke was screwing his wife," I said, "why the chummy scene around the outdoor shooting range? If I was Luke, that would have been the last place I'd want to hang out, particularly with a brother who hated me.

"There's also the question of why Margaret separated herself from the children and grandchildren. That separation occurred at roughly the same time Abigail learned she was pregnant. An affair wouldn't have been enough for Margaret. There had to be something else."

Hannah glanced at her watch. It was time to meet Emily Reasoner.

Emily was the person I considered the least likely to have committed either murder, and she proved to be an unenlightening interview.

She did confirm her unpleasant kitchen interaction with her brother-in-law, adding a few details Matthew had left out.

"I knew there'd be trouble when I smelled the alcohol. You shouldn't speak ill of the dead, but Luke was a slimy asshole, even at the best of times. When he was sober, he managed to keep his true self hidden. I think that was more due to fear of his brothers than any self-control. When he was drunk, you just tried to stay the hell away from him. I could usually manage that, but I never heard him sneak up behind me that evening in the kitchen.

"When I finally did hear something, I turned around and saw him leering. I genuinely think he wanted to see what I would do. Maybe he thought I'd be interested, but

I got out of there immediately. I'll never forget Luke grabbing my ass as I edged past. I was tempted to slap him, but I figured the bastard might like that. I never told my husband about the ass part. I figured Matthew might kill him. The Reasoner men all have tempers."

Hannah followed up. "If Luke tried coming on to you, I imagine he might have done the same thing to Abigail. Did she ever tell you about anything similar happening to her?"

Emily shook her head. "Abigail and I may live in the same house, but we rarely talk. It's not that she's unfriendly. We're just very different people. Abigail is ambitious, a quality I've always admired, even if it's not one I share. She always has her sights set on the next conquest. When Matthew and I began dating, he was very open about the fact that they had been an item before she married Joshua."

"Did that worry you?" Hannah asked.

"Not really. Matthew told me he quickly realized Abigail wasn't for him. I know guys say that when they're talking about former girlfriends, but there was something about the look in Matthew's eyes that made me believe him. I don't think he ever quite trusted Abigail's motivations. In truth, I can't blame him."

I asked Emily about her mother-in-law. "We know Margaret separated herself from her family not long before her death. Do you have any idea what drove her to take that step?"

Emily frowned, wondering, perhaps, just how much she should say. "When Margaret first announced she would be eating in her room, Matthew and I tried to speak with her. Margaret could be intimidating as hell, but I always liked her. I didn't want to see her spending her last few years locked away on her own.

"Margaret invited us in readily enough but refused to say exactly what was wrong. She appeared almost stunned, like she didn't know what had hit her. I talked to Matthew afterward, and he thought maybe old age was finally catching up to his mother. Thinking back, I'm not so sure. The old lady still seemed pretty sharp. Whatever was bothering her, it had shaken her so badly she was afraid to say it out loud."

I looked at Hannah, who had no further questions. Just as we were leaving, Hannah glanced at her phone. Dr. Ho had texted to tell us the results were in from Luke's autopsy.

Our next interview was with Abigail. While we were anxious to talk with the family's new grand dame, Hannah and I decided it might be helpful to have the ME's feedback before our meeting. Hannah returned to our suite while I knocked on Abigail's door to tell her we would be late.

Abigail seemed annoyed, but that could have been a perceived insult to her social status. She finally agreed to wait a half hour.

Hannah had already turned on the TV before I

rejoined her in our room. When I entered, she dialed the ME's number.

Dr. Ho answered on the first ring, and Hannah put him on speaker. "You people bring me the most fascinating cases. I'm sorry it took so long to complete Mr. Reasoner's autopsy, but I wanted to make sure I got this correct."

Hannah looked at me. "Luke Reasoner died of a gunshot wound. I wouldn't have thought that'd be all that difficult to diagnose."

Clearly excited at his find, Dr. Ho almost chuckled. "You're correct. Luke Reasoner did die of a gunshot wound. The thing is, he would have died shortly afterward even without the shot. You asked me to look for something explaining why Mr. Reasoner might have stayed asleep when his assailant entered the room. The autopsy showed no drugs, though Mr. Reasoner had ingested a substantial amount of alcohol. It was what someone mixed in with that alcohol that would have killed him eventually. Crazy as it sounds, Luke Reasoner was drinking antifreeze."

Antifreeze? What the fuck was going on?

Hannah's reaction was more practical. "I know some homeless are known to drink antifreeze when they can't get their hands on alcohol. We need details. What does antifreeze do to the body, and how long has someone been poisoning Luke Reasoner?"

Dr. Ho returned to clinical mode. "It's hard to do

better than antifreeze if you're trying to poison an alcoholic. It's clear, odorless, with just a slight sweet taste. You put some in a bottle of booze, and the average drinker wouldn't notice a thing.

"Antifreeze is made up of ethylene or propylene glycol as well as methanol. By themselves, those products are more or less nontoxic. In the body, however, they metabolize very quickly into some very nasty byproducts. The symptoms of antifreeze poisoning can vary, but they tend to mimic those of alcohol intoxication. Those include impaired judgment, dizziness, disorientation, fatigue, and lack of balance. Mr. Reasoner was lying face down in his bed when he was shot. Given the toxic mix he'd been drinking, that's not really a surprise."

He stopped there, so I repeated Hannah's other question.

"How long would you guess he'd been drinking the stuff?"

"All those chemicals will eventually destroy your kidneys. Based on the extent of the kidney damage I saw in Reasoner's autopsy, I would guess he'd been drinking antifreeze for the last few weeks, though not consistently. From the number of bottles we saw in the room and the few in his trash, I'd say that intake was substantial. I'd like to analyze the remaining bottles to see if they were tampered with as well. Whether they were or not, however, my opinion stands. The signs are unmistakable."

Nothing with this family was ever easy. "Take us back to the gunshot wound," I said. "Can we assume the Ruger we found next to Luke Reasoner was the murder weapon?"

"It was. There was a single shot fired, and his death would have been instantaneous. As I mentioned, I'd assume that particular gun was chosen to avoid waking up the other household members. The time of death I gave you still holds, with Luke Reasoner likely shot between 5:00 and 6:00 a.m. I'd guess the earlier end of that estimate. Based on the placement of Mr. Reasoner's arms, it was clearly murder. There's no way he committed suicide."

"I'm asking for your opinion," Hannah said. "Why would someone choose to short-circuit the poisoning process with a gunshot?"

I'd considered that as well. "We're assuming the same person who shot Luke Reasoner also poisoned his alcohol supply. Knowing how many people disliked the man, that's a dangerous assumption to make. There's also one other possibility we should consider."

Hannah waited, and I continued. "It's possible they got tired of waiting. Somebody once said impatience can make wise people do foolish things. You mix impatience with hatred, then you've really got something."

We thanked Dr. Ho, and Hannah promised to arrange for the remaining liquor bottles in Luke's room to be sent to his lab for analysis. Before proceeding to our interview with Abigail, I had another question for Hannah.

"Do we have confirmation the murder weapon came from the Reasoner's gun closet?"

Hannah checked something in her notebook. "I spoke to Summers. While he wouldn't say for sure, the Ruger does match one of the weapons the Reasoners had purchased and stored there. I also asked Joshua, and he verified Summers's answer. He said the Ruger was purchased by his father a few years before he died. That would make sense. Ruger apparently stopped making that model in 2005."

"Did Summers tell you who had access to the closet?"

"Yes, and it's as bad as you might expect. The closet is always kept locked, but every family member has a key. That includes Lydia and Mark. The only nonfamily member with a key is Summers himself. It was a tradition for family to receive firearms training on their thirteenth birthday. Margaret's husband would bring in an instructor, and the entire family would watch."

For my thirteenth birthday, I just got a Timex. With that thought, Hannah and I went downstairs to meet Abigail Reasoner.

We knocked on the door of the master suite, and Abigail called to us to enter. Once inside, we found the Reasoner corporation's very pregnant marketing executive working at a large desk on the side of the living room area. I wondered briefly about the arrangement. From our previous visit, I knew the suite included two studies, both with their own desks and desktop computers. How many workspaces did one couple require?

Abigail looked up as we entered. While she motioned us toward a couch, she made no move to follow. Hannah and I waited impatiently as Abigail continued typing.

Finally, she closed her laptop and joined us, sitting on an old antique rocker that reminded me of the one my mother owned. She gestured back toward her laptop.

"We're about to undertake a major change in our detergent branding, hoping to broaden our appeal beyond the 1950's stereotypical American housewife. If I didn't have to meet with you, I'd be at headquarters strategizing with my team."

Hannah looked dumbfounded. I was just pissed.

"I apologize," I said. "We probably shouldn't have let something so minor as your brother-in-law's murder get in the way of your new branding campaign. Since you've deigned to give us some time, do you think we could get on with our questions?"

"Luke's death was and is a tragedy," Abigail responded, unapologetic. "Sometimes in the face of such situations, I find it easier to cope by sticking to business."

Hannah jumped in. "Let's start with your brother-in-law. What kind of relationship did you have with

Luke? Several sources have told us he could be a bit…aggressive with women, including those that were married." I would say Hannah was aiming for good cop/bad cop, but neither of us had the patience.

Abigail hesitated for only an instant. "I'm not sure what you're implying, but my relationship with Luke was always cordial. He never did anything that I would describe as improper."

"He was handsome, however," Hannah continued. "No disrespect to Matthew or Joshua, but he was considerably more so than either of his two older brothers. It's not surprising he was successful with the ladies, at least based on his social media accounts. Are you sure he never tried anything with you?"

Abigail hesitated a bit longer this time—she wasn't sure what we had heard.

"He may have occasionally said some things. It was just Luke's personality. I never took any of it very seriously."

I figured it was my turn. "What about Joshua? Did he take any of it seriously?"

"Joshua occasionally found his brother annoying, but he loved Luke. There was never any serious bad blood between them."

"Are you sure?" I continued. "I have a brother I've also found irritating. I never punched him in the middle of a newspaper interview."

Abigail's face had a hunted look. Not used to being

challenged, she wasn't good at hiding her annoyance.

"The incident you're referring to occurred during a difficult family period. All of us were on edge, including Luke and my husband. Joshua later apologized, and the two came to an understanding."

An understanding—an interesting way of putting things. I figured the next question should also be mine. Hannah might need plausible deniability should she face blowback from the police department.

"This difficult period between Luke and Joshua, wasn't that also about the time you found that you were pregnant?"

Abigail's face turned beet red, but her outburst was, if anything, a disappointment. "Just what are you implying?"

I had insulted a Reasoner, but I'd spent a good part of my childhood insulting grade school nuns. I figured if I could survive that, I could survive anything. Luke might have been a dickhead, but murder was murder. I saw no reason to back off.

"I'm asking if your relationship with Luke went beyond brother and sister-in-law. I'm asking if your husband was aware of that relationship, something any jury would consider a motive for murder."

Abigail stood up so quickly I was almost afraid for her unborn child.

"Get the hell out! And I'm not just talking about my suite; I want you both out of our house right the fuck now."

"No!" It was a single word, but the force of Hannah's response appeared to shock Abigail into silence. Hannah stood to face the new Reasoner matriarch and advanced on Abigail until she was only inches away.

"This is a murder investigation. While the death of two family members may be inconvenient, you don't call the shots here. You want Terry and me out of the house? That's fine—wish granted. We'll continue this interrogation at the Cleveland Twelfth Precinct. I'm sure you'll enjoy that. Besides the cops, you can always count on a reporter or two hanging around to see what stories they can find. A Reasoner hauled in for questioning on a murder? That'll be like Christmas come early.

"I'm sure those reporters will want to speak with you, and I'm sure I'll get any number of questions. While I usually like to keep these things quiet, I would consider it my civic duty to respond to any and all inquiries from the press."

Hannah then sat back down. "But all of this is completely up to you. Should we continue this down at the station house?"

This was fun, and I was more than a little turned on.

Abigail sat as well, her face still beet red. "My husband promised the family would cooperate here at the house. We've done so up until now and will continue to do so. I hope you can understand why I might react to these sordid...insinuations."

While I was enjoying the front seat to female fight club, I figured this was a good time for me to jump back in.

"They may be insinuations, Mrs. Reasoner, but you have to look at things from our perspective. We have your brother-in-law, who was notably handsome and not above chasing married women. That included women in his own family.

"Then you have yourself, a beautiful woman in her own right, a woman who had been trying to get pregnant for some time. Suddenly, you're successful, an event that just happened to coincide with your husband smashing his now-dead brother in the jaw without warning.

"You may not like it. You may view our questions as rude and salacious. But can you understand how this looks to us? Detective Page and I are suspicious by nature. That's one of the things that makes us good at our jobs. Based on those suspicions, we can't help thinking there are things you're not telling us. If we can find out the truth now, that will save us from asking these same embarrassing questions again in the future."

Abigail stood once more, and I reminded myself to be careful. As a marketing executive, this woman lied for a living. Based on how far she had come, I knew she was likely very good at it.

"First of all," she said, "I never had an affair with Luke. I love my husband, and I would never consider sleeping with another man. You're right that I've been hiding something from you. I have no wish to speak ill of the dead, but Luke did come on to me, quite aggressively I should say, one evening while Joshua was out of town.

"My brother-in-law was very fond of liquor. I'm sure you noticed the number of bottles in his room. While I don't drink as a rule, I do appreciate an occasional glass of wine, particularly those from vintages you might describe as exclusive. That is the one passion Luke and I shared.

"Luke had commissioned a representative to bid on a particularly rare collection from the wine department at Christie's. The wine in question was from the private collection of a man named Nicholas Kotovsky. I knew about the bid. Luke had told me weeks before, but I'd forgotten until the evening in question.

"I won't bore you with all the sordid details, but Luke saw me downstairs and told me the wine had arrived. He asked if I wanted to share a glass in his room. I should have said no, but I had a genuine interest in the vintage, and Luke had never tried anything untoward before that night.

"I followed Luke upstairs, not expecting more than a single glass of wine, but I realized my mistake when I stepped into his suite. After pouring the wine, Luke handed me a glass and stepped between me and the door. I didn't say anything, but I remember the smile on his face. It was creepy, the look you'd expect from some vagrant in an alley. I finished the wine, and Luke poured me another. He held it out to me, but I said no. Instead of backing off, Luke stepped even closer. I knew I was in real trouble when he reached out and cupped my left buttock. It was the kind of move you'd expect from a seventeen-year-old, but that was Luke in a nutshell."

"How did you get him to back off?" Hannah asked.

"I told him I would tell Joshua. He begged me not to. Luke had always been afraid of his older brothers. He said he'd had too much to drink that evening and lost control. I didn't say anything but just pointed to the door. Luke finally backed away and let me leave. He never said another word about that night."

Liars have a number of tells, the most common of which is to be overly generous with detail. They believe those elements will make their story more believable, but they typically only make it easier to disprove. I suspected Abigail had put a lot of thought into this rendition. It was just enough to trip her up.

Without that extra detail, it wouldn't have been a bad effort. Anyone who met Luke even once might have believed it. It wasn't dissimilar to the tale we heard from Emily Reasoner.

I decided to let the lie go for now. Instead, I asked about Joshua.

"I assume you told your husband. What was his reaction?"

"Joshua has a temper. All the Reasoner men do. I debated whether I should tell him at all, but I finally figured it was best that he knew. I waited until he got home. Joshua was furious. He was ready to march up to Luke's room, but I talked him out of it. The next day was that newspaper interview in the great room. I guess seeing Luke just waltz in was too much for Joshua. The punch was inevitable, but I think it was also cathartic. After confronting his brother, Joshua forgave him rather quickly. A week later, I saw the two of them and Matthew on the tennis court. Joshua was just watching, but there were smiles all around."

I glanced at Hannah, and she motioned me to continue. It was time to circle back.

"Returning to the incident in his room, you said Luke held out a second glass of wine. When you didn't take it, he stepped closer and cupped your left buttock. You have a strangely exact memory, not to mention your use of the word 'buttock.' Most women would have just said, 'He grabbed my ass.' Who knows? Maybe that's your marketing background.

"My question is this—if Luke was holding a glass of wine, I assume he was doing so with his dominant hand. My memory for detail isn't bad either, and I remember from our meals that your brother-in-law was right-handed. Depending on which hand he used for the grab, that would make it either the messiest buttock squeeze in history or the most awkward. Just how did he grab you that night?"

Not used to having her veracity questioned, Abigail returned to furious mode.

"I'm not sure what I said," she huffed, backtracking almost immediately, "but Luke put the wine glass down before approaching me. There was nothing in his hand when he grabbed me."

Hannah wasn't about to let it go that easily. She glanced at her notebook. "You told us he poured another glass and held it out to you. It's interesting that a woman so careful with her language would be confused on that point."

Abigail again stood up. "You asked me to remember an incident that took place months ago, and I did my best. Now, unless you have any other questions, I must insist that you leave."

As we walked out the door, I had one more question. "Who do you think killed your mother and brother-in-law?"

Abigail sighed. "I have no idea. Maybe it was one of the servants. Margaret and Luke could be pretty hard on them sometimes. Whoever it was, I can say for certain it wasn't me or my husband."

"I can understand you declaring your own innocence," Hannah said, "but how do you know it wasn't your husband?"

"I am a light sleeper. If Joshua had gotten up in the middle of the night, I would have known."

That reasoning might have had merit if everything else she'd told us wasn't such utter bullshit. Hannah and I left and went back to our room.

After turning on the TV, Hannah said, "Nice catch on the buttock thing. Not exactly court-admissible, but she was clearly lying."

"Buttocks are my specialty, starting and ending with your own. All kidding aside, it was an oddly formal turn of phrase—not exactly an anachronism, but odd nonetheless."

Hannah chuckled briefly. "Where does that leave us?"

"I can't prove it, but I think an affair was highly likely. Abigail is someone who goes after what she wants. She started with Matthew and moved on to Joshua as soon as she realized what he could give her. She made that move quickly enough, though my reporter source claimed there was no love lost between husband and wife. If it was a marriage of convenience for Abigail, why not take advantage of Joshua's business absences to screw around with the younger, more handsome Reasoner?

"I know we talked about this, but that really might explain how Abigail got pregnant after years of trying. If Joshua knew of their liaison, that explanation wouldn't have to necessarily be true. Just knowing his wife and brother had previously screwed around, you couldn't blame Joshua for coming to the logical conclusion regarding the father of his child. That would explain the punch. The Reasoners learned from childhood that affairs don't matter within the family. Luke as the father of Joshua's only child? That would have mattered to

Joshua quite a bit—"

I was interrupted by Hannah's "Easter Parade" ringtone, and as Hannah reached for her phone, I said, "My mother forced me to watch that musical every year, and I still have nightmares of Judy Garland and Fred Astaire. Can't you change it to something normal? Even rap would do."

"You hate rap and every other song not written by some blues musician in the 1940s. Be glad it's not closer to July fourth; I still have John Phillips Sousa stored in my cell. You should also be grateful I don't change my text tone. I will start if you keep harping on it."

She was right. Two bad songs would be much worse than one, and God knows what text alert she might choose just to annoy me. I decided to keep any further musical opinions to myself.

The call was from Franklin Aimes, and Hannah put the detective on speaker. The department computer expert was to contact us when he'd finally worked his way through the Reasoner's inventory system.

"This shouldn't have taken so long," he started, "but everything in that system is coded. That includes the chemicals, the people ordering them, the places they're shipped from, and the locations they're shipped to. I've been in systems used by criminals that were less convoluted. Fortunately, the number of carbon monoxide tanks used by the company is pretty small. Once I figured out how the CO containers were coded, I filtered out those above sixty pounds. I figured no one planning a murder would want to lug anything larger across an unfinished attic floor.

"I finally found two forty-pound tanks of carbon monoxide that were sent to the Reasoner mansion two days before Margaret Reasoner's death. To tell you just how unusual that is, there wasn't even a destination code in the system to signify the mansion. One of the inventory clerks made one up and added it in for this delivery. That's part of the reason I had a problem—it turns out 'BH' stands for 'Boss's House.' That code, by the way, is the only one in the system for a destination outside of the Reasoner corporation itself."

Aimes wasn't done. "The insanity doesn't stop there. More than two hundred Reasoner employees are authorized to initiate orders from the system, and a handful don't even work for the company anymore. The manager I spoke to admitted that was a problem. He said the system is due for a midyear audit in late June."

"Codes or not," I said, "I assume you would need some sort of security clearance to enter an order. I'd think that should be trackable. Who entered the order for the two carbon monoxide containers you tracked down?"

"That's just it." Aimes sounded exasperated. "Your level of security in the system is based on your login credentials. The highest level is reserved for managers and directors in the company, but certain line personnel also have permission to enter equipment and supply orders.

The order you're looking for? It was requested by one Alan Masters, a foreman listed as an employee in the detergent division. I spoke with human resources and three people who worked in his area. All of them said Alan Masters left the company years ago. His name was used, but this is not our guy."

"Who the fuck is running this company," Hannah said, "that they allow such slipshod standards in their IT department? Hell—could Terry or I step in and order something? What if it was an explosive?"

"In fairness," Aimes said, "this is an issue for virtually every organization above a certain number of employees. You pick your company, and I'll bet you'll find at least a few people who should not have computer access. Hospitals, factories, even defense contractors—that's why cyber security is such a big business these days."

Hannah looked at me. "How the hell will we figure out who ordered those tanks? Whoever pulled this off was more thorough than I hoped."

I'd been considering that problem, and I thought I had a solution. There were some things you couldn't hide via computer. I leaned closer to Hannah's phone.

"Detective Aimes, thank you for all your work on this. I wonder if there's one more thing you can track down for us. You said the company doesn't typically deliver to sites separate from one of their factories. I'm guessing for this delivery, they called a service, some firm that's used to transporting dangerous chemicals. Can you find out what firm they used? Once you do that, we need to know the name of the employee who dropped off the two tanks."

Hannah looked at me, suddenly realizing where I was headed. "If we can find the person who made the delivery, we can ask him who accepted the containers. Once we know that, we'll have our killer."

"Exactly. Is that doable, Detective Aimes?"

"It might take me a day, but it should be possible. Pray the Reasoners used a small firm because they might not have as much turnover. A company with a lot of customers? That might be more of a problem. I'll try to track this person down, but I'll need you to send me current pictures of the Reasoner family members."

"That'll be easy," Hannah said, "You'll get the pictures from me in the next hour."

"One more thing," Aimes added. "I'm getting good reports on Tomas. He's even done pretty well on his range work, and I know that worried him. The department is bleeding computer people because there isn't one of us who couldn't make more in the private sector. Given his skills, Tomas should make it out of the academy without a problem."

I'd never used Detective Aimes's first name; doing so seemed almost presumptuous. However, this was one of those situations where a last name just didn't seem to cut it.

"Franklin, I really want to thank you for everything you've done for Tomas. Given his past, I know that took a certain amount of trust."

"No thanks necessary," he replied, seeming touched, "and my computer exploits before entering the force weren't all that much different from Tomas's. I'll let you both know what I find out regarding the chemical delivery."

Hannah ended the call. Rather than eat an uncomfortable meal with the Reasoners, we decided to grab a pizza at a restaurant Hannah knew of.

We picked up the pizza and returned to our room. Hannah, a slice in hand, said, "You did well today. You poked a gigantic hole in Abigail's story, and you came up with the idea of letting the deliveryman identify who accepted the CO tanks. You did so well, I'm tempted to allow you to squeeze my left buttock."

This day might not end so badly after all.

"I was actually hoping you'd allow me to squeeze both buttocks. I believe in equal opportunity when it comes to those things."

As she removed her clothes, Hannah said, "As long as you aren't holding a glass of wine, I'll let you squeeze whatever the hell you want."

CHAPTER TEN

DAY FIVE

HAVING COMPLETED ALL but one of our interviews, Hannah and I designated days five and six in the mansion for tying up loose ends. Besides our remaining interview with Mark Reasoner, our unresolved issues included a meeting with Margaret's lawyer, an appointment we had rescheduled from the previous day. We also intended to conduct a more thorough search of the Reasoner's attic, though our odds of finding anything relevant were slim.

In addition, we planned a visit to the Bridle Path Bridge. Bernie's death there was not officially part of our purview, but I felt I owed a visit to her and Annabelle. Bernie had died shortly after realizing something was badly off at the Reasoner mansion. Knowing Bernie and her instincts, I was guessing she'd figured out what had driven Margaret to divorce herself from the family. That was one of the key remaining questions in our case, something Margaret herself had refused to answer.

We also needed to hear from Detective Aimes about the person who delivered the carbon monoxide to the Reasoner home. Assuming Aimes was successful, the driver's identification should tell us who was responsible for Margaret's death.

We started with Margaret's lawyer. Adam Cheevers was the lead partner in the firm of Cheevers, Loeman, and Blanque, a boutique Cleveland law firm specializing in estate planning for the very rich. Arriving five minutes before our ten o'clock appointment, Hannah and I waited for Cheevers in the firm's ornately designed outer office.

Half an hour later, there was still no sign of Adam Cheevers, and Hannah was getting restless. Cheevers's secretary also appeared nervous. We didn't fit the profile of their clientele, and she likely hoped we'd be safely tucked away in a conference room before anyone else arrived.

The secretary was rescued a few minutes later as the man himself came striding out of his office. Cheevers, tall and in his early sixties, greeted us like long-lost cousins. Interestingly, he was holding an Egg McMuffin.

Brushing the remains of his breakfast off his designer suit, he said, "You have to excuse me; I've grown addicted to these. I usually eat at least three every morning."

I wondered about his cholesterol but decided that was none of my business. Cheevers escorted us into his office, giving me an interested glance as he did so.

"I am really excited to meet you, Mr. Luvello. I've read about your exploits, and one of my clients told me about your interesting past."

I suspected Ray West but decided not to ask. The Margaret Reasoner portion of this investigation was time-limited, and we were already on day five.

Hannah started things off after taking a seat in one of the three leather chairs. "We shouldn't take up much of your time. We're here about Margaret Reasoner and the codicil she inserted in her will. Let's start off with when that was done. After that, we'd like to hear her reasons for making the change."

"Judge Cramer, the representative Margaret selected as her primary arbiter, called earlier this week to tell me you two would be in touch." Cheevers chose his words carefully. "He has held Margaret's privilege since her passing, so attorney-client confidentiality is not an issue.

"Confidentiality aside, there's not really much I can say. Margaret came to my office on September 12th of last year to discuss her will. I assumed it was a routine review. Margaret was in the habit of meeting with me yearly to discuss the individual details of her estate. Like many of my clients, she liked to tweak things occasionally. Sometimes, she would add a charity or take one off, that sort of thing. Harold had left the entire Reasoner estate to Margaret after his death. The changes Margaret made were typically minor, particularly when compared to the estate's overall size. With Margaret's advanced age, I was in the habit of inviting a second lawyer to join us for these meetings. I told Margaret that was routine, but I did so just in case there were any questions later about her mental state.

"I knew something was off during that visit when Margaret told my secretary she wished to speak only to me. When Margaret told me what she was considering, I thought my cognitive concerns had proven valid. I won't bore you with the details of the change—you are aware of those already. Still, the thought that someone in Margaret's family might be trying to kill her seemed ludicrous, if not insane.

"Margaret's demeanor, however, was almost icily calm. There were certainly no outward signs of any impairment. She had done a fair amount of research on her own regarding the wording of the codicil. I tweaked what she suggested only slightly. I would guess maybe 90 percent of the language was hers.

"After we were done, I asked Margaret if she wanted me to make anyone in her family aware of the addition. Margaret, being who she was, looked at me as though I was insane. She had already spoken to Judge Cramer and her alternate representative. I'm assuming the judge might have been the person who helped her with the original wording. With no reason not to, I added the codicil and filed the revised will with the Geauga County Probate Court."

I asked the next obvious question. "Did Margaret give you any indication who in her family she viewed as a threat?"

He shook his head. "She did not. I suggested she call the police, but she just waved me off. Given her rather grim mood, I didn't think of asking anything else. I would say our meeting lasted no more than thirty minutes. That was the last time I ever saw Margaret Reasoner, though I understand her death was from natural causes."

Neither Hannah nor I corrected Cheevers. Doing so would have led to a number of inquiries neither of us had any time to answer. Before we left, I had one more question.

"You said you didn't contact anyone ahead of time about the change in Margaret's will. Tell us who you notified after she died."

Cheevers grabbed one more Egg McMuffin out of his top desk drawer before replying. "I contacted Joshua Reasoner and Judge Cramer as per Margaret's instructions. The judge was aware of the codicil; Joshua was...surprised. Using some very colorful language, he accused me of acceding to the wishes of an obviously demented older woman. I told him his mother did not appear demented in any way. When we left the conversation, I assumed Joshua might seek outside legal guidance to see if there was any avenue to contest the will. I heard nothing if he did so."

After thanking Cheevers for his time, we left his office and returned to Hannah's car.

"That man," Hannah said, "must either have a sky-high cholesterol count or the most amazing metabolism I've ever seen. I've never eaten more than one Egg McMuffin, and that was on a bet."

"You do, however, eat toaster pastries every morning."

"Toaster pastries are fine dining compared to those things. Besides, you eat them too."

She had a point, and I moved back to the case.

"I'm not sure we learned much. It's interesting Margaret kept Joshua as her primary family point of contact. I don't know if he wasn't involved in whatever dispute was eating at her or if she just felt she had no other choice."

Hannah shook her head. "You're forgetting option three. Margaret may have wanted to throw the codicil in her oldest son's face."

We drove back to Hunting Valley, past the Reasoner estate, until we reached the Bridle Path Bridge. The bridge was only five minutes away from the mansion, and we parked along a small drive off Fairmount Boulevard near the entrance.

Not big enough for cars, the Bridle Path Bridge served as a walkway for pedestrians, bike riders, and the occasional city dweller on horseback. The latter was not as unusual as one might think. The White North Stables in Hunting Valley was one of the premier equestrian training facilities in the state of Ohio.

Dodging the occasional horse dropping, Hannah and I made our way to the middle of the bridge. At only sixty feet across, it provided a picturesque view of the stream that ran below, as well as a small waterfall some distance away. The drop from the bridge to the water was maybe forty feet, easily enough for a broken neck.

Based on the medical examiner and police reports, Bernie had fallen or been pushed from roughly the point where Hannah and I were now standing.

"I brought the police report, but I can't help thinking she was pushed." Hannah peered down at the water, voicing my thoughts. "The pictures the cops took showed Bernie lying on her side, her body leaning on one of those rocks we're looking at right now. Without the rock, Bernie would have been lying on her back."

"I know the cops said suicide," I said, "but how many suicides have you seen where the person jumped backward? The whole thing doesn't make sense. Bernie's outlook on life wouldn't have allowed her to admit defeat that way."

"Assume she was pushed," Hannah replied. "I have trouble picturing an assailant sneaking up on her. The mansion also isn't visible from here. That means she was likely planning to meet someone."

"I agree, but the obvious question is, who? It would have had to have been someone she trusted, maybe someone from the staff. Bernie never went anywhere without her gun, and she was a hell of a shot. If it was a Reasoner family member, I can't believe she would have let them get close enough for a shove."

With nothing else to go on, Hannah and I returned to her BMW. We picked up some lunch and drove back to Shadow House. Not for the first time, I thought about the mansion's rather grim moniker. We were only on day five of our stay, but I was having difficulty thinking of the Reasoner mansion by any other name.

We returned to the house just before our scheduled meeting with Mark Reasoner. We knocked on his door, interrupting Mark just as he looked to be finishing up a video game, a new release called *Titan Overlord.*

While Mark's demeanor seemed low-key, I was re-minded of the attempted rape story we heard from Olivia during our meetings with the staff. Unfortunately, there was no way we could bring up that episode without breaking Olivia's confidence. I also doubted Mark was our killer, though he was undoubtedly slimy. Margaret's murder took a great deal of intelligence and planning, two traits that didn't seem present in Judith's son. While Luke's shooting appeared sloppy, the antifreeze in his system suggested another layer to the killing that may have also made it more complicated than it first appeared.

As planned, Hannah started with something we'd asked all the Reasoner children.

"Mark, you know why we're here. Why don't you start by telling us about your relationship with your uncle and grandmother."

Mark mumbled a few unintelligible words before finally answering. "I didn't have a relationship with my grandmother. We got along well enough, don't get me wrong. She always gave me gifts for my birthday, asked about my studies in high school, that sort of thing.

"But our talks were always very surface level. I was maybe thirteen when Grandpa Harold died. A few months after the funeral, I asked Grandma about the company and one of its detergent product lines. I remember being very proud of myself. I researched my question beforehand because I didn't want Grandma to think I was an idiot.

"I will never forget the dismissive look on her face when I finally did ask. Grandma just said she would talk to me later, and then she walked away. We never did talk, of course. Lydia, Uncle Luke, and I—Grandma thought we were the mental morons of the family. She would give us money when asked, but there was no real relationship. We never seemed worth Grandma's time, though she did try to argue with me when I decided not to go to college."

I was curious about who he'd left out. "What about your mother? She had nothing to do with the Reasoner corporation. How did your grandmother treat her?"

"My mother may not be involved with the company, but she represents the respectable social side of the Reasoner family. Whenever mother went to an art function or purchased a painting, Grandma would ask her who was there and who she spoke to. Grandma once tried to talk Lydia into taking more of an interest in the arts. She said it was important for every wealthy family to have a presence in those circles."

"You said you and your uncle were the same in your grandmother's eyes," Hannah said. "Did you and your Uncle Luke have any sort of relationship?"

Mark smiled for the first time. "I always liked my uncle, and I wouldn't mind pulling the trigger myself on the person who shot him. When I turned sixteen, he took me for a ride in his Corvette. I remember we stopped at this small house, maybe a half hour away. Uncle Luke told me he wanted to introduce me to a friend.

"It turned out the friend was a woman, someone I found out later owed Uncle Luke some money. I never learned her name, but she was cute and in her midtwenties. I also remember she had a young kid running around her kitchen.

"The woman must have been prepared for us to arrive. As soon as we got there, she sent her kid off to his room to play. After that, she led me up to her bedroom while my uncle waited downstairs. That was the first time I ever had sex. I know it sounds kind of sleazy now, but the woman didn't seem to mind. Uncle Luke called it my birthday present, and I never saw the lady again."

I couldn't have been happier not to have been born rich. Still, I had another question. Whoever ordered the carbon monoxide must have had some knowledge of the company or at least known others that worked there. While I was almost certain that wasn't Mark, I needed to make sure.

"You said you never went to college, but did you ever have a summer job or an internship at the Reasoner corporation?"

"I worked two summers in the shipping department. We sent huge pallets of detergent pretty much everywhere across the United States. There were a few European shipments, but those were pretty rare."

I asked if he ever placed orders through the company's computer system.

"I never got near one of the computers. I used to complain about that because computers were the one thing I was pretty good at using. All the shipping supervisor wanted me to do was haul boxes. I'm pretty sure he didn't like having a Reasoner working in his area. The grunt work was his way of pushing me to quit."

Hannah spoke up. "You and your sister are still in your twenties. Is it lonely being tied up in this house so much?"

Mark sneered, reminding me of his late uncle. "I have a car and an allowance probably five times what you make in your cop job. The money gives me access to a far less lonely life. You asked about Uncle Luke? That was one of the things he taught me. I won't speak for my sister, but she's always been a bit agoraphobic. She has a car, but I can't remember the last time she used it. I always imagined Lydia haunting the corridors of this house, floating down the stairs in one of her nightgowns. She and I rarely talk these days. She always turns away whenever she sees me."

I looked at Hannah, but neither of us had anything more to ask. We left Mark's room and made our way down the second-floor corridor past our suite, headed for a date neither of us was eager to keep. We needed to do a more extensive search of the Reasoner attic.

I told Hannah about the rat traps, and she shook her head. "What kind of rich person's house has rats?"

"They're not my favorite creatures, but I worry more about the traps. Be careful sticking your hands in any dark corners."

Hannah and I had both brought pocket-sized Fenix flashlights. Their 1,200 lumens were strong enough to both illuminate and blind a potential attacker, but I was doubtful the rats would be impressed.

Hannah agreed to take the left side of the attic while I took the right. Before we began, I made my way down the entire floor and turned on all the overhead lights.

"I'm hoping the noise I made will scare off whatever might be hiding up here."

"The rats, maybe," Hannah replied. "But God only knows what else they have hiding up here."

What they had hiding turned out to be a fascinating mix. Opening box after box, we took a tour through Reasoner family history. Hannah found a photo album with old two-by-three-inch snapshots of Edward Reasoner and his family in front of the original mansion. As he stood next to a child and a woman I assumed was his wife, those photos had clearly been taken in happier times. The shadows had yet to arrive.

Next to a collection of old children's toys, I found boys' clothing that appeared well over fifty years old. I turned to Hannah.

"These clothes would be guaranteed to bring you grief in any schoolyard in America."

"Remember who you're talking about," Hannah said. "These kids had tutors. None of them would have gone anywhere near a schoolyard unless it was to drive past on their way to the country club."

Farther down the attic, we found more modern keepsakes. Most were still photos and clothing items, though we also found a rather imposing collection of hunting knives. I held one up to show Hannah.

"Maybe," she said, "we should take one in case we find a rat or our killer."

I shook my head. "I don't know about the rats, but I strongly suspect our killer is residing downstairs. This might be the safest place we can be right now."

We continued searching until we reached the far end of the attic. We had now spent three hours upstairs. Even in late March, the heat was stifling.

That far end of the attic was also devoted to clothing, many of those items stored in large plastic boxes as much as five feet in length. They were, Hannah told me, the type of storage often devoted to old dresses or formal gowns.

It was the dress lying crumpled behind one of the last attic boxes that told me we might have discovered something important. I tried to pull out the box in front of the dress. It was made of metal, and whatever was inside made it far too heavy for my efforts. I turned to Hannah.

"I need your help with this one. Either the Reasoners have taken to storing suits of armor, or the item in this box is no dress."

Hannah came over, and between the two of us, we managed to drag the metal box out of the corner. Hannah then reached for the dress behind it and almost lost her hand in the process.

The *snap* from the trap under the dress was immediate and terrifying. I was inspecting our box when it happened, but Hannah told me it came within an inch of her fingertips.

"I hate this fucking place," she said with a grimace. "One more inch, and I would have had to learn to shoot with my left hand. I would have still been better than you, but the margin would have been much closer."

She was probably right—my lack of marksmanship had been proven on multiple occasions. I moved to Hannah's side to offer assistance, but she brushed me away and returned to our metal box. The trunk was likely more than fifty years old, though it was sealed with a modern cable tie.

Most cops carried multiple weapons, and Hannah was no exception. As with other cops, only some of those weapons were legal.

Having almost lost her hand, Hannah was in no mood for delay. The switchblade she removed from her pocket was a nasty little affair. With a four-inch blade, it cut through the tie in no time.

"Sometime," I told Hannah, "You'll have to tell me where the hell you got that thing. I know you can't buy them here."

"I would tell you, but then you'd want one. One piece of advice John gave me when you weren't around— never, ever let you carry a knife."

The fact that he was right wouldn't keep me from seeking revenge on John later. For now, though, I was concentrating on the box.

In truth, I expected to see nothing. I had always assumed whoever killed Margaret had long ago ditched the

CO containers they'd used. I couldn't have been more shocked, therefore, to find myself looking at two metal tanks lying side by side and easily visible underneath yet another old dress. I looked at Hannah, who was equally stunned.

"Jesus shit," she said finally. "I was beginning to think these were like the holy grail."

Hannah and I both put on gloves, and I heaved one of the tanks out of the box. Stamped just over the supplier's name was a serial number next to a metallic sticker with the Reasoner corporation logo. While the serial number and logo had multiple scratches, the circled *R* was unmistakable. We had our means. Now we just needed our killer.

Each tank appeared to weigh about thirty pounds. When full, I guessed the gas would add another five to ten. Hannah hoisted the second tank out, and its markings were identical to the first.

"Why do you suppose," Hannah asked, "the killer left the tanks here? Why not just take them out the same way they were brought up here?"

I had wondered the same thing and thought I had an answer. "In a word—disposal. These tanks aren't biodegradable. If you toss them in some trash bin—not easy to do given their size—there's a fair chance they might be identified. Look at the scratches on both tanks. I think someone went to a lot of effort to try to hide the serial numbers and Reasoner company logo. With both of those still visible, our killer may have been afraid the tanks would be found. Keeping them hidden up here might have seemed safer, at least until he or she could have come up with a disposal solution."

Hannah had finished taking pictures and was already on her phone. Her first call was to Franklin Aimes, still busy seeking the identity of our elusive carbon monoxide delivery driver. After ending that call, she turned again to me.

"The delivery company is cooperating. Aimes has a name for the driver, a woman named Amy Caster. Unfortunately for us, Amy is currently on vacation at her sister's cabin in Pennsylvania. They gave Aimes her cell, but the Wi-Fi at her location is apparently spotty. That's a problem since Aimes not only has to speak to her, he needs to send her the Reasoner family pictures to complete an identification."

Hannah next called Captain Slovitz, who arranged for a patrol car to pick up the carbon monoxide tanks and log them into evidence. The captain immediately asked to be put on speaker, his booming voice echoing off the attic's bare walls.

"Tell me just what the hell you two have so far."

Hannah gave him the bullet-point version. That included the details behind our attic discovery of the CO tanks and Aimes's difficulty contacting the delivery driver.

After promising to send a black-and-white to pick

up the tanks, the captain asked, "Is there any chance that Aimes gave you the location of the cabin? My brother is a cop in PA, and his family camps all over the state. A phone call is probably not going to happen; many of those campgrounds are in the hills. You tell me where she is, and I can have George contact one of his PA cop buddies to track down your driver. They can also show her the Reasoner pictures and let you know if she makes an ID."

Hannah checked her notes. The driver's name is Amy Caster; her sister is Shirley Caster. It looks like they're staying in the Buttonwood Campground."

I was checking Google as Hannah spoke. "The campground is in a city called Mifflintown."

The captain rarely appreciated my uninvited interruptions, but today he was insult-free. "Send me the pictures, and I'll call George and explain what we're looking for. I'm not sure how long it'll take him, but I'm betting he can help us. If we're lucky, I'll call you back tonight. Otherwise, we're looking at tomorrow morning."

Hannah thanked Slovitz and ended the call. After texting Aimes to let him know of our conversation with the captain, she said, "It looks like we're on hold until either Aimes or Slovitz gets back to us with an identification."

With nothing else to do, we finished our attic search. Closing the last box, I said, "The Salvation Army would have a field day with some of this stuff. I'm amazed so much of this just sits here."

"For all you know, they do donate some of it. The stuff up here may be the things they can't imagine some poor person wearing."

Rather than sit and wait for the patrol car, we moved the CO tanks to the elevator and locked them in our suite. It was now close to seven, and neither Hannah nor I felt like going out for dinner. With some trepidation, we decided to eat once more with the Reasoner family.

"What are the odds," Hannah said, "the tanks will still be here when we get back?"

To our knowledge, no one had witnessed our finding or carrying them to our suite. Still, Hannah had a point. We positioned the tanks in our bathroom, and I grabbed a camera from my suitcase.

Designed to be worn on clothing, the camera would work just as well stuck to a bathroom window blind. The miniature battery would last at least ninety minutes, plenty of time for us to finish dinner.

Hannah and I then went downstairs and joined the already-seated Reasoner clan in the dining area.

Joshua seemed surprised to see us and almost sputtered as we arrived. "We weren't expecting you this evening, but there's plenty of food. Dinner is braised pork chops. I'm hoping that meets with your approval. I'm also hoping we can get an update on your investigation."

I looked at Hannah, who simply shrugged. We were expecting a black-and-white sometime within the next five minutes, and that was hardly something we could hide from the family. Hannah would need to supervise the handoff of the tanks, so the update would be mine.

The Cleveland police car, visible through the dining room window, arrived even faster than we expected. Hannah excused herself, ignoring the alarmed looks from the others. I waved my hand to draw their attention.

"We told you about our theory regarding Margaret's death. Based on input from the medical examiner and the hole drilled through your grandmother's ceiling, we believe someone released carbon monoxide into her bedroom. The gas entered through the smoke detector on the ceiling.

"The thing you don't know—Detective Page and I found two spent carbon monoxide tanks in your attic just before we came down for dinner. Those tanks were hidden in a large clothing box on the far-right side of the attic. Both were marked with the Reasoner company logo."

"Bullshit!" This came from Matthew Reasoner. The rest of the family remained quiet.

I chose to ignore him. "We couldn't confirm the identity of the employee who ordered the tanks. It appears the code used to request the shipment belonged to someone who left the company some time ago. The delivery location, however, was definitely here. We are taking steps to discover who received those tanks when they arrived. I'm hopeful we'll have a name by tomorrow morning. The cop car we saw arriving is here to pick up the containers."

I waited then for the inevitable questions. They started with Joshua.

"How do we know this isn't some kind of setup? I got a call at work today from some reporter wanting information on Luke's death. When I told him the death was being investigated, he then brought up my mother. By the terms of your NDAs, none of this was supposed to get out."

Two deaths under his watch, and he was worried about bad publicity.

"The nondisclosure agreements we signed covered Detective Page and myself. A leak could have come from anywhere, including the medical examiner's office and the Hunting Valley Police Department. Neither Detective Page nor I spoke to your reporter. As to the idea this was a setup, the evidence the tanks were delivered here is clear-cut. They were also stored in your attic, a location where few individuals except your family have access. Once we get word on who accepted delivery, that should settle the issue for good."

Joshua wasn't mollified, but he did remain quiet. The next question was from Lydia Reasoner.

"Beyond a retainer, what was your goal in taking

this case, Mr. Luvello?”

Lydia’s inquiry was, to say the least, not what I was expecting. Hannah, returning just in time to hear it, looked as flummoxed as me. Sensing this was somehow important, I paused before responding.

“I’m here to find the truth. I have the same motivation in all the cases I investigate. I want to know what really happened to your grandmother and uncle.”

Lydia appeared only vaguely satisfied. “I always figured the truth had layers, like the cemetery where my grandparents are buried. The writing and designs on their tombstones are each so beautiful. Everything on the marble is supposed to be true—their birthdates, the dates they died, and even the little poems in between.

“Beneath the stones, we have a different truth—the rotting corpses that decay no matter how much the mortician talked you into paying for a casket. What do you think is most real, the headstone or the rot underneath?”

Judith frantically tried to wave her daughter into silence. I was fascinated, not so much by the question as by the person asking it. I remembered our interview with Lydia and the sheer nightgown she wore for the occasion. She was a curious mix, half childlike ingenue, the other half temptress. I was convinced she knew far more about the goings on at the Reasoner mansion than her family gave her credit for.

This was also the second time Lydia had alluded to the rot that plagued her family, the first being when she told us that everyone in it lied. Just what did she know?

Lydia waited for my answer, ignoring her mother's attempts to short-circuit our conversation. I figured I owed her an honest response.

"You started by asking about my goals for this investigation, and I said my aim was to find the truth." Gazing at each face around the table, I suddenly felt tired. "At least one person here, possibly two, committed murder. You want my truth? That annoys the fucking hell out of me. All of you like to pretend your family name means something. From what I've seen, it doesn't mean shit. Luke may have been a bastard, but you lost a brother, for God's sake. Unless I've missed it, not one of you has even inquired about his body and a potential funeral.

"That doesn't even address your mother. She was killed by someone who took the time to drill a hole through her ceiling and pump in carbon monoxide. Death by CO gas may be painless, but you still have a sociopath in your midst. I get no sense that any of you care, except to keep that fact out of the newspapers."

Hannah looked at me in surprise. Usually, I was the calm one in our partnership. As for the Reasoners, I was likely the first person to give them such a thorough dressing down in their own home. They stared at me, and I stared back. This family could destroy me, but I was no longer in the mood for pretend niceties.

I returned my gaze to Lydia, wondering if she would

ask anything further. Margaret's granddaughter appeared pleased with my response, as if I had validated her judgment somehow. Instead of speaking, she simply nodded. I swung my gaze then to Joshua and waited for the fallout.

Sounding almost guilty, he said, "I know we can be an unusual family. Insular is one word I've heard to describe us, though I disagree with the implication. Whatever you may think, I do miss my brother. We had our disagreements, but I loved him just like I loved my mother."

His voice then took on a new edge as he continued. "Do not think you know us, Mr. Luvello, just because you've stayed here for five days. You believe we're arrogant? I would say your presumptions are equally so. I would think such arrogance could be foolhardy, if not dangerous, for a man in your profession."

Was that a threat? I chose not to respond, though I continued staring in his direction. Finally, his attention returned to his dinner.

Hannah and I finished our meal in silence, the Reasoner clan now quiet as well. We polished off the best pork chops I had ever tasted and then returned to our room. Tomorrow would be our last full day at the Shadow House. Given my little outburst, we'd likely eat that day's dinner at one of the local restaurants.

Hannah turned to me when we returned to our room; she didn't even bother to turn on the TV. "I know you've got that whole 'eat the rich' thing going sometimes, but are you sure that was smart?"

I wasn't sure, but I also wasn't sorry. "The truth is, I find this place exhausting. What you heard tonight had been building for some time. Right now, I just want to solve these two murders and get the hell out of here."

Hannah considered me thoughtfully. "You said two murders. What about Bernie?"

"I haven't forgotten about Bernie. If we find who killed Margaret and Luke, I'm hoping that'll tell us who pushed Bernie off the Bridle Path Bridge."

Hannah turned on the TV and said, "Now, onto the bigger question. Just what was Lydia Reasoner trying to tell us? That girl knows something. I just can't figure out whether she's the smartest person in the family or the most insane."

I was wrestling with the same question. "It's the weirdest thing. Lydia reminds me of someone, but I just can't pin down who. It's been driving me crazy ever since our interview in her suite."

Hannah's raised her eyebrows. "She reminds you of someone? How many beautiful girls in slinky nightgowns have come on to you during one of your cases?"

"Only the rich ones, particularly since my voice got deeper. For whatever reason, the poor ones never seem to care."

"So, you credit my rich mother and father with the fact that you and I hit it off. I'll have to tell them that. I'm sure they'll take it as a compliment—knowing how they feel about you."

She was joking, I think.

CHAPTER ELEVEN

DAY SIX

OUR SIXTH DAY at the Reasoner mansion started with Hannah and me grabbing some muffins from the refrigerator by the breakfast nook. We ate breakfast in our room and discussed the day ahead.

Looking at my notes, I said, "We need one more conversation with the medical examiner. He initially hedged on his carbon monoxide finding based on the circumstances surrounding Margaret's death. Given what's happened since—the discovery of the tanks and the hole drilled into Margaret's room—I want to make sure he no longer has any doubts."

Hannah had her own follow-up list. "The captain promised us an answer by this morning from the deliverywoman in Pennsylvania. Getting in touch with Slovitz can be difficult, so let's start by calling Aimes."

Hannah's ringtone sounded seconds after her statement. She was wrong about Slovitz. Not only would he not be hard to get ahold of, both he and Aimes were on their way to the Shadow House.

Hannah talked more loudly than usual, as if she was having trouble hearing. She finally ended the call and turned to me. "The signal sucked, and I could barely understand him. You can bet they found something. The two of them wouldn't be coming all the way over here if they hadn't."

I wasn't sure about the Reasoner's protocol for unannounced visitors, but I was sure some sort of violence would be involved. I informed Lawton Summers of the captain's arrival. I figured Summers would alert the appropriate Reasoner.

A dark Chevy Impala, the go-to for unmarked police cars in every city, pulled into the side lot just ten minutes later. To my surprise, the captain's car was followed by a Hunting Valley black-and-white and the tan Bentley favored by Joshua Reasoner. Perhaps my visions of a shoot-out weren't so farfetched after all.

Slovitz and Aimes disembarked from the Impala, and the captain took a long look at the outside of the mansion. Chief Reilly got out of the Hunting Valley cop car, the first time I'd seen him since the day Luke was killed.

The captain and Reilly shook hands. Along with Aimes, they then joined Hannah and me as we waited outside. Joshua had pulled his car into the covered lot the Reasoners had designated for their personal use.

Captain Slovitz moved straight to Hannah while ignoring me pointedly. Glancing at Chief Reilly, he said, "I invited the chief because this is his turf, and I thought he should hear what I have to say. I assume the guy who came in behind us is a Reasoner. Is there any chance we can go inside before he or she sticks their nose or something where it doesn't belong?"

Summers stood behind us, likely listening in. Without a word, Hannah led the group past him and into the small movie theater downstairs. Aimes whistled when he saw the setup.

"Don't get too carried away," the captain said. "With any luck, we'll be out of here before the rich shits hear what we found."

We sat in the theater's front two rows, and the captain pulled out a picture. We were then interrupted by rich shit number one.

"Lawton said we would be having another police visit," Joshua said in his best lord of the manor tone. "Is there any reason I wasn't informed directly about your arrival?"

Slovitz looked pissed. If he had been at all worried

about the politics of this situation, that worry was long forgotten. "We're here to discuss evidence in a murder investigation, an investigation in which you are a prime suspect. You can either get out of this room or get hauled in on an obstruction charge. Right now, those are your only two options."

Joshua turned to leave, but before exiting, announced, "I'm going to call my lawyer!"

Slovitz sounded amused. "And tell him what, exactly? We're here investigating two murders that took place on your property. You and your lawyer will find out the details of the evidence when we're ready. Until we reach that point, you need to get out."

Slovitz turned back to us when Joshua finally left. "According to the Pennsylvania cops who interviewed the woman driver, she had no problem identifying the individual who accepted delivery of the tanks. While some of the other pictures looked close, this is our man."

He showed us the photo from the file he was carrying. The driver had identified Luke Reasoner.

Hannah looked at her captain. "I know you said the driver was certain, but is there any chance she made a mistake?"

"The first thing we did with those tanks you found was dust them for prints," Aimes replied. "You said you lifted them from the bottom, so we concentrated on the handles and the sides. Whoever brought them upstairs did a good job of wiping the handgrips, but they must have reached out at some point to steady one of the tanks. I'm assuming that was due to the unevenness of the attic floor. Luke Reasoner had been arrested several times for various petty offenses, most of which he committed while drunk. The prints they took then matched the prints on the tank. The driver also said something else. The handoff of the tanks occurred just outside the entrance to the estate. That arrangement would make sense from Reasoner's perspective. It would be out of sight of the staff or any family members who happened to be looking outside."

"It seems like we're halfway home," I said to Hannah.

Chief Reilly spoke up. "I'll talk with the ME, and we'll change Margaret Reasoner's cause of death to homicide. The surviving Reasoners will raise holy hell, but we'll also list Luke as her killer. You should contact the Cranberg Institute, Mr. Luvello. They're about to become a hell of a lot richer."

Reilly turned to Hannah. "Luke Reasoner didn't kill himself. That means we still have one more killer to find. Where are we on that murder?"

Hannah glanced quickly at me. "While it was money that got us involved, everything else about this case has been personal. The ME told us Luke was being slowly poisoned with antifreeze long before he was shot. Antifreeze mimics the effects of alcohol, including disorientation and loss of muscle control. Eventually, the victim just falls asleep and dies. I don't know why the killer suddenly changed their timeline and shot Reasoner instead. We suspect that may have had to do with our involvement, though I'm not at all sure why."

I thought I might have an answer, but I had no direct evidence to prove whether I was right. We needed to talk with the ME and one other individual. Because Hannah was the lead detective in Luke's murder, I would need her permission to try.

I'd been silent, and Hannah stared straight at me. She knew me well enough to know I had something. She also knew I wasn't ready to share it just yet. I would try to stay on more solid ground until we were alone.

"We need to talk to the ME at least one more time," I said. "I want to know what he found in those other liquor bottles he took from Luke Reasoner's room. I also want to see if there are any fingerprints on the bottles, though I suspect our killer would have been too careful to leave any behind.

"We should start with what we do know. Luke Reasoner killed his mother. He did so shortly after she cut herself off from her family. You have to assume the reason for that divorce started with Luke, particularly given the timing of Margaret's murder. Luke killed Margaret to protect his inheritance.

"I think Luke's own murder can be tied to whatever he did to piss Margaret off. This woman would forgive anything, infidelity included, to preserve the Reasoner's good name. Whatever Luke did changed that dynamic, not just for him but for the entire family."

Reilly looked puzzled. "Explain that last part."

"You need to think about Margaret's actions before her death. She not only stopped talking to her children, she became a virtual recluse in her upstairs suite. Margaret was not a woman prone to overreaction. The family legacy was everything to her, but suddenly she was willing to give that up.

"I think whatever Luke did, somehow others became involved. I suspect Joshua had a role, at the very least."

Reilly began to edge noticeably towards the door.

Slovitz turned to Hannah. "Reilly, Aimes, and I need to get out of here, but when do you guys think you can wrap this up? My boss, the Cleveland chief, called me before we drove over here. He's been getting calls from the Reasoner lawyer, who reminded us that our mansion invitation was not open-ended. Tomorrow is supposed to be your last day out here. The lawyer also said he's been talking to experts who would dispute the ME's finding about the gunshot wound. They will present this as suicide brought about by guilt over Luke Reasoner's role in the death of his mother. The family's apparently willing to take that hit and the loss of Luke's portion of the Reasoner inheritance. They would gladly do that to avoid an even larger scandal around a double murder."

I glanced at Hannah. "The suicide thing makes no sense. Margaret's carbon monoxide killing was very real, but the way it was done was far more convoluted than Luke's execution. If the family's willing to admit to the circumstances of Margaret's death but not Luke's, there's something way more damaging hidden in Luke's murder."

The captain shook his head. "I'm not saying you're wrong, but my question remains. When can you wrap this thing up? Technically, the two of you can continue once you leave here, though Luvello's part of the case is finished. Your access to family and evidence will also be more limited after you go. The family has a team of lawyers who will make sure of that."

I looked at Hannah. "I want to talk with one more person besides the ME. If he tells us what I expect, we might be able to finish this up tomorrow. It will require us bringing the whole family together, but I doubt they'll object if they think they'll be rid of us afterward."

Slovitz appeared surprised, but he asked no further questions. The concept of plausible deniability was likely foremost in his mind.

Hannah and I walked Reilly, the captain, and Aimes back to their cars under the watchful gaze of Joshua, now peering through the great room window. After we watched them drive away, Hannah turned to me immediately.

"Any chance you'd care to clue me in on what you're thinking? If not, could I at least hear the identity of the mystery person you want to talk to besides the ME?"

"Let's go back to our TV-sound-insulated suite. I promise then I'll let you know exactly where I'm headed."

Hannah just shook her head. "At least tell me who else we need to talk with."

"Remember Dr. Resnick, the police psychologist you spoke with after you shot Michael Grieve? You said he gave you his cell phone number. I need you to call him, though you can wait until after we speak to the ME."

Hannah laughed, clearly thinking I was joking. After hearing my plan, I was afraid she might start asking Dr. Resnick some questions about me.

Stepping inside our room, Hannah turned on the television. Our noise barrier du jour was, coincidently, another *Columbo* episode. Even with the TV on, I motioned Hannah to the bathroom. Knowing the implications of what I was about to suggest, I figured we could use all the cover we could get.

Sitting to the side of the massive double sink, I explained my theory and my plan for the following day. The former had the advantage of explaining both murders as well as Margaret's behavior in the month before her death. Its disadvantage was simple—none of it was provable.

As far as my plan for tomorrow was concerned, crazy didn't even begin to describe it. Hannah was fine with my theory about the killings. The plan, not so much.

"If this doesn't work," Hannah said, "you'll give the Reasoners a free look at our best hypothesis. That would be a gift for any lawyer, and the Reasoners will hire a veritable legal army."

"That's true, but I'm not sure we have another option. I think there's a reason Luke was executed when we were on the premises. That aside, this is a criminal case, and you're the cop. If you think my plan is bullshit, we'll try something else."

Hannah shook her head. "I'm not saying it's bullshit, just incredibly risky. Let's talk with the ME and Dr. Resnick. If they don't think you're nuts, we'll give it a shot."

With Hannah's okay, I tracked down Joshua, catching him just before his planned return to the office. As I expected, he had no problem with my proposed family meeting set for noon the next day. To get rid of Hannah and me, he would have acceded to just about any request I made. My only condition for the meeting—every family member had to be present.

"What about Lawton and the staff?" Joshua asked.

It was an unexpected question, but I saw no upside to their presence. If things went truly south, they might also get in the way.

"We'll meet in the great room without the staff. Given the topic of conversation, I would even suggest you send them home for the day. There's no telling what one of them might overhear."

I figured the potential for gossip would terrify him, and I was right.

"I'll have Lawton stay in his room upstairs," he said. "We'll send the rest of the staff home.

He looked at me straight on. "I expect tomorrow's meeting will finish our business. What you discovered here was horrible. My brother Luke was a very troubled soul, and it goes without saying I was aware of none of it. Whatever his motive, the idea Luke would kill our mother is devastating to the entire family."

It sounded like a press release.

"You should also know," Joshua continued, "that I have spoken to my lawyers. While they have advised me to fight the terms of my mother's will, I've decided it would be best to put this matter behind us. Your client, the Cranberg Institute, will get the money they are due. I hope that will satisfy both you and them."

I couldn't help asking. "Does it bother you at all that someone killed your brother?"

Joshua had hoped the promise of money would settle all our differences. That hope dashed, his face hardened. "Those same lawyers have consulted experts who dispute the finding of homicide in my brother's death. If you have proof otherwise, then present it tomorrow. If not, I'll expect you and Detective Page to leave our home as soon as your presentation is concluded."

"I promise you we will leave, one way or another." I gestured to the kitchen. "It's unfortunate; I'll miss the food here. Your cook really is excellent. Does he do weddings, Bar Mitzvahs, that sort of thing?"

Hannah was right. I had a gift for pissing people off. Having no wish to eat with the family, I grabbed some food from the always filled refrigerator by the breakfast nook. I took our dinner upstairs, where Hannah and I sat down to eat and make our first phone call.

CHAPTER TWELVE

DAY SEVEN

WE WOKE UP on our seventh day at the Reasoner mansion expecting fireworks. Hannah opened her suitcase to choose an outfit for our noon presentation and pointed to her gun.

Given what we might be facing, I said, "Take it, and I'll take mine. We've already had one person get shot, and there's a whole closet full of weapons a couple of rooms away from where we'll be meeting. If our theory is correct, at least one more family member might still be at risk. While I don't like any of them, I don't want another murder on our watch."

Hannah had a shoulder holster as well as one that hid inside her trousers. The latter was useful in situations like today, where we didn't want to advertise we were packing weapons. For Hannah, that was unusual. In my line of work, it was an everyday occurrence.

Hannah and I holstered our weapons, both of us wearing loose-fitting shirts to hide the fact that we were carrying. We then ate breakfast, though neither of us were hungry for more than leftovers from the previous day's dinner.

Chewing on the remains of a well-cooked steak, Hannah wondered again if we were doing the right thing.

"The captain's right," I told her. "And please don't tell him I said those words. If we don't resolve this today, there's a good chance the Reasoners can delay any further investigation into Luke's death. Reasoner money can pay for any number of experts who will say the situation isn't clear-cut. You, Dr. Ho, and I can testify to our dying day that Luke's murder wasn't a suicide. The very idea is ludicrous based on the position of both the body and the gun. Even granted all that, a friendly judge might derail any additional investigation due to self-interest alone.

"We need to end this thing today. Since this is my theory and your job is more at risk, I'd like to take the lead in making our presentation. That's especially true since I might be slightly overstating our evidence. Beyond that, there's also my gift for pissing people off, something you've noted ever since we met. That may be the key to getting our killer talking."

"You can do the presentation," Hannah said, "but be careful what you say. If your lie is obvious, they'll clam up and toss us out before we even get going."

"I'm going to limit my dishonesty to Abigail's affair. That was the betrayal that set this whole thing in motion. If we can get her or Joshua to admit to that, I think we're home free."

"Home free?" Hannah asked incredulously. "What you're accusing them of is far worse than a single affair. If this gets out, the damage to their reputations would be catastrophic. Don't think they won't realize that. While your theory has the virtue of explaining both murders, you're also relying on a psychological profile that we don't even know is accurate. Even Dr. Resnick thought it was iffy."

"I'll grant you 'home free' was too optimistic, but we're running out of time. Let's see what happens. If nothing else, we can take bets on how soon Joshua's head explodes."

We finished our leftover breakfast steak, and Hannah and I discussed the other variables.

"What if," Hannah asked, "the other murder has already been set in motion? Given how insane this case has been, it could be anything from another poisoning to an electrocution. We're also assuming the killer has no interest in the two of us, but that might not be the case.

That may be especially true if we get in the way of whatever else they have planned."

"All we can do is be ready. That and our guns will have to be enough."

It was nearly noon, and I reached to turn off the TV. Before I touched the control, Hannah grabbed my arm. I figured she'd thought of something else, but she pointed to the screen.

"This is an old *Boston Legal*. I always had a crush on William Shatner."

Wonderful—now I was competing with Captain Kirk.

With Hannah's reluctant acquiescence, we finally went downstairs after I grabbed a small file from my briefcase. On the first floor, we found the whole family seated on the two large great room couches, both now tilted to face two center chairs. I glanced at Hannah—we were to be that afternoon's entertainment. After they heard what I had to say, I wondered if they'd be feeding us to the lions.

We moved to our designated seats, but I remained standing. Bernie was right. The shadows were circling, and I could sense their presence all around me. Unfortunately, they were no longer offering their advice—this was now my show. Carefully studying each member of the family, I began my presentation.

"Five months ago, Margaret Reasoner died in this house. I was sent here to determine if that death was due to natural causes.

"As you now realize, the answer to that question is 'no.' Margaret Reasoner was killed when someone decided to pump carbon monoxide into her room from the upstairs attic. The tanks used to deliver that gas were hidden in an old clothes box, and we were able to track those containers to a delivery here, accepted by Luke Reasoner. That left no doubt. It was Luke who killed Margaret."

I started to pace. "Those are the things we know, along with the fact that Luke himself was murdered just days before we discovered his role in Margaret's death. Much of this you'd already been told, and these facts are indisputable."

"Those details did, however, leave us with one obvious question—who killed Luke? To add to that mystery, whoever shot Luke likely did so, knowing he was already being poisoned. Luke was facing a slow, inevitable death due to the gradual ingestion of antifreeze slipped into his whisky. That last point is important—the poison wasn't found in his bourbon or wine bottles. I'll talk more about that inconsistency later.

"To uncover Luke's murderer, we needed to discover the motive. As it turned out, the genesis for both killings occurred over seven years ago when Margaret first stepped into the offices of the Salinger Detective Agency. Margaret was convinced her family might be trying to kill her, but none of us at that meeting could figure out why. My partner, Bernie Moffitt, thought

Margaret must be crazy. That's saying something because Bernie was the most suspicious person I'd ever met.

"Bernie did some preliminary follow-up and then essentially dropped the case. She picked it back up again about six months ago when she became convinced, for reasons I could never fathom, that Margaret might not be as paranoid as she first appeared."

The Reasoner family had remained remarkably quiet during the first part of my talk. It was only now that Joshua started to twist noticeably in his seat, suddenly taking an interest in the mansion's only wood-burning fireplace. It was time to take a swing.

"As far as I knew, Margaret never told Bernie what had precipitated her concerns. I left the Salinger firm shortly after that initial meeting. Until a few weeks ago, the case had become a distant memory.

"Bernie never told me why she became suspicious of your family, but she did find something. For reasons unknown, my old partner never bothered writing that something down in her case notes. I don't think she trusted Harry Salinger not to leak what she found to Joshua or someone else in your family. Bernie grew so paranoid over that possibility that she didn't even include the information in the separate case file she kept in her home.

"I thought I'd have to find that reason by myself, at least until I opened a gift Annabelle Moffitt brought me, a gift purchased for me by her mother just before she died. The gift was a book, a first edition of Raymond Chandler's *The Big Sleep*. Annabelle had found the present in a box with Bernie's private case notes. Bernie and I were different in many respects, but we both loved old-time detective stories. I thought the book was Bernie's way of letting bygones be bygones."

I pulled an old hardbound copy of the Chandler novel from the file I'd brought downstairs. It was by no means a first edition, but it was the best I could get from the Cleveland Heights bookstore near our home. Assuming the family didn't look too closely, I hoped it would suffice. Lydia nodded approvingly as I displayed the novel for all to see.

"Hoping it would help fill in any downtime, I brought the book with me for our excursion in your home. I never opened it until two days ago, and it was then I saw the note Bernie had written to me on the inside cover. Among other things, that note mentioned the sexual relationship Bernie had discovered between two members of your family, something she thought I should be aware of if anything happened to her."

I looked directly at Abigail. "While I would normally see no need to advertise a family indiscretion of this sort, it is crucial to what we are meeting about today. That's true, isn't it, Mrs. Reasoner? Maybe you should just tell the room. Your husband has known for some time."

Joshua Reasoner almost flew off his seat on the couch. I wasn't sure whether it was to defend his honor or his wife's. In truth, I really didn't care.

"You bastard! Get the hell…"

Hannah didn't let him complete another word. "Sit the fuck down! May I remind you this is a police investigation? You will sit down, shut up, and let us finish. One more interruption, and I will gladly arrest your ass."

Joshua wavered. He badly wanted to hit me, but he couldn't be sure what Hannah might do. Abigail stood then and started to speak.

"If your purpose is to humiliate me, Mr. Luvello, you've done so nicely. Yes, I had an affair. As you are no doubt also aware, that affair was with Luke. My indiscretion occurred roughly seven years ago. I am not proud of what I did, but I confessed my infidelity to my husband. I was young and stupid, and Joshua, quite understandably, nearly filed for divorce. While that wasn't a proud moment in my life, it doesn't mean either of us was responsible for Luke's murder."

Young and stupid? Given Abigail's age at the time of the affair, seven years ago would have put Joshua's wife in her midthirties. The fact that she wasn't directly culpable didn't mean she bore no fault at all.

I turned once again to a still-seething Joshua. "You were considering a divorce. I bet that alarmed your mother. Seven years ago coincides perfectly with Margaret's first visit to the Salinger agency. I'm guessing Margaret learned about the affair, and you two fought. It wasn't that Margaret had any great love for Abigail, but you would have been in your late forties, and your mother worried you might never find another wife. Unmarried and childless wouldn't do for the new head of the Reasoner corporation. Your mandate was not just to run the firm. With Matthew then divorced and Mark's less than stellar prospects, you needed to produce an heir of your own."

I was prepared for a negative reaction from Mark, but he appeared at peace with his place in the family.

I continued on. "Just how badly did you threaten your almost eighty-year-old mother? The argument must have been epic, though Margaret clearly won. Bowing to the inevitable, you made peace with your mother, brother, and wife. Being the dutiful son, you and Abigail then went to work making a baby.

"But that didn't happen quite the way you thought it would, did it? You tried for years. As rich as you are, I'm guessing you hired the best fertility experts to speed things along. Finally, with Abigail in her early forties, a miracle happened.

"Only it wasn't a miracle for you, was it, Joshua? All the bad memories came rushing back, and you wondered if your wife hadn't come up with her own way of speeding along the process."

"I'm going to destroy you."

I had glanced away from him before the words were spoken. They were uttered in a low, almost guttural tone I assumed had come from Joshua Reasoner. It wasn't until I turned back to the couple that I realized I'd been threatened by Abigail. She knew where I was going, and Abigail wanted me to back down before the rest of her family heard what I was implying. Scanning the room, I wasn't sure that would matter as much as she thought. Not a single family member appeared surprised or upset.

"You might try to destroy me, but that may not be as easy as you think. As a private detective, no one can fire me. You can try to influence potential clients, but I'm good at what I do. There will always be those who'll pay for my services." I gestured to Hannah and added, "Before you go to the effort of also threatening Detective Page, you might want to wait and listen to the rest of what I'm going to say. Your family has a far greater problem than the questionable lineage of your newborn son."

I wasn't sure of the rest of the family, but Abigail possessed no weapon. Based on the color of her face, there surely would have been shots fired by now.

I shook my head. "Seven years of trying, who could blame you for turning once again to an alternate partner. To be fair, I'm not sure that you really did. Child or no child, a new affair might have seemed too great a risk.

"Whether you were guilty or not, however, your husband thought you might be. That was why he punched his brother during a newspaper interview, an interview that took place just after you learned you were pregnant."

Now it was Matthew Reasoner's turn to speak. "Unless you're going somewhere fast, this needs to stop. You may not like us—a lot of people hate the Reasoners in this town. That's still no reason to humiliate my brother and his wife, even"—he glanced at Hannah—"if it's being done under the auspices of a police investigation."

I held up my hand. "You want me to get to the point, and I promise you I will. All of this, the initial affair, Abigail's pregnancy, and Joshua's doubts concerning the paternity of his child will lead us to who killed your mother and brother. I know hearing this is difficult. If the situation wasn't so unusual, I wouldn't be discussing these things in front of the entire family. It is taking us somewhere, however, and I ask that you bear with me a little bit longer."

Matthew nodded reluctantly, and I turned to Joshua once more. "Your disagreement with your brother didn't end with a punch. I believe you confronted him soon after that and ordered him to stay away from your wife."

Abigail turned to her husband. "This is all so stupid. I told you the affair was long over. If you didn't believe me, the blood test should have told you for sure."

I looked at Joshua. "It did tell him. That was one of the reasons for his eventual reproachment with Luke, something I saw evidence of at the gun range soon after Detective Page and I arrived. I say 'one of the reasons' because I believe there was more to it than that. That's true, isn't it, Lydia?"

Lydia appeared calm, as if she'd anticipated being drawn into the discussion at some point. Her mother, however, had not.

Judith's confusion was evident. "What the hell does my daughter have to do with any of this?"

I ignored her. We were getting to the climax of my presentation, and all would be won or lost in the next ten minutes.

"Let's go over the timeline one more time," I continued, feeling even more like a shit. "Abigail is now six months pregnant. Joshua's fight and later confrontation with his brother occurred just after Abigail learned she was expecting. What exactly happened in your conversation with your brother, Joshua? Did Luke tell you he was once again screwing your wife? Whether or not it was true, I think he hated you enough to throw that in your face. To you and everyone else, Luke was the Reasoner marked for failure, the family member whose only claim to importance came from his money and good looks. You were in the opposite position. A success in business, you had no confidence at all in your physical appeal. Your wife had betrayed you once. With her biological clock winding down, who's to say she hadn't done so again?

"This was Luke's best chance for revenge. Unlike the situation seven years ago, your mother was older, weaker, and no longer able to keep peace in the family. All Luke had to do was tell you he'd gone back to sleeping with Abigail, and there was a better than even chance your son was his. That would have been bad enough, but then he made you an offer.

"Luke was a predator at heart, a man who made up for his personal insecurities by picking targets within his own household. Whether those conquests were voluntary or involuntary made no difference to him. Luke had already gone after both of his brother's wives."

Matthew's head swiveled at the mention of his wife. I thought he might object, but then I remembered he knew about Luke's attempted seduction.

"If Luke was going to lay off your wife, he wanted a substitute, another family member he could enjoy at his leisure. His sister was out of the question, but his beautiful niece? I wouldn't be surprised if Lydia had been in his sights all along."

I turned to Lydia, who appeared to be experiencing a strange sort of calm. "I'm sorry, Lydia. When I spoke about all the coincidences occurring around the start of Abigail's pregnancy, I deliberately left one out. When we searched your suite the morning after your uncle was killed, we found your birth control pills. The prescription was written about six months ago, just after Abigail learned she was pregnant. The pills could have been for a partner you'd met outside your home, but your brother told me you are agoraphobic. While Mark is less than reliable in many ways, I believe he had no reason to lie in that instance."

Lydia simply nodded. This sort of public family

shaming was what she wanted all along.

"I think you wanted me to find the prescription, and I also think you were sending me a message the day Detective Page and I came to interview you. You greeted us that morning dressed in a sheer nightgown, like a teenager attempting a seduction. I remember thinking you reminded me of someone I'd met in a previous case. It took me a while, but it finally came to me. It was a child who had been abducted and abused by her stepfather. A psychologist told me seductive behavior is often seen in abused children. I can only apologize to you for not realizing it sooner."

Turning back to Joshua, I continued, "Your brother wanted to make you complicit in his sexual depravity. Luke threatened you, didn't he? I'm not sure whether you found out before he began raping Lydia or after, but Luke offered you a choice between your niece and your wife. You couldn't accept the humiliation of being the cuckold once again, particularly within your own household. You told your brother you wouldn't interfere."

Judith stood up then, staring at her brother. "Tell me this is a lie. Tell me you wouldn't pimp out your own niece to her goddamned uncle!" Judith's voice rose with the last word. I glanced at Hannah and saw her hand move carefully to her side within inches of her holster. Joshua, now clearly panicked, said not a word.

"He offered me a drink." Lydia's voice sounded hollow. It was as if she'd been rehearsing her words for so long that they no longer had any meaning. "Uncle Luke invited me to his room. He told me he'd bought a first edition Jane Austen he wanted me to see.

"Before he handed me the book, he poured me a glass of whisky. It tasted a little strange, but I didn't think anything of it. It wasn't until much later that I found out he'd dosed it with GHB, the date rape drug. Everything was a blur from there until he woke me up at five the next morning. He told me I needed to get out before the rest of the household got up. I remember looking down and realizing I was naked. I just panicked. I couldn't remember anything after the drink he gave me.

"I asked Uncle Luke what happened, and he told me I got drunk and seduced him. I was still groggy, and I couldn't think straight. I just stood there, feeling this sense of pure terror, like my whole life had turned upside down. I remember him watching me for a few seconds, and then he showed me his phone. He'd taken pictures of me. I didn't remember any of them, but I was smiling in most of the shots. That made me think he might have been telling the truth.

"Uncle Luke threw my clothes at me and told me we could talk the next evening. He said I should come by around 3:00 a.m. so no one would see me. He also said he needed to think about what he would tell my mother. I begged him not to say anything, and he said he wouldn't until we had a chance to talk.

"I went back to his suite the next evening. I was so embarrassed by what I had done. I couldn't imagine what would happen if anyone else in the family found out. Uncle Luke told me that didn't need to happen. Family relationship aside, he said we clearly had a connection. He wanted to explore that. With my imagination and sense of adventure, Uncle Luke said I should want the same thing.

"I'd love to tell you I said no, but I was too scared. Our arrangement was once a week. Every time I came close to backing out, Uncle Luke would offer me another drink of whisky. He said only a child would refuse a single drink."

Lydia turned to her mother. "I always panicked when I tried to leave the house, and I started to think maybe Uncle Luke was right. Maybe this was the only way I could experience what a real woman should already know."

As gently as possible, I asked, "When did you realize you were being drugged?"

"It was about a month after we first slept together." Lydia's voice again turned matter-of-fact. "When I went to his room that evening, Uncle Luke was already drunk. He also hadn't been careful—he'd left the bottle of GHB by his liquor cabinet next to the alcohol. The next day, I got my courage up, and I went to talk with Uncle Joshua."

She faced Joshua. "I remember that conversation very well. You said you would talk with Uncle Luke, but then you asked me if this was something I really wanted spread around the family. You told me about your own situation with Aunt Abigail. You said I was old enough to understand the concept of sacrifice."

Her mother had heard enough. I was honestly surprised Judith had lasted that long. With a sound approaching a growl, she launched herself from her seat across the room and leaped on her older brother. Judith had no weapon, but she did possess some of the longest fingernails I had ever seen.

Joshua's attempt to stand limited the damage to only his left cheek. Abigail screamed, but she made no move to protect her husband. I'd watched Abigail's reactions throughout my presentation. The horror on her face told me she really hadn't known.

Joshua stood before his family, blood pouring from the cut on his cheek. He pointed to me. "Don't tell me you believe this bastard. I tried to help Lydia. I spoke to Luke, and I tried to get him to stop."

Matthew stood up, maybe six inches away from his older brother. "Sit the fuck down," he snarled. "We'll listen to the rest of what Luvello has to say. Right now, I'd say his credibility beats yours by a fucking mile."

Matthew turned then to his sister, who appeared ready to strike one more time, and said more gently, "Let's hear the whole story. You can take your revenge after that, and no one will try to stop you."

Joshua sat, but it was now Abigail's turn.

"I really didn't know," she almost whispered to

Lydia. "God help me, I didn't have a clue any of this was happening. The baby was Joshua's. We had a blood test and everything. The thing between Luke and me ended years ago."

I still had more to say, quite a bit more, actually, and turned back to Lydia. "After you realized your uncle Joshua would do nothing, you then told your grandmother. Margaret had always been the one to solve the family's problems. After you spoke with her, Margaret realized she finally had a situation she couldn't, in good conscience, just cover up."

I returned to Joshua. "Your mother spoke to you, didn't she? She couldn't let the situation continue, and I'm guessing she wanted to throw Luke out of the house. She was your mother, but you couldn't have that. A banished Luke would have no reason to keep his affair with your wife quiet, and he could also cast doubt on the fatherhood of your son. I'm not sure what you threatened your mother with, but I'm guessing that's when she cut herself off from the family. She couldn't bear to look at any of you, and she was too old to handle the problem alone.

"You may have thought that would end things, but I'm sure it didn't take Luke long to figure out what prompted so dramatic a change in your mother. You probably told him not to worry, but Luke knew his inheritance might be at risk. He decided to kill Margaret, but it would have to be in a way that would pass muster with the medical examiner. His choice of carbon monoxide was clever, brilliant, really, particularly with the ME at the time so close to retirement. If Luke hadn't decided to hide the tanks upstairs, we might have never figured out which family member had pulled this off."

"I never thought my grandmother would die," Lydia said sadly. "Part of me feels like I killed her myself. I didn't know how Uncle Luke had done it, but I figured she didn't just die in her sleep."

"That," I said to Lydia, "brings us to our final murder. You guessed your grandmother had been killed. As revenge for that and your debasement, you decided to take care of your uncle Luke yourself. Being you, his killing would have to be done in the most literary way possible.

"We found out about Luke and the antifreeze, and Detective Page and I wondered about the killer's choice of poison. When I began to suspect you might be responsible, I remembered you saying you read detective novels, specifically those by Karin Slaughter. You mentioned the Will Trent series.

"I'd never read any of Slaughter's books, but I was curious enough to pull up the plot summaries. In one of her Trent novels, Slaughter wrote about a sports agent who covered up for a serial rapist. The killer snuck antifreeze into the agent's drink for revenge. Antifreeze poisoning is extremely slow, and it eventually shut down the agent's organs until he was entirely helpless. That feeling of helplessness was exactly what you wanted for your uncle. Dr. Ho also told us you only tampered with the whisky bottles in Luke's room. From your perspective, that was only fitting. That was the alcohol Luke used with you to hide the GHB."

Her mother immediately protested. "My daughter would not kill anyone. If you want to blame my bastard brother, no one in this room would stop you. My daughter is off-limits. Whatever you think she did, no jury would ever convict Lydia once they realized what Luke had done to her."

The truth was, Judith might be right. The high-end lawyers she could hire would have no problem constructing a sympathy defense. Lydia, however, wasn't aiming for an exoneration or a coverup. Her plan to murder her uncle would not be complete without the humiliation of her entire family.

We were almost there, and I continued. "You mentioned the Slaughter novels deliberately, didn't you, Lydia? You hoped my partner and I would understand the connection. I think that's also why you shot Luke after you visited his room and realized the antifreeze was finally doing its job. We wondered why a killer would first poison and then later shoot their victim, particularly with two detectives sleeping just rooms away. The truth is, you shot Luke *because* we were there. You were afraid Luke's death by antifreeze would be covered up just like Margaret's from carbon monoxide. You couldn't have that because you wanted your family's rot exposed for all to see. You weren't emulating a detective novel— you were aiming for Greek tragedy."

Lydia nodded, pleased. "I figured you'd get it. From the time I first read about you on the internet, I knew you'd be the perfect hero for my little story."

Judith, still in a state of shock, stared disbelievingly at her daughter. "Why didn't you tell me?"

Lydia looked at her sadly. "This wasn't an art show, Mother. This was more gothic horror. It was something I needed to deal with in my own way."

Lydia then turned to Joshua, still in the process of wilting under the unforgiving stares from his family. "The villain always dies, so there needs to be one more death. You realize that, don't you? You can't live here anymore. Once this gets out, your time at the company will be over." Her voice almost gentle, Lydia added, "Everything really is over. It's just a matter of knowing when your part is done."

Hannah and I observed Lydia carefully, paying particular attention to her hands. Rather than reach for a weapon, however, Margaret's grandchild surprised us one more time. In one fluid movement, she stood and dashed quickly up the grand stairway.

"This is her show," Hannah said to me. "We're just bit players. Let's get moving before she decides to commit suicide."

We raced after Lydia, now maybe thirty feet ahead, after first warning the others to remain downstairs. I expected Lydia to head toward her suite as she reached the top of the stairs, but she turned left instead.

I wasn't sure how Lydia had arranged it, but the elevator door already stood open, awaiting her arrival. Lydia stabbed quickly at the buttons, and the door closed before we reached it, the elevator headed for the attic.

Hannah was already in the process of recalling the elevator to our floor when I remembered the size of the lift.

"We have to assume Lydia might be carrying. I didn't notice any sign of it, but that doesn't mean she isn't. We'll be can't-miss targets once the elevator door opens."

Hannah considered the problem. "If she's going to shoot, she'll fire straight in. You lie down on the floor, and I'll crouch to the side, away from the entrance. It's the best we can do, though I don't think she intends to kill us."

I did as Hannah suggested. After getting in the elevator, I withdrew my weapon and lay prostrate on the floor.

Hannah was right. Whatever Lydia's intentions, they didn't include shooting us. The elevator door opened without incident, and we faced the attic once again. Hannah and I turned on what lights we could and began our search.

We moved some of the old boxes we'd inspected just days earlier as we stepped carefully on the loose floorboards. As we maneuvered our way forward, I wondered if Lydia didn't have one more surprise, maybe a second exit that Summers hadn't bothered to tell us about on our first-day tour.

My fear was misplaced. Lydia rose from behind a large mound of boxes as we reached the end of the attic. From the annoyed expression on her face, I half expected her to deliver a lecture regarding our inappropriate presence in the storage area.

Instead of a lecture, Lydia cocked her head. "Did you hear a noise?"

I had heard a sound—a sharp crack, somewhat muffled by our attic location. I glanced quickly at Hannah. Someone had fired a weapon. Whoever had done so, we both knew the target.

Lydia also understood, and I realized this was why she'd led us away from the first floor. "We can go back downstairs now." Her voice was deadly calm.

We'd been played by an expert. The three of us ran to the elevator, Lydia following along quite willingly. Hannah pressed the button, and we proceeded to the first floor.

We were greeted by chaos. I knew before we turned the corner that Joshua would be the victim. My only uncertainty was whether the oldest Reasoner had shot himself or fallen victim to his sister.

It turned out to be suicide. The entire family, except for Judith, was gathered just inside the entrance to Joshua and Abigail's suite. Matthew stood next to a crying Emily, who tried, in turn, to comfort an even more disconsolate Abigail. Matthew turned, hearing us behind him.

"While you were upstairs, Abigail and I spent all our time trying to keep Judith from scratching Joshua's eyes out. Joshua eventually went back to his suite, and I figured he was trying to get the hell out of the way. I thought he and I could talk about next steps when things had a chance to calm down." He paused and continued, "I didn't even know he kept a gun in his suite."

Abigail choked back her tears and turned to a still-calm Lydia. "Even I didn't know, but you did, didn't you? You told him there needed to be another death." The tears came even harder then. "My husband was not a villain. Whatever he was, he was not a villain. You should have killed me."

I wasn't sure if she really loved him or was just upset about the almost certain end of her privileged company life. I fixed my eyes on Summers as he joined us by the master suite. Another puzzle piece fell into place.

I yanked him aside, away from the others. "Did Joshua really keep a gun in his room, Lawton, or did you put one out in the open where he could find it? You know everything that goes on in this household. Was it you who told Bernie what Luke was doing to his niece? I was driving myself crazy trying to figure out what Bernie saw on her mansion tour that convinced her something was wrong. It never occurred to me you might have simply told her.

"I could never guess how she found out, and Bernie never talked about the discovery in her case notes. She was protecting you, wasn't she? Was the gun your way of bringing things to a close?"

Summers gazed at Lydia with a fatherly affection. "It's a house manager's job to protect everyone in his purview, particularly those with no one else to defend them. Instead, I acted like a coward and relied on your ex-partner to do my job for me. With her death, I knew I'd have to handle it on my own.

"You provided the proof I was never able to obtain. I overheard what was said before you ran upstairs. Miss Lydia was absolutely right. There was only one ending to this story. My way just hurried it along."

Judith returned downstairs just as Lawton finished speaking. Her tears had ended, though I suspected the guilt never would. Judith moved to console her daughter, and Lydia accepted her embrace without hesitation.

Hannah and I entered Joshua's suite. We now had one more dead body to deal with, a burden that would largely fall on Hannah as the only official presence on the premises. Joshua lay on his bed. If you ignored the hole in his head, his expression was almost peaceful.

"I know I shouldn't," I told Hannah. "But I almost find myself feeling sorry for him. The rot in this family just ate away at him eventually."

Hannah shook her head. "He allowed his brother to rape his niece. You shouldn't feel sorry for him at all."

I knew she was right. We moved away from Joshua, and Hannah pulled out her phone to start making calls.

She turned back to me fifteen minutes later after her third hurried conversation.

"Dr. Ho should be here in five minutes. I thought he might question my sanity when I told him what happened, but he didn't seem shocked at all. For all their money, it's incredible how little people thought of this family.

"I also spoke to Chief Reilly. Whether he wanted to be involved in this case or not, he is in it now up to his eyebrows. Reilly's on his way, and we should hear his siren any minute. He's also bringing Officer Styles. He said Styles was quite impressed with you. I'm guessing Reilly figured including him would make the case's transition back to Hunting Valley run a little more smoothly."

"What about Slovitz?"

"Slovitz said this little clusterfuck might follow me for the rest of my days. He reminded me for the fiftieth time how crazy I am for getting back together with you."

"I'm surprised he let you off the phone that quickly."

"He said he needed to call his chief because he'll be the one handling the political fallout. I'm not to go near a newspaper reporter until he gives his okay. He said the same order goes for you, at least if you want to live. I reminded him you hated being in the news. He told me you need to remember that feeling and hold on to it, big time."

I would, but I reminded Hannah about our other problem. "What about Lydia? She admitted to shooting her uncle. On top of that, she also copped to his poisoning."

Hannah shook her head. "I mentioned that to Slovitz, and he said we should bring her into Cleveland. That's assuming Reilly agrees, but he almost certainly will. Hunting Valley can handle Joshua's suicide, but a murder case of this magnitude is on a totally different level. Slovitz also suggested I call my mother to get her perspective. Mom would die for a high-profile case like this, but my involvement likely means they'll assign it to somebody else.

"Do you think there's any chance they'll convict her?"

"That's really a mom question, but my guess is a deal will be made. Judith will hire a boatload of lawyers for her daughter. As guilty as Judith feels right now, that much is certain. I think they'll plead Lydia out based on some kind of reduced capacity. The opinion writers will call it rich person's law. They'll be right, but she'll also get some well-deserved sympathy. Lydia is a young woman victimized by an asshole, a woman who finally decided to strike back. The movie rights alone will be worth millions."

I thought of Patrice Clairview, the *Plain Dealer* reporter who first alerted me to the friction between

Joshua and his brother. While I couldn't give Patrice any direct information, I at least owed her a heads-up. Slovitz might complain, but I would call Patrice after the Hunting Valley cops showed up.

As if in timing with that thought, we finally heard the blare of a police siren. Hannah and I made our way past the Reasoner family, now being herded respectfully away from Joshua's door by Lawton Summers. Abigail was still crying. Her infidelity started all this, something I assumed at least part of her now realized.

We met Chief Reilly and Officer Styles as they disembarked from the cruiser. The dark-blue medical examiner station wagon pulled up behind them in the driveway. Dr. Ho joined us, his assistant pushing a stainless-steel gurney that would soon be holding Joshua Reasoner's body.

The chief joined both of us. Hannah had given him a run-through of what had occurred over the phone, but he and Styles appeared more than a little shocked.

"I heard you two were relentless," Reilly said to Hannah. "I wasn't sure until this moment just how true that really was."

Captain Slovitz had called Reilly after his conversation with Hannah, and the chief agreed his team would take charge of Joshua's suicide. He also agreed Hannah and I could transport Lydia to the Cleveland Twelfth Precinct.

"The powers that be have decreed they will be

holding a press conference later this evening," Reilly said. "Just so you understand how big this case is, those powers include the mayors of Hunting Valley and Cleveland, plus two representatives from the Cleveland prosecutor's office. The Cleveland police chief will also be there, but I was told my presence will not be required."

He turned to Hannah. "I asked about you and your partner. These murders would never have been solved without the two of you. I know that, and your captain does too.

"However, the unique and unofficial circumstance of your presence here means that your name will not be mentioned. If someone asks about you, the story will be a partial truth. You were the officer assigned to assist my department once it was determined that Margaret Reasoner's death was actually a murder.

"Mr. Luvello, Ms. Clairview from the *Plain Dealer* has been burning up the phone lines asking anyone and everyone about your role. She already stumbled upon your connection with the Cranberg Institute. The press conference will acknowledge that connection while going into as little detail as possible. You are, of course, free to elaborate as much as you might wish. Raymond West from the Cranberg board of directors has already given her some background. Still, those powers I mentioned are hoping you will stick with your usual practice of avoiding the press as much as possible."

"That," I said, "will not be a problem."

"Captain Slovitz had planned to tell you all of this himself, but he gave me permission to drop the news. Due to the outcome of this case, he now has, as he put it, 'meetings with assholes and dickheads' running well into next week."

"The captain does have a unique turn of phrase," Hannah said.

The three of us turned then to watch along with the surviving and now-mute Reasoner clan as Dr. Ho's assistant wheeled the body of Joshua Reasoner out of the mansion. Dr. Ho followed, his right hand gripping a recording device as if holding a deadly weapon. I noticed Judith and Matthew talking on their respective cell phones. In Judith's case, it sounded as if she might be speaking with a lawyer. Matthew, the only surviving Reasoner son, was talking with someone at the company. Life, for the Reasoners, was moving on.

Hannah and I went back inside the mansion to collect Lydia. The youngest Reasoner appeared calm as Hannah read her Miranda rights and slipped on the handcuffs. With Hannah's acquiescence, Judith would accompany her daughter to Hannah's precinct.

Hannah suddenly seemed uncertain what to do with me.

"I know you have to take Lydia back to the station house and write this disaster up," I told her. "I also need to contact the Cranberg Institute and give them my report. Once that's finished, my part in this is done. If you don't mind, I'll hitch a ride with you to the station and grab an Uber back to the house."

I looked around the great room, a feature Edward Reasoner had planned in such great detail. "This place sickens me. There's too much death here; it's like it's seeped into the walls. Let's go upstairs, grab our stuff, and get out of here. I don't know about you, but I want to go home."

CHAPTER THIRTEEN

ANNABELLE

I MET WITH Annabelle Moffitt the day after Hannah and I left the Shadow House. At 9:00 a.m., Annabelle parked her green Subaru Forester behind my Passat on the drive leading to the Bridle Path Bridge.

The Cranberg Institute had been my official client for the Reasoner case; my unofficial client was Annabelle. I wouldn't have even known there was a case to begin with without her afternoon visit to my home. I owed Annabelle closure, particularly given what had happened to her mother. Thinking about my own questions, I hoped Annabelle could give me some closure of my own.

I had promised Chief Reilly I wouldn't speak about the case to outsiders, but I didn't consider this meeting to be a violation of that pledge. Someone else might have thought it odd that Annabelle might agree to meet me at the location where her mother died. Given what we had to discuss, I don't think we could have met anywhere else.

After a quick greeting, we walked slowly, almost solemnly, to the bridge itself. I turned to face Annabelle when we reached the bridge's midpoint. I had a lot to tell her and at least one thing to ask. I started by handing her a dollar.

She looked at me quizzically. "What is this?"

"I am officially hiring you as my lawyer on the chance I might someday face liability for the events that occurred at the Reasoner mansion. The dollar is your retainer. I believe that makes our conversation privileged. Is that correct?"

Annabelle nodded, now understanding. I told her everything then, starting with the first day of our arrival at the Reasoner mansion. The only details I withheld were those related to certain aspects of Hannah's police role in the investigation, aspects I thought Hannah might wish to keep private. When I got to my presentation in the great room, Annabelle whistled.

"You told them my mother left you a book implicating Abigail in an affair? That was a ballsy move. What would you have done if she had denied it?"

I'd wondered that myself. "This whole case was about guilt. Abigail's guilt over the affair, Joshua's guilt over his niece, even Lawton Summers's guilt over what he had allowed to happen in his household. Despite what TV will tell you, there are very few true sociopaths in this world. Most guilty people want to confess. Their lies alone can be exhausting. Even with someone as calculating as Abigail, I was betting she was tired of hiding the truth."

Driving to the bridge that morning, I wasn't sure how Annabelle would react to my story. Rather than appearing triumphant, she looked only tired.

"What about Lydia?" she asked suddenly. "Do you think there's any chance she does jail time?"

"A pretty, young, rich girl abused by her uncle with the best legal representation imaginable? I think she will spend some time in an institution, after which she'll leave a free woman. Despite my sounding cynical about her circumstances, I also think that might be the most just outcome. Lydia planned this out to a remarkable degree, changing her strategy on the fly after Hannah's and my arrival. Her run up the stairs after my presentation was designed to get the two of us away from Joshua. She knew what her uncle would do if left to his own devices. Guilt is a powerful thing."

"It's ironic," Annabelle said. "With her brains, Lydia might have been better qualified than Joshua to run the

Reasoner corporation. That would never happen in a million years now, but it'll be fascinating to see what she does after her legal problems are over."

Annabelle had no more questions. Now it was time for me to ask one of my own.

"I've been straight with you through this entire case, even agreeing to take it for the bullshit reason you gave me when we first met. Now I need you to be straight with me. Why did you kill your mother?"

I expected shock, an angry denial, even a quick retreat. Annabelle simply stared at her shoes for a long moment. What I said earlier was true. Guilt is a powerful force.

Now looking at the water below us, Annabelle appeared about to speak. She stopped herself suddenly, however, and turned back to me. She looked at me pointedly from head to toe.

I knew where this was going. "You're wondering if I'm wearing a wire. I'm not, but feel free to frisk me if you think I'm lying."

Annabelle hesitated, making no attempt to hide the tears forming in her deep brown eyes. She had killed her mother, a mentor who taught me everything I knew. Even with that, I couldn't help feeling sympathetic.

"What I said about guilt is true, Annabelle. You're not a sociopath, and I think you've been dying to tell this story since the first day we met. Joshua Reasoner held on to his guilt until it killed him. I don't want that for you, and I know your mother wouldn't either."

The tears came for real now. "How did you know?"

"At first, I assumed one of the Reasoners killed your mother. I even considered Lawton Summers, back when I thought he was nothing more than a loyal Reasoner foot soldier.

"It was the location that threw me. Your mother was a lot of things, but she wasn't trusting, and she wasn't stupid. There's no way Bernie would have agreed to meet any of the Reasoners at a spot this isolated.

"Lydia would have been the only possible exception, but two things play against her as a suspect. The first is her agoraphobia. I found out about Lydia's condition from her brother. Mark is a moron, but he wouldn't have any reason to make up that detail. Lydia would have also considered your mother an ally, someone as dedicated to taking down her family as she was. No—Lydia was definitely out.

"After ruling out Lydia, I thought maybe the Reasoners hired someone at the Salinger Agency. Most of the people working there are legitimate, if barely competent, private detectives. There are a few, however, who wouldn't hesitate to get involved with some rough stuff, even if that stuff included pushing someone off an isolated bridge.

"The more I thought about it, the more that scenario didn't make sense either. Your mother didn't trust anyone at the agency. I figured that out pretty quickly when she and I started working together. There's no way she would allow anyone working for Harry Salinger to get that close to her on a bridge.

"There are only two people your mother would have trusted. One of them was me, and you were the other. Why don't you start with why you two were meeting that day."

Annabelle went back to looking at the water. "Mom and I had talked over the phone the night before we met on the bridge. It was a Friday, and that Sunday was my son Anthony's first birthday. I'd told Mom about the party three weeks before, but she kept putting me off. She said things were finally breaking on the Reasoner case, and she needed to keep an eye on the mansion. My mother had contacts everywhere, including the Reasoner corporation. She'd heard about an unknown chemical shipment to be sent directly to the house. Mom didn't have a date or time, but her contact told her it would be arriving sometime that week.

"Based on what you told me, I'm guessing that shipment was the carbon monoxide Luke Reasoner used to kill his mother. Mom didn't know anything about Luke's plan, but she did know about some chemical dumping going on at the corporation. Mom assumed this shipment had something to do with whatever illegal crap the Reasoners were involved in.

"Mom knew she couldn't protect Margaret's life twenty-four seven. The mansion was too isolated and well-guarded for that. Her plan was to obtain proof of illegality at the corporation and use that as a threat to short-circuit any family murder attempt. Mom never spoke to me about Lydia, but I'm guessing she thought the same strategy might work for that situation. Joshua may not have wanted to see his wife and brother's affair made public, but his legal liability related to chemical dumping might have made kicking out his brother seem an acceptable risk. If Luke became a problem later, Joshua could always buy him off.

"Though she didn't know what you dug up, Mom always guessed Margaret's murder wouldn't be straightforward. There was too much money involved to openly kill the head of the Reasoner family."

So, Bernic had essentially figured things out. Not the how, maybe, but she knew to expect something out of the ordinary.

After a brief pause, Annabelle continued with her story. "Mom didn't think she could, in good conscious, quit watching the house until she figured out what that shipment was. I asked how her conscious felt about missing her only grandchild's first birthday party. I said a lot of other things as well, hateful things she didn't deserve. I told her she was a lousy mother all the while I was growing up and that I wasn't surprised she'd be the same sort of grandmother.

"Even over the phone, I could tell how much I hurt her. I felt like shit, but I couldn't take it back. Mom finally asked me to meet her the next day on the Bridle Path Bridge. I had never heard of this damn place before that. Mom had found it when she was scoping out the area. It's only five minutes from the Reasoner mansion, but isolated enough so we were unlikely to be seen. From Mom's perspective, that was perfect. She could meet with me and drive quickly back to the house to continue keeping an eye on things. I didn't even know where the hell the bridge was, but Mom gave me directions on how to get here.

"We were supposed to meet at two. I arrived early, but Mom was already here waiting. Seeing her standing there, I just got angry all over again. Mom tried to hug me, but all I could do was shove her away. It wasn't a hard push, and I swear to God I never meant to hurt her; I was just so pissed.

"Mom stumbled backward after I shoved her, and I think her foot hit a rock. If you look at the sides of the bridge, you can see they aren't that tall."

I did look, and Annabelle wasn't exaggerating. The Bridle Path was built in the early 1900s. The bridge had celebrated its centennial in 2020. Built before the advent of strict safety guidelines, the sides were brick and no more than thirty inches high.

Annabelle continued. "I couldn't have stopped her if I'd tried. It was like a slow-motion video. Mom staggered backward, hit the side, and fell over. I reached for her, but I was too slow, and our hands never quite touched. Even with that, I never thought she'd fall. This was Mom, right? I figured she'd grab the edge of the bridge or do almost anything to keep herself from going down."

"But she did fall. What happened afterward?"

"Mom hit the ground just before I got to the side myself. When her body landed, it made the most sickening thud you could imagine. I looked down over the side, telling myself it couldn't be her. I figured she'd stand up, shake her head, and swear at me for pushing her. I would have given anything for that to have happened.

"Instead, all I saw was her lying there. Her head had hit a rock, and her neck was bent at this strange angle. That's the image I still dream about. My husband wonders why I sometimes wake up screaming at night. I told him I still dream about Mom, but I could never tell him what really happened. Who would want a murderer raising their one-year-old child?

"That's the full story. I ran down to the bottom of the bridge, hoping Mom was okay. Her heart wasn't beating, but I called 911 and told them I'd seen a woman fall off the Bridle Path Bridge. I didn't leave my name or hang around for them to come. I wondered about my footprints, but this was fall in Cleveland. It rained all that morning and for five days afterward.

"I know leaving the scene makes me a coward as well as a killer. I spent months telling myself Mom's death was the Reasoners' fault, that she never would have been on that damn bridge if she hadn't been so obsessed with that family. That might all be true, but it wasn't one of the Reasoners who shoved her. That was me, only me."

Annabelle was sobbing even harder now. As for me, I believed her story. I'd been around enough death and guilt this past week to realize the dangers in the path Annabelle was headed on. I owed it to Bernie, if not Annabelle herself, to try to keep that from happening.

I shook my head. "I don't think you're a coward or a killer. When you talked me into taking this case, you said it was based on my reputation and the need to avenge your mother. Your mother was obsessed; every great detective is. You inherited that same obsession while I absorbed it secondhand. You hired me, even knowing how good your mother thought I was. You knew I might figure out what happened between you and your mom. You were willing to take that risk to clean up the Reasoner case. You risked discovery because it's important to your mother's legacy. Even more, you were praying I'd figure things out because you needed someone to talk to. Does any of that spell coward to you?

"You're not a killer either. Your mother's death was accidental. If you think I'm wrong, imagine an impartial jury viewing the whole thing on tape. Do you think anyone watching would think your mom's death was intentional? You're a lawyer, Annabelle. You understand culpability. You reacted in a perfectly understandable, human way without knowing what would happen afterward.

"This guilt you're feeling will eat you up if you let it. I told you what happened to Joshua Reasoner. He finally reached a point where he couldn't face himself, and neither your mother nor I would want that for you. You hired me because you knew your mom would want a resolution to the Reasoner case. Your perseverance made that happen, but now you owe her one more thing."

I held her by the shoulders, making sure our eyes met. "You need to live, Annabelle. Go home and love that husband and little boy of yours. It's what your mother would have wanted more than anything."

Annabelle hugged me then, a gesture I think surprised both of us. "Do you really think she'd forgive me?"

"I know she would. Your mom's death was a tragedy, not a crime. If you two had met anywhere but on this bridge, none of it would have happened. Go live your life, Annabelle. It really is what Bernie would have wanted."

She nodded and turned to walk away. Stopping before she reached the end of the bridge, she looked back and shook her head.

"Mom said you were the only other investigator she knew who was ever worth a damn. Are you sure you won't have your police detective partner come and arrest me?"

I wouldn't, but I needed to think about what I'd say to Hannah. I could tell her I let Bernie's case go, but Hannah wouldn't believe that in a million years.

I decided to tell my girlfriend the truth. Hannah was a cop, but there was nothing about the evidence in this case that would even remotely constitute proof in a court of law. Knowing how I felt about Bernie, Hannah would also trust me if I told her I'd concluded Bernie's death was an accident. Hannah understood justice, and she also understood guilt. She wouldn't choose to take the case further.

I turned to Annabelle. "If I had you arrested, your mother would haunt me for the rest of my days. While normally I might enjoy her company, I wouldn't look forward to having Bernie call me 'poof' for my remaining years."

Annabelle nodded as if that made perfect sense. I nodded back and followed her, stepping for one last time off the Bridle Path Bridge.

EPILOGUE

THE AFTERMATH OF the Reasoner case was as messy and vicious as the case itself. Hannah and I tried to stay out of it as best we could.

Lydia Reasoner never came to trial. Represented by eight lawyers hired by her mother, Lydia's fate came down to a sanity hearing in the Shaker Heights Municipal Court, the venue holding criminal jurisdiction over cases in Hunting Valley.

Judge Martin Steeples, one of the last remaining Reasoner allies in any level of municipal government, presided over the case in a closed sanity hearing. Having been subpoenaed myself, I watched Judge Steeples pay rapt attention as the court-ordered psychiatrist testified to Lydia's dissociative disorder, a condition that arose after she was preyed upon by her uncle. The psychiatrist's testimony came directly after my own.

My tale, a dry rendition of the facts of the case, was not nearly as gripping. I started with our arrival at the Reasoner mansion, emphasizing the events that occurred on the day that Joshua died. The judge seemed interested in how we had drawn our conclusions, and I tried to enlighten the court as best I could.

The proceeding could not have been better choreographed, and it ended with Judge Steeples ruling that Lydia wasn't competent to stand trial. Another judge might have considered Lydia's deliberate actions in killing her uncle and reached a different conclusion. Judge Steeples had been maneuvered onto the case, however, through Reasoner money and influence. His conclusion was never really in doubt. He sentenced Lydia to six months at the same Columbus mental institution as her father.

The judge's ruling was issued without Lydia having the opportunity to testify. That outcome was viewed as favorable by all except Lydia herself, a woman who wanted nothing more than to tell her story.

The hearing was closed to reporters and anyone outside the Reasoner orbit except for witnesses. No one else would know Lydia's involvement in her uncle's death or the vile circumstances that led to that tragedy.

I approached Lydia as she was escorted from the courtroom. Understanding what she had been aiming for, I knew she would be disappointed. As Lydia was about to walk past, I asked her female guard if she could give us just one minute. The guard agreed and stood in the background as Lydia and I spoke. Lydia, initially grim, brightened when she saw me.

"I'm sorry, Mr. Luvello. I'm afraid I didn't give you the literary ending I promised."

I waved my hand. I had something else in mind and needed to speak before her guard reentered our conversation. "You're not headed for a prison, so I'm guessing they'll let you keep your cell phone. Would you mind giving me your number?"

Lydia looked surprised, but she gave me the information. "Don't tell me you're going to call, Mr. Luvello. Won't Detective Page get jealous?"

"I have something else in mind. You can thank me later if it works."

The judge had issued a gag order on all participants in the trial, so I could say nothing myself. That order did not, however, keep me from making a phone call. I had spoken to Patrice Clairview three weeks before Lydia's hearing, limiting our discussion to the Michael Grieve and Federal Reserve cases. Being the skilled newsperson she was, Patrice also dug for information about the Reasoners, Joshua and Luke's deaths having already made the papers.

After Lydia's hearing, I contacted Patrice a second time. With the gag order in mind, I told her nothing about the hearing. I did, however, give her Lydia's cell phone number. I provided nothing else, just an assurance that she would hear far more about the case from Lydia than she would from me.

The articles that arose from their conversations were as explosive as the events that led up to them. Threats to sue were made and then dropped, the individuals making those threats coming face to face with the risk of legal discovery.

There was nothing I could do to shield Matthew Reasoner from that fallout. A basically decent man who appeared to have no knowledge of the interaction between his two brothers, Matthew was still caught up in Lydia's story.

The sensational details in the Clairview articles stunned the Greater Cleveland community. A wealthy family had turned its back while an older uncle terrorized their pretty young niece. Pitchforks were raised, and retribution was demanded. Matthew, though not directly implicated in the scandal, was doomed from the moment he took on Joshua's duties as president of the Reasoner corporation. The futility of that attempt became apparent as the family's notoriety spread. With the Reasoner stock price falling by the day, Matthew stepped down from his new position just two weeks after he assumed it.

Based on the last article I read, Matthew and Judith Reasoner planned to sell their shares in the company. Matthew intended to invest the proceeds from his sale of Reasoner stock in an entirely new venture, an innovative redesign of the miniature batteries used in many electronic devices.

With their interest in the Reasoner corporation soon to end, Matthew and Judith still owned the Shadow House. The two siblings had controlling interest in the Reasoner mansion, and I heard they intended to put their longtime home on the market. Based on the terms of the estate, they were able to initiate the sale over the objections of Abigail, who had inherited Joshua's share. When the family finally left, I wondered if the shadows would as well. After all the fun they had during our visit, I suspected they might stay.

Never really a part of the family and now a minority shareholder, Abigail tried desperately to hold on to her position at the Reasoner corporation. As with Matthew, that proved impossible after the wave of negative publicity generated by the Clairview articles. Abigail was forced to resign as marketing vice president soon after she sold Joshua's shares.

Facing ongoing negative publicity regarding Lydia and the fate of their company, the Reasoners had no interest in also battling a charity. After a remarkably short negotiation, the Cranberg Institute was awarded forty million dollars, the perceived value of Luke's portion of the Reasoner estate. Some in the community argued the school should also receive Joshua's inheritance. With no evidence Joshua was involved in his mother's death, Margaret's arbiter quickly shot down that argument.

I spoke to Ray West a week after the Cranberg settlement. Though nothing had been finalized, he told me the school wanted to use the Reasoner money to open sister institutions in Columbus and Cincinnati.

While trying to minimize my involvement, I had my own non-Reasoner concerns. An event I had looked forward to for some time was finally happening. For better or for worse, I finally had my surgery.

It might seem counterintuitive, but the scariest part of any surgical procedure can be the moment you wake up. I'd just survived a multiple-hour phalloplasty procedure, the second of several operations scheduled for the coming months. I woke up in my hospital room to find my ever-inquisitive girlfriend peering under my bed sheet.

"Please tell me they didn't forget anything down there."

Caught in the act, Hannah looked guiltily in my direction. "It's hard to tell. Don't forget you have a lot more to go. They started with the main equipment—remarkably impressive, by the way—but you still need some of the add-ons."

You would think I had just purchased a power saw. In truth, I knew what Hannah was referring to. Today's procedure was actually the second in my long list of transition procedures, the first being my outpatient top surgery two weeks prior. The "add-ons" would include a scrotoplasty, the implants for which would be inserted in about six months. It would be a long transition, and I had some thoughts.

"You know," Hannah added with a smile, "I had to chase your mother and John out of the room just before you woke up. John wanted a peek, and I think your mother was also curious. I told John that peeking was a privilege reserved only for me. He and your mother are now down in the hospital cafeteria. John wanted me to tell you that the surgeons mixed up the graft. He told me to say they used the forearm skin off a patient with a Jonas Brothers tattoo."

I shivered, even knowing it was John. "The tattoo sounds horrifying, and thank you for defending my honor. While we're here alone, though, there is something serious I want to talk with you about."

I gathered myself because I really did want her opinion. "You know I've been getting more case referrals than I know what to do with, and they tell me it's going to take three months before I can return to full activity. What would you think if I took on a partner?"

Hannah looked more than a little surprised, and with my well-earned reputation for privacy, I really couldn't blame her.

"The two of us working together full-time?" she joked. "One of us would kill the other within a week—a few days if you got too annoying."

She was probably right, but I had a different thought.

"I was thinking about Officer Styles. Do you remember him from the Reasoner case? He contacted me a few weeks ago to ask if I could offer career advice. The kid is bored as hell working for Hunting Valley, and he knows it'll be a lifetime before he gets another case as interesting as the Reasoner's. He's also intelligent, a little naïve, but smart nonetheless. He's young but no younger than I was when I went to work with Bernie.

"Even with my work restrictions, I could go with him on a few cases, talk him through the basics, and show him what to look for. It gives me a practical solution to what I'm facing in the coming months because I really don't want to turn down all the new clients."

Hannah looked dubious. "Isn't this the kid with a girlfriend he met at the church choir? Do you really think he'll want to work with some of the shitty clients you deal with?"

"I think he knows there's a great big world outside of Hunting Valley. Most importantly, he doesn't want to be bored. I can appreciate that because it's the same reason I got started. Church or no, I think he'll jump at the chance. In a weird way, I also feel I owe it to Bernie. She took me in as a raw kid. Based on appearance alone, she had no reason to think I'd be successful. This is my way of paying her back."

Hannah hesitated only for a second. "I like the idea of you having a partner. Talk to the kid and see what he thinks. With no dependents in his life, this might be the perfect time for him to make a change."

I had one week before I'd be discharged from the hospital. I figured I would call Ken Styles after I was out. We could meet and discuss the particulars, assuming he was interested.

Hannah sat back down to let me rest and finish whatever paperback novel she'd brought with her. Suddenly nervous, I wondered if John and my mother had carried out their part of the plan.

"Before you get settled," I said, "I wonder if you could hand me John's earbuds. He agreed to let me borrow them and said he'd put them in the drawer next to the bed."

Hannah looked surprised. "I didn't know you cared for earbuds."

She wasn't wrong. John had once suggested earphones as an alternative, but I could never find any that fit comfortably.

Hannah opened up the drawer and pulled out the small box John had placed in there while my mother distracted Hannah. Opening it, Hannah suddenly stopped cold.

"What the hell is this?"

Not exactly the reaction I was looking for. "If John did his job, that should be a ring."

Hannah held it up as if afraid she might be mistaken.

I thought I should explain or at least ask the

traditional question. "You and I have faced so much death together. I thought it might be time to experience a little life. I'm not in a position to get down on one knee, but is there any chance you would consider marrying me?"

Hannah still looked stunned. Perhaps placing the ring in an earbud box wasn't the best idea. Finally, she found her voice.

"Are you sure this isn't the anesthesia? Do you really want to do this?"

"I thought I did. Your reaction is telling me I may have been mistaken."

She bent over to kiss me then. It was a warm, deep, wonderful kiss.

"Yes, I'll marry you, idiot. I'm amazed you'd want to marry me, but I'm allowing no takebacks."

I leaned forward as much as I could. "No takebacks will be requested now or ever."

I pointed to the ring, now safely on Hannah's finger. "That ring belonged to my grandmother on my mother's side. My mom knew I was spending all my money on this procedure. She suggested, in her usual subtle way, that it was something I should keep around in case I ever decided to make an honest woman out of you."

Hannah told me she loved it, but I noticed her again looking at my groin. "Are you sure that thing doesn't work yet?"

"I am unfortunately sure, and it might be a little awkward even if it did. By now, I'm guessing you'll find John and my mother waiting outside the door."

Mortified, my ordinarily unflappable fiancée virtually ran to my hospital room door. Mom and John were waiting, and they rushed forward and offered their congratulations. I hugged them both, trying not to scream when John grabbed the forearm with the incision. They'd put up with a lot from me over the years. Whatever good I'd done in my life, I owed mostly to the people in this room.

My mother stepped out to call Tomas and my brother Paul, both of them already alerted to my intentions for that day. I took a moment to breathe then, and I noticed someone else.

It might have been the aftereffects of the anesthesia, but I could swear I saw Bernie sitting in the chair Hannah had just vacated. My old mentor was smiling, the first time I'd ever seen her with that expression.

Iain Thomas once wrote, "Everything has changed, and yet, I am more me than I've ever been." Lying there in my hospital bed, I suddenly understood the truth behind that statement. In the midst of all the future shadows in my life, that truth would need to be enough.

ACKNOWLEDGEMENTS

Shadow House would never have been completed without the support of everyone at NineStar Press, particularly my editor, Elizabetta McKay. Elizabetta, you took a chance on an unproven writer and saw this series through to the end. Without your advice and patience, Terry Luvello would never even have earned his detective license.

I would also like to thank Michelle Guzowski and Denise Vonderau. Your input was essential to the series, and it was very much appreciated.

About Joe Rielinger

Joe Rielinger lives in Cleveland, Ohio, with his wife, Lisa, and their two fun-loving, though often borderline crazy golden retrievers. With a lifetime love of mystery, crime, and detective novels, Joe is currently working on *Beneath the Mask*, a new crime novel. When he isn't writing, Joe likes to cook, read, and pretend he might someday learn something about training his two dogs.

Email
jarielinger@gmail.com

Facebook
www.facebook.com/jrielinger.author

Twitter
@JAR_author

Website
www.joerielinger.com

Other NineStar books by this author

Terry Luvello, PI Series
And God Laughed
Deepfake

CONNECT WITH NINESTAR PRESS

WWW.NINESTARPRESS.COM

WWW.FACEBOOK.COM/NINESTARPRESS

WWW.FACEBOOK.COM/GROUPS/NINESTARNICHE

WWW.TWITTER.COM/NINESTARPRESS

WWW.INSTAGRAM.COM/NINESTARPRESS

www.ingramcontent.com/pod-product-compliance
Lightning Source LLC
Chambersburg PA
CBHW060233100726